FOR THE BLESSINGS OF A FRIEND

Jean (and Marvin)

Thanks for being a great aunt and uncle and a blessing to me!

Susan
7-2001

FOR THE Blessings OF A Friend

by

SUSAN NYSWONGER McCRACKEN

FRIENDS UNITED PRESS
RICHMOND, INDIANA

© 2001 Susan Nyswonger McCracken

Printed in the United States of America

Book and cover design: Susanna Combs

Library of Congress Cataloging-in-Publication Data

McCracken, Susan, 1950-
   For the blessings of a friend / by Susan Nyswonger
   McCracken.
      p. cm.
   ISBN 0-944350-55-0
   1.   Women missionaries—Fiction. 2. African Ameri-
cans—Fiction. 3. Quaker women—Fiction. 4. Freedmen—
Fiction. 5. Kansas—Fiction. I. Title.

PS3563.C352485 F54 2001
813'.54—dc21   2001023897

*This book is dedicated to all people
who have faced prejudice and injustice
and have been able to forgive and discover
that of God in each of us.*

*A special thanks to my daughter, Alisha,
for once again lovingly and patiently
using her editing skills to help create
the final product.*

Contents

FOR THE BLESSINGS OF A FRIEND

CHAPTER 1

'THIS LITTLE *Light* OF *Mine*'

"*P*lease, ma'am . . . please! Jist a loaf a bread! Even a crumb!"

"An angel! She's an angel sent from God! Oh, glory be to the Lord! She's come to save us!"

Julia felt the panic rise within her. Her skirt was being tugged . . . hands of all shapes and sizes reached out to grab her own . . . a sea of desperate faces swarmed around seeking to swallow her. The scream in her throat threatened to unleash itself on the swirling crowd but somehow she kept it inside. Frantically Julia searched for Elizabeth among the faces. Where was the woman who was supposed to protect her from this unruly mob of ragged refugees? She felt herself falling, falling, into a deep pit with hundreds of black bodies careening toward her. She couldn't breathe. Help! Help! she screamed.

Jerking awake, Julia threw off the blanket that had somehow managed to wrap itself around her head. The scene of the dream, however, would not go away and the feelings of hope-lessness lingered in her mind. Similar dreams had plagued her repeatedly since arriving in Topeka to begin her evangelistic work with the black refugees. Would she ever manage to put the terrors of that first day from her mind? The sea of black faces imploring her for food, with a belief that somehow she, a mere eighteen-year-old girl seeking to answer God's call on her life, had come to save them from their wretched plight. Men, women, and children in tattered shirts and pants or rotting dresses. No food, no clothing, no homes. For some, only black stubs remained where frozen fingers and toes had snapped off as they struggled north to freedom during the previous winter. They were free from the bonds of slavery they were born to but chained with a new form of servitude: brutal living conditions and a life that was in many ways a living hell.

Pulling the covers tightly around her body, Julia shuddered at the sights and sounds of the throngs of suffering refugees that seemed to constantly trudge through her mind. Although it had been three months since she arrived with Elizabeth Comstock on the train from Iowa, it seemed like three years. Had she done the right thing? She had been so certain of God's call last spring. All the pieces had snapped into place at the last minute: the confirmation of the Holy Scripture and friends who affirmed her decision. Then came the last-minute opportunity to ride with neighbors to the train station to meet Elizabeth when it had appeared there was no possible way she could get there. Her decision to travel with Elizabeth to Kansas to help provide for the needs of the Negro refugees seemed to be blessed by God. Unfortunately, nothing had prepared her for the throngs of Negroes who swarmed the depot the day she and Elizabeth arrived.

Three trains continued to arrive daily in Topeka, each from a different point of departure, carrying carloads of men, women, and children whose lives as slaves had ended with the war but whose misery was far from over. Some estimated there were twenty thousand refugees in the city already. Twenty thousand homeless, helpless, penniless starving black refugees. How was one eighteen-year-old supposed to make a difference in their lives?

Julia thought of the others who labored with her. Quite naturally Elizabeth was the first to come to mind. Elizabeth Comstock. Had God ever created a more perfect human? As a traveling Friends evangelist, Elizabeth had recognized the great need of the black refugees who poured into Kansas and other free states. She had traveled from one Friends Meeting to another, from the East Coast to England, to get supplies for simple living: blankets, quilts, plates, dishes, and money for food. Julia remembered the first time she had heard Elizabeth speak at the Iowa Yearly Meeting of Friends and how her heart had been stirred by her powerful words. Elizabeth had spoken with honesty and openness, and she seemed to have an endless capacity for love. She had asked Friends to put aside their petty quarrels about holiness and the Inner Light and focus on the starving and needy of this world. "When you can do that," she had said, "you will be fulfilling Christ's words in the scriptures: 'when ye have done it unto the least of these, my brothers, ye have done it unto me'."

Working with Elizabeth in Kansas had seemed to be God's call. Yes, Elizabeth was a powerful speaker, but it had not been her words that had persuaded Julia to join the work with the refugees. God had spoken to her, of that she was certain. But if God had been speaking to her then, where was God now? Why didn't she feel God's presence each day as she worked in the Kansas Freedmen's Relief Association, which Elizabeth had founded in Topeka?

What am I expecting? Julia chided herself. Manna from heaven? God could only provide through the hands of those willing to do His work. Elizabeth's hands. Laura Haviland's hands. John Watson and his wife's hands and the hands of the staff at the Relief Association. Her hands. Even John Stanley, the most self-absorbed man Julia had ever met, occasionally volunteered his time at the Association when they were desperate for extra hands. But would it ever be enough? Could they ever provide enough food and clothing for the river of refugees flowing into the city? They were in constant need of additional supplies. Could they possibly train all of the refugees so they could find employment and make a decent wage? The outlook was grim, at best.

Julia rose from her bed and moved to the window of her upstairs room to capture the view of the street below. Though the sun had yet to creep above the horizon, a crowd began to mill about in the narrow street in front of the Relief Association. There were men with no jobs and women whose husbands waited in the South to escape the prisons where many of them sat for trivial crimes like voting for a Republican candidate. And children. She saw children with sunken bodies and hunger written all over their faces.

Julia quickly turned away, determined not to fall into a state of despondency so early in the morning. Dressing quickly, she made up the bed and sat for a few moments of quiet time before starting the day. She knew Maggie, the woman from whom she rented her room, would have something ready for her to eat when she got downstairs. Right now, however, she needed a bit of time with the Lord to help soothe the agitation the dream had aroused. Dropping to her knees beside her bed, Julia laid her doubts and fears at the feet of the only One who could possibly bring her the peace she needed. Only an hour remained before she would be expected to bring a message to the refugees gathered for morning worship. A message of hope and faith. Faith was certainly something she needed more and more as each day passed, faith in a God who promised to supply every need of every believer, a God who knew the number of hairs on each person's head. Would this God not also know and meet the needs of each former slave that was seeking a new life? Yes, it took a lot of faith to believe that God would supply all their needs. She pushed back the doubts that were never far away. *I must live for just today. Let God use me however He sees fit.* With new resolve to be faithful to God's calling, Julia rose from her knees and headed downstairs to see what Maggie had prepared for their morning meal.

Later that morning as Julia waited for Meeting for Worship to begin, she carefully scanned the faces of the refugees who were

slowly entering the large room. Attending worship was a requirement of those living at the Kansas Freedmen's Relief Association,
and one regular worshiper in particular had stirred Julia's heart. As
she searched the crowd, however, she was disappointed not to see
his face. Julia's thoughts returned to the events of a few weeks
earlier.

Since the day Elizabeth had established the Freedmen's
Association, masses of refugees had come to the center, located
in North Topeka, to receive whatever supplies they had need
of: food, clothing, dishes, and bedding. In addition to her job
of speaking at worship each morning, Julia spent a good por-
tion of her days keeping an inventory of the supplies that came
in on the trains from Friends across the Eastern United States,
as well as distributing supplies to the refugees who came for
assistance. She would never forget the morning she had first
met Hosea.

Hosea was the blackest Negro Julia had ever seen. His skin
was so black it shone like a candle in the night pierced by two
dark eyes. He seemed to be about her age, as near as she could
tell, but that's where their similarities ended. Hosea was a head
taller with shoulders twice the width of Julia's. Through the
tattered shirt Julia could see bulging muscles, no doubt the
product of years of manual labor. Hosea's face spoke of the
injustices and indignities he had endured in his short life. The
angry curl of his lip and the guarded eyes telling the story of
his past. John Brown, the general superintendent of the Association, had quickly moved to speak to the young man and
inquire of his needs. John was also a Negro, and although his

life had been one of unusual cultivation for a black man, the link of their ancestry would provide a bridge to the young man Julia could never hope to cross.

"What is it you might need this morning?" John asked. His voice pleasant but not overly so, not wanting to make Hosea uncomfortable.

When there was no reply, John continued. "Are you alone or do you have a family? Do you have food? What about clothing? If you can tell us your needs we can prepare a package for you."

Hosea looked first at John and then Julia as if trying to understand what this fiery, red-haired girl was doing with an obviously educated black man who had never known the struggles of slavery.

"Why yous got dis lily-white chile out here?" Hosea's first words were directed toward John, but his eyes were focused on Julia.

Julia's head jerked up, and the shirt she had been folding fell back into the box she was unpacking.

"Yes um . . . I's talkin' 'bout you. You ain't got no place here. Dis is fer us po' black folk who ain't had life easy like you has." Julia could see a flash of anger in his eyes as he spoke.

"Even you, Mista Black man . . ." he continued, turning to John, "you's had life purty easy yourself, now ain't ya? Mus' be a nice life jist sittin' here givin' tickets to us po' black folk who need you alls help."

Julia could see John bristle for a moment, but soon he regained his composure. "What is it you might be needin' this morning, sir?" he asked again.

7

Hosea seemed a bit surprised by John's calm manner. Looking once again at Julia, he seemed to be considering whether or not to resume his assessment of her. Finally turning away, he began to tell John his immediate needs. "I's needs food 'n' bedin'."

"What about shelter?" John asked. "Do you have a place to live? We have room in the barracks right now if you would care to live there until such time as we can provide some training for you. Unless, of course, you have a family and have already arranged a place to live."

Anger rose within Hosea as he thought of the choices that lay before him. Having spent his first few days camping by the railroad tracks with other refugees, he had finally decided if he wanted a new life he would have to accept the training he had heard the Quakers offered at the Association. He had wrestled with the dilemma. He was loath to accept anything from the white man, but trapped in a way of life with no future if he lived from hand to mouth by the tracks. But he still could not understand why someone would offer him a place to stay, and training. He figured there was something the white man would require in exchange . . . like one's soul, perhaps. He had seen enough of the white man's treatment of blacks in the South to know that they never gave you anythin' without a price. But this wasn't a white man offerin' these things . . . it was a black man like him. And what was the lily-white girl doin' here? She surely didn't live here. Which must mean she was one of the workers. But why? There must be a million things a pretty white girl could do besides work with filthy dirty starvin' black folks like him!

"Sir?" John spoke again, bothered by the conflicting expressions displayed on the face of the young man standing before him.

"Hosea be da name. Jist Hosea. I ain't got no famly. I 'scaped by the skin o' my teeth and snuck on a barge comin' up the river. Then I walk da las' two hunerd miles."

Julia quickly looked down at the young man's feet and saw they looked healthy enough. Somehow she had expected to see badly injured feet from all the walking.

"Da path ain't bad—least not 'till winter sets in," Hosea said when he saw Julia's downward glance.

Trying to conceal the blush on her face, Julia quickly turned back to her folding project.

"So, would you like to stay in the barracks until you can get established here in Topeka?" John asked again.

"Don' know what y'all mean by 'stablished', but I reckon dis place be as good as any." And better than the railroad camp, he thought bitterly.

"Fine. Just go to the second window down and Julia will give you two sets of clothing for these blue tickets. A bell rings for meals, but the next meal is several hours away. If you need something to eat now, go on to the next window and give the woman this red ticket."

Hosea stared at the writing on the tickets the black man had just given him. He had been a house slave in the south, a position of privilege for young black children. As a companion for the massa's son, he had learned a little about reading as he watched the boy do his lessons each night. Longing to be able to read, Hosea had paid close attention to his young master's daily assignments. He felt a sense of pride that he could read the words 'clothing' and 'food' on the tickets he now held in his hand. He knew few of his people would know what the words meant.

Moving to the first window, Hosea stared once again at the strange young girl folding and sorting the clothing. Bet she has a nice white daddy and momma that gives her everthin' she ever wants, he thought bitterly. Then why is she workin' in a place like this? he asked himself again.

Julia took the tickets Hosea silently offered her and gave him her most winsome smile. "I'll be right back," she said after surveying his height and weight to estimate the size he might take.

In a few minutes she returned with two shirts, two pairs of pants and socks. "These should help thee," she said, smiling again. "Is thee moving into the barracks?"

Hosea continued to stare at Julia, again wondering her motivation for handing out clothing to poor refugees like him, and why in the world she called him 'thee.'

"I am sorry," Julia finally said when there was no response from the young man before her. "It really is none of my business. Thee may take the red ticket to the next window and they will give thee some food." She quickly turned her back on the boy, not understanding why he refused to speak to her. Maybe he is not used to talking to white people. Maybe he is embarrassed. Or maybe he just does not like me. It is his problem, not mine.

"These ain't da right size." Hosea's voice interrupted her thoughts.

"Oh, I think they will be fine." Julia was irritated. Who did he think he was, anyway? She had been doing this work for many weeks now, and she could size up a person in one easy glance.

"You think you's so almighty. How would you know what size I wear? You didn' put your purty lil' hands on me, now did ya?!"

This time Julia's blush failed to recede quickly as she felt the warmth spread all the way down her neck. "What size do you think you need?" she asked stiffly, dropping the Friends' preferred 'thee'.

"Oh, I 'spose one size bigger oughta do it." Hosea's voice had lost some of the anger that had laced his earlier words, and now there appeared to be a twinkle in his eye.

He thought he had made a fool of her, did he. Julia was determined to find the clothing as quickly as possible and get the arrogant young man out of her sight. All she was trying to do was help, and he was certainly in no position to make demands. After all, he was practically begging for food and clothes.

"Thank ya, ma'am." Hosea's words were mocking as he picked up the pile she would have liked to throw at him.

"I expect I will be seeing thee at Meeting for Worship each morning," Julia called as he moved on to the next window.

Hosea looked back incredulously. "I don' reckon ya will, Missy. I don' do church. An why's you always sayin' 'thee'?"

"The members of the Society of Friends—or Quakers as some call us—use the plain language of England because we believe everyone is equal in the eyes of God. And worship is a requirement of those living in the barracks," Julia added, glad for once to have something on this overbearing young man.

"Then I bes' be movin' on," he said.

"Oh, do not do that! I mean, worship is not that unpleasant. It only lasts an hour. Then you go right to training for a trade." For some reason Julia felt the need to somehow atone for not helping Hosea feel more at ease in his new surroundings. Besides, the sooner he learned a trade, the sooner he could support himself. Perhaps he just needed someone to encourage him a bit since he did not have a family.

Hosea stared at Julia for a long time. Shaking his head he finally moved on without another word. Julia had no idea if he would leave or stay, but she hoped he would choose to live in the barracks and begin training for work offered in Topeka.

It had been several weeks since Julia's first encounter with Hosea. After talking with some of the other refugees at the Association, Hosea had decided living in the barracks with the daily worship requirement was better than trying to make it alone on the streets. He usually came to worship late, shoulders slouched, head down, and the minute the final amen was spoken he was the first one out the door. Julia tried to make eye contact during her messages, but only once had she seen the poor soul even look up. Something heavy was troubling him, of that she was certain. But how did a person minister to someone like Hosea? How did a woman of her background find the link to understand what a slave had survived?

As Julia's thoughts returned to the worship service that was about to begin, a pang of loneliness enveloped her as she thought of the many worship services she had attended with her family at Salem Friends Meeting. What did her family think of her now?

Her father, community physician in her home town, so capable, so proud of his family, yet so determined she would not answer what she knew was God's call on her life. Charles Jones was a model doctor, model husband, model father—almost. Why had she not been able to persuade him that coming to Kansas as an evangelist to the refugees was God's plan for her life?

Her mother, Rebecca, was probably taking care of Julia's eighteen-month-old sister, Rachel, right now. Did her mother think of her often? Did she worry about her? Although Rebecca had been reluctant to give her blessing to Julia's mission, she knew that God had touched her young daughter in a special way, blessing her with many gifts including the desire to follow His will for her life. Surely her mother would rest in the assurance that God would protect her strong-willed child.

Julia thought of her brother, David, no doubt back in Salem practicing medicine with their father. He was surely making plans to marry Hannah; sweet, simple Hannah who wanted nothing more than to be a good wife to David and the mother of his children. Hannah, who thought Julia was brave and talented. Hannah, the girl Julia had never much cared for while growing up, even though she was the daughter of her mother's best friend. When it had come time to leave for Kansas, however, Hannah had been one of her strongest supporters.

Finally Julia's thoughts rested on the two young men who had been a part of her life the past two years: Jonathan White and Will Clark. Two men anyone would consider perfect marriage prospects. Will, of course, was now engaged to be married. Had Jonathan also found a woman to replace her? But I told him I only wanted to be friends, Julia reminded herself. Still . . . would she someday have a chance to find yet a third man who might want her for his life partner?

Seeing Hosea enter the meeting room for worship brought Julia back to the present. As usual his dark head was bowed, seeming to convey the message that being anywhere was preferable to being here. I have to reach him, Julia thought fiercely. I have to! Please God, give me Your words today that somehow Hosea might know that Jesus died for him, too. He needs you. I need you.

CHAPTER 2

'EVERY TIME
I Feel
THE *Spirit'*

*W*orship. What did God desire from His children? Julia yearned to know the answer. Each day the one hundred or so refugees living at the Association made their way to the required worship service. Each day they left with many of the same dull expressions on their faces. Julia was baffled. Were her words of so little value that not one black man, woman, or child was moved? And the singing. Were not Negroes known for their spirited singing? Were there not stories of slaves singing haunting spirituals long into the night? Perhaps if she knew some of the songs that moved these people worship would be more meaningful.

Julia's worship experiences had always been in the silence. Friends traditions taught that in the quiet of silent worship the Holy Spirit 'spoke to one's condition.' Julia understood that to mean the Spirit would reveal areas of sin in her life if she would only ask and wait for a response. But had she not been called by God to be an evangelist? Julia chuckled at what the elder members of the Salem Friends Meeting might think if they could see her standing before a crowd preaching the gospel of hope and salvation each and every day. A Salem Friends member in good standing preparing messages to deliver to those gathered for worship? No, Julia thought, the elders of her home meeting would find it difficult to approve of her current occupation. Most of them firmly believed silent worship was the only true form of worship for a believer.

Seeking the advice of the one she admired most, Julia made her way to Elizabeth's office at the close of one particularly dull worship service. In her full black dress with her hair parted and pulled back, Elizabeth was a large woman, who presented an imposing figure to anyone entering the room. Her voice, however, was gentle and full of compassion and put even the most fearful at ease. Elizabeth's face brightened as she saw her young protegé enter.

"Julia! How delightful to see thee! Was Meeting for Worship Spirit-filled this morning?"

Julia, slow to answer, moved to sit on the wooden chair across from her friend's desk. "What does worship mean, Elizabeth? I mean, true worship. What does God expect of poor black souls forced to sit through a service led by a young white girl? And what about the Friends belief that God speaks out of the silence? We spend precious few minutes waiting for God to speak to individuals in that way." Julia's voice was laced with raw emotion as she sought the answers to her nagging doubts.

Elizabeth sat for a moment considering how best to answer the queries of the searching soul sitting before her. Finally she began to share what worship meant to her.

"Worship of Almighty God is doubtless the most exalted exercise of which the human mind is capable. The traditional Quaker method of worship is the most exacting of all methods in the demands it makes upon the mind and spirit. It is doubtless true that some persons are incapable of meeting these demands, having difficulty keeping their thoughts on the divine. But it is in that silent meditation that the human spirit can readily find answers for all of life's questions from the voice of the Holy Spirit that speaks to our individual needs.

"In addition, when Friends believe the Spirit requests them to share a spoken word with those gathered for worship, there is often a genuine response of community and the spiritual level of the Meeting is lifted to a higher plane. Of course, Friends have always respected other forms of worship if the lives of those worshiping reflect the benefits from such worship."

"But if silence is so powerful why did thee become an evangelist?" Julia's question produced a smile that reflected the love Elizabeth felt for her young friend.

"Thee knows that evangelism has been my life's work. Naturally, I was raised in the silence. I grew to appreciate every facet of sitting and waiting for the moving of the Holy Spirit. But I also sensed a growing apathy among Friends. While the silence was meant to be a time of deep communion between man and God, it seemed to have become ritual for many. Men sat on their side of the divider, women on the other, often silent for several hours without anyone speaking a word for their group. Singing, of course, was frowned upon by the elders. They felt if everyone sang the same words there would be little meaning for individual worshipers, and rather than be true worship it would become a ritual.

"I believe God can use the spoken words of an anointed evangelist just as easily as God can speak to Friends in the silence. And for some who have not come to Meeting with their spirits prepared to receive from God, the spoken word may be what they are able to receive that day. Does this make sense to thee, Julia?"

"Yes, I believe I understand what thee is trying to say. But why do the refugees sit and stare at me rather than being moved to worship by my words?"

Elizabeth's smile was once again gentle. "My child," she began, "thee has been here at the Association for how long? Six weeks?"

"Four months," Julia said emphatically. "And worship should be meaningful after that much time!"

"Ah . . . that helps me see thy dilemma. Julia, my dear, worship, like many things of the Spirit, is something one must put energy into for some time before one sees the fruits of his or her labor. Tell me . . . can thee feel the Spirit in worship?"

Julia's mouth opened, but no words came out. She shifted in her seat before answering. "Sometimes when I bring the message I have prepared God seems to be right there beside me. But other times it is as if I am alone. When we sing I try to exhort the others to sing from their hearts and not just their mouths, but they do not seem to understand. I just wish I knew some of the songs they sang in the South. And the refugees never speak out of the silence . . . it is as if they are waiting for me to bring the message and the silence is just something they must endure."

"I suppose thee has spoken to the group about the meaning and purpose of sitting in the silence?"

"Yes, that was one of the first things I did when I came."

"Then tell me a little about the order of worship. I wish I had been able to attend more of your services. It seems that mornings are the times when we are so overwhelmed with those needing supplies that I have difficulty leaving the office."

"We usually sing a few hymns. "Abide With Me" seems to be one that everyone knows and enjoys. And then I read some scripture verses that will go with the message I have prepared. That is followed by silent worship. When the Spirit seems to say it is time for me to speak, I rise and say what I have prepared for that day. When I am finished we sometimes sing a song—if there is time—and I always offer a benediction."

"What does thee suppose would happen if thee waited until the close for silent worship? Perhaps thy words would encourage a brother or sister in the Lord to share what the Spirit has impressed upon their hearts."

"I suppose I could try that," Julia said doubtfully. "But I think they would be wanting to leave and would have a difficult time sitting and listening for the Spirit."

"Ah . . . perhaps thee has a point. Julia, I assure thee I will make this a matter of prayer. Perhaps God is speaking to all of us on this matter of true worship. In the meantime, why not consider rearranging the order of worship to see if our friends seem more receptive to the leading of the Holy Spirit after thy message."

"I will give it prayerful thought. Oh, Elizabeth, I do so want to be an effective evangelist for God. I do not want the words to be just my words. I want the refugees to know what it feels like to have God's Spirit commune with their spirits!"

"And it will happen, my dear, please do not lose hope. We both know God has called thee to this work, even on days when He seems distant. Faith is the key to our work here, because faith simply means believing in God's promises even when we see no evidence of them."

Julia thought again of Hosea and the times she had seen him in worship. There was certainly no evidence that God was anywhere near that young man's life. Would worship ever speak to his condition?

"I thank thee for thy words, Elizabeth," Julia said as she rose to leave. Elizabeth walked with her to the door, embracing her as a mother would a precious child.

"Thee is doing a fine work, Julia. I am so proud of thee for choosing to follow God's call to evangelism. All God asks of thee is to be faithful. It is God's work to move the hearts of sinful men and women, not ours."

Julia smiled sheepishly. Yes, she supposed she wanted her words to move those in worship each day instead of letting the

Spirit do the work. From now on she would turn each Meeting for Worship over to God. Somehow her step felt lighter as she left to go work in the distribution center.

As Julia worked the next day, an idea wormed its way into her mind and refused to go away. No, she protested, impossible. No, I cannot do it. No, God, do not even ask me. It will never work. But the thought would not leave.

This is the worst idea I have ever had, she chided herself as she made her way to find Hosea that evening, still not convinced of the wisdom of her mission. But if I can just learn the songs the refugees like to sing, she argued with herself, then perhaps they will feel more like they are a part of the worship service.

Julia's pace slowed as she approached the barracks. The barracks consisted of eight cabins built in a circle around a courtyard. Each cabin housed sixteen men, or women, and children. It was Julia's hope that Hosea would be in the courtyard talking over the day's events with some of the other young men there. She knew she could not go inside the men's barracks, but the courtyard would be a safe place to talk to him—or so she thought.

As she approached the open area she could hear shouts of 'get 'em!' and 'knock 'em out!' Quickening her steps, Julia's heart began to pound as she saw what appeared to be a fight in the center of the courtyard. Pushing her fears aside, she carefully worked her way through the spectators gathered to lend encouragement to their favorite fighter.

Oh no! Julia thought as she got closer to the brawl. She was certain one of the men rolling on the ground was Hosea. The fight seemed to be over by the time she finally managed to make her way to the front to see exactly what was taking place. Hosea was lying on the ground with blood everywhere: his face, hands, clothing and the ground. Forgetting any sense of propriety, Julia rushed to kneel beside the still body. "Hosea . . . can thee hear me? It is Julia. The evangelist." She had no idea if he knew her name or even what an evangelist was.

Opening one eye, Hosea's next words would be seared in her memory for some time. "Go home, lily-white perfect preacher girl. You make me sick ta my stomach!" and with that he rolled over and began to retch, a combination of his blood and evening meal spilling on the ground. Though splatters of vomit hit Julia's shoes and skirt, it was his words that soiled her. Why did he hate her? Was it because she was white? He always used those same words—lily-white—to describe her. Or was it because she was a woman? Or an evangelist? Was this her reward for trying to show him kindness?

"Ma'am, I think it'd be best if you jist headed on back to headquarters. We alls can take care o' Mr. Hosea, here." The voice came from an elderly gentleman standing close to Hosea, and although the words were quietly spoken his steely tone spoke of the seriousness of the situation.

Julia looked at Hosea, then at the elderly man, then back at Hosea. No, she thought, I will not leave. He needs proper care and there is only one place he can receive it: the infirmary.

"I would appreciate two of you gentlemen helping me carry Hosea to the infirmary where he can be examined. He will return when he is fully recovered."

"I said ya best leave us alone, ma'am," the stooped graying man repeated his wishes. "You ain't gots no business being down here in da first place."

Fear rose in Julia's throat as she looked at the surly faces surrounding the man who appeared to be their leader. Looking him straight in the eye Julia repeated her request as calmly as possible. "I need two gentlemen to help me. Who will it be?"

The group of men looked at the elder for guidance. A battle for authority was being waged. Could the old man not see Hosea needed help? At that moment the vomiting began again and the decision was made.

"Jacob, John, give Hosea a hand here. He mightin' be hurt inside and we ain't got no way ta check it." The man's words set the others into motion and in a matter of minutes Hosea was lying on a bed in the makeshift infirmary. The men reluctantly left Hosea in Julia's care, though heads were shaking as they headed back to the barracks.

"Thee must lie still," Julia admonished. "The doctor will not be here to make rounds for another hour. Where is thy pain? I can get thee a cold cloth—"

Hosea rose on an elbow and once again made his feelings known. "I don' wan' your help. Jist leave me be. I ain't gonna die and that's all dat matters. You always be stickin' that nose o' yours where it don' belong!"

"That is not so!" Julia's tone spoke of her frustration. "I am merely trying to help you. And why were you fighting, anyway?"

A slight twitch of Hosea's mouth preceded his next words. "What happen' to them fancy 'thees 'n' thous', miz preacher woman?"

Julia blushed. "Oh, well, sometimes I forget." And sometimes I rebel against Friends teachings, she thought to herself. Julia had always had trouble using the "thees" and "thous" of her heritage, and had been chided by her parents on numerous occasions for not using the plain language.

"Ya don' seem like the type to furget that easy, missy."

Again Julia felt her cheeks grow warm. "Well, if there is nothing I can do for thee I will let thee rest until the doctor comes." Having decided that her gesture of mercy had no respectful recipient, Julia quickly left the infirmary and headed for her office rather than be further insulted.

When the doctor arrived to do his evening rounds, Julia met him at the door and asked if she could join him. "I don't think this is proper work for a young woman," he began to protest. "You know all the patients are in that one big room, and it is difficult trying to keep diseases from spreading from one patient to another."

Dr. Samuels was a godsend, having volunteered his time at the Association for over a year now. Elizabeth had learned of his empathy toward the refugees when she shared the needs of the mission at one of the Topeka churches. Her description of the ill and lame refugees persuaded the elderly doctor to help with the sometimes-heavy load of patients needing medical attention.

"I will not be any trouble, I promise," Julia pleaded. "My father is a physician and I have worked with him in his practice numerous times." That was stretching the truth a bit, but as a teenager she had gone with her father on a few house calls back in Salem.

"All right, but please stay back away from the patients. Some have illnesses even I don't recognize. You wouldn't want to contract some disease and have to go home, now would you?"

"No," Julia said meekly.

The doctor quickly moved from patient to patient, making note of progress or regression. Finally he approached Hosea. "What seems to be the problem, young man?" he asked.

"Better ask da missus. She da one that drug me here."

Dr. Samuels looked curiously at Julia.

"I . . . well . . . I mean, he got in a fight and there was blood everywhere and he was retching something fierce. I wanted thee to check him and make sure there were no internal injuries."

Old Doc Samuels had been in the business of treating patients for thirty-five years and he knew the chances of internal injuries from a fight were slim, especially considering the young man seemed to be in little pain. But Julia seemed genuinely concerned, so he went ahead with the examination.

"I think you'll be just fine," he said closing his bag.

"I knowd there weren't nothin' wrong with me 'cept a broken nose," Hosea said contemptuously. "Miss high'n mighty here think she know so much 'bout me. She da pain, Doc."

Dr. Samuels smiled, moving on to the last patient. Julia looked once more at Hosea. Surely this was not the time to ask him to teach her some of the Negro spirituals. Would he ever want to talk to her again after she had insisted he come to the infirmary?

"Hey missy . . . " Hosea called to Julia as she turned to leave.

"My name is Julia. Not 'Missy,' not 'lily-white girl,' just Julia."

"Whooeee! You gots a little temper to go with that fiery red hair, Miz Julia!"

Julia blushed again. Why was it he always knew the exact words to irritate her so? She would not let him get the best of her. "I am sorry thee does not appreciate my efforts on thy behalf. I was merely trying to help thee. Someday thee will respect my work here at the Association."

"Oh, I respect ya, all right. I respect that perfect little body and that hot temper you gots." Then, as an afterthought, he added, "'N' I respect what ya do at worship."

Julia stared at Hosea. Was his comment about worship sincere or was he making fun of her again? Did she dare ask?

"What do you mean?" she finally managed.

"I ain't gots no use fer God, an' I ain't gots no use fer that there worship you alls make us go to. But I gots to admit you is one fine sight up there in front o' all us poor niggas."

Turning quickly, Julia marched toward the door, head high, tears threatening to spill down her cheeks. What gave him, a black man, the right to speak to her like that? Impossible boy.

That is all he is. Just a little boy in a man's body. Why had she ever thought he might help her with songs for worship? She would be glad when he had mastered his skill training and was out of the barracks. Not that she saw him that much anyway. But at least she would not have to see his bitter head bowed in worship each day.

"You is good at prayin'." Julia barely heard the words spoken to her back. She would never believe another word Hosea spoke to her. Never.

Julia ran into the street, not looking anywhere but straight ahead. The darkness was a welcome hiding place for her wounded soul. The sobs that wracked her body were for all the doubts and fears about this new life, all the loneliness of having left family and friends hundreds of miles away, and for all the imperfections she felt within herself.

After walking for what seemed like hours Julia finally headed back toward Maggie's, still plagued with doubts of her worth in this foreign state. Where was the happiness one was supposed to receive when doing God's will? "Abide in Me"—what did that song really mean? How did one abide? How had the refugees learned to abide in God when their very lives were threatened? Perhaps there were lessons to be learned in this new home. I will be happy if I survive, she thought as she reached her new home. Any wisdom gained will be an additional bonus.

CHAPTER 3

'Sometimes I FEEL LIKE A *Motherless Child'*

*F*all passed quickly. Winter announced itself sharply one morning in December when howling winds and swirling snow greeted Julia as she looked outside the Hollingsworth home. She was so grateful there had been a room available for her in Maggie's home where Elizabeth boarded when she was in Topeka. Though not very large, Julia's room was cozy and furnished in a simple way that reminded her of her own room back home in Salem. The hand-pieced quilt on the bed, the bowl and pitcher sitting on the wash stand in the corner, and the plain wooden rocker by the window seem to envelop her with comfort when she retreated to the room each evening. Living with Maggie, Elizabeth, and Laura Haviland, the other woman working at the Association, had provided a sense of family that kept Julia from succumbing to homesickness.

Watching the swirling snow reminded Julia that the chills of winter were upon them, which would not be good for Elizabeth's health. Whether it was the deep cough or the struggle to breathe that was the more worrisome Julia was not sure, but she knew this kind of weather was bound to worsen the elder woman's condition. She felt an urgent need to keep Elizabeth from walking to the mission in the snow. Hurrying back upstairs she knocked lightly on Elizabeth's door and waited for a reply.

"Come in," a weak voice called.

Julia quickly opened the door. "Good morning, Elizabeth," she greeted as cheerfully as possible. 'A merry heart doeth good like medicine' was a proverb her father had taught her at an early age. He believed those who were ill needed someone outside their misery to help them feel better. 'A cheerful person is a miracle worker' he often said.

"I am fine, dear." The pale face and barely audible words betrayed the message.

"I am afraid winter is here this morning," Julia began. "I do not believe thee should try and work at the Association this morning."

Elizabeth's smile was indulgent. "I know thee thinks I am weak, Julia, but I will be just fine once I get moving." As Elizabeth threw off the covers and sat up she was instantly consumed by a coughing fit. The cough was deep, doubling her over as she gasped for air.

Julia moved closer to Elizabeth, fervently wishing there were something she could do to ease her pain. After many minutes had passed the coughing finally subsided. Elizabeth wiped her eyes and blew her nose. "That was a good one, was it not?" She tried to laugh, though the effort was feeble and threatened to start another round of coughing.

"It was indeed a good one, and thee will stay in this house today if I have to barricade the door!" Julia hoped her words were convincing, though she knew Elizabeth was indeed a strong-willed woman.

"Julia, God's work must go on. If He wishes me to continue to assist the Negroes, then he will supply the strength I need. Did thee know Governor St. John is coming this week to see the mission? Oh, I suppose I should not call it 'the mission,' but it truly is a mission to those we serve."

"When will the governor arrive?" Julia asked, thinking of all the little jobs that needed done before one so important should visit. Not only were there large areas in the warehouse that needed cleaning, but the storage area needed to be examined from one end to the other, sorting and rearranging the clothing and supplies that were shipped by train daily. There were also leaves to rake, and the barracks needed to be inspected for cleanliness.

"The telegram I received yesterday said the governor should arrive in a week or two. That does not give us much time, but in some ways that is better. The governor will truly see how we live from day to day. I want him to know that we still need his support. I cannot begin to tell thee, Julia, how very much the governor has contributed to our work. Why, nearly every time he is asked to speak to a group of people across this state he mentions our need for food, clothing, bedding, and dishes. Many days we receive a shipment of goods from a city where the governor has spoken about our work."

"Does thee know the governor—personally, I mean?" Julia asked.

"We are not close friends, if that is what thee is asking. But we have spoken on several occasions when I have been at the capitol building, and he toured our site when we were first beginning the work."

"Then thee must feel very proud of thy work." Though Julia meant it to be encouragement, her praise had the opposite effect.

"Oh, my dear, if thee only knew!" Elizabeth's words were so emphatically spoken that she nearly lapsed into another fit of coughing. When the cough was stilled again she returned to the concerns that weighed so heavily on her heart.

"Julia, if thee never has to feel the plight of these poor souls then thee will be blessed. And yet, when one fully understands the enormity of the problem, one cannot help but become involved in the work. Refugees come to me daily begging for the things I cannot give them. Yesterday, for example, a young man begged me on bended knee to give him the forty-one dollars it would take to bring his wife from Alabama to be with him. I did not have it to give to him. The stories of cruelty and wrong-doing these people tell cause me many a sleepless night. Oh, how I long to have the money to give to all who ask; an abundance of clothes for every man, woman, and child who arrives with nothing but rags on their thin bodies; the food to fill the bellies of the starving babies, not to mention their mammas and daddies. So many arrive ill that the money for medicine alone depletes the funds sent by Friends for our work. Sadly, far too many survive the journey only to fall victim to the ravages of their diseases. And once they pass on, the undertakers will not remove their dead bodies without pay—not that I can blame them—so more money is needed.

"But I tell thee, Julia, though mere living is a struggle for many of the refugees, they are still so grateful, so trusting, so affectionate. Why, some days they nearly squeeze the air right out of me with their hugs of thanksgiving. I would stay here forever to help them if I could." Elizabeth paused, her mind seeming to take another journey, far away from the day-to-day trials in Topeka.

"Some days I long for the temperate climate of my home country. The weather in England is so pleasant compared to the blistering heat of summer and frigid cold of winter in these parts. I am certain I would not have this cough if I were not exposed to these extreme temperatures."

At that moment Elizabeth looked older than her sixty-plus years, with the cares of so many and the enormity of providing for the refugees resting on her shoulders.

"But enough of such dismal talk. There is work to be done." Elizabeth rose from the bed, determined to accomplish as much in the day as was humanly possible.

"But Elizabeth," Julia began to protest, "I believe thee should—"

"Nonsense, dear. Thee will come with me today and begin to learn the details of my work. Someday perhaps thee will be able to manage the office in my absence."

A sense of dread filled Julia. "Thee will always be here!" she said firmly, as if strong words would make it so.

Elizabeth chuckled. "Doest thou believe I am ageless, to be carried off to heaven in a chariot some day like Elijah in the Old Testament? No, my days here are numbered. All I must do is listen to the daily protests of my body to know that someone will soon need to rise up and take over the work. I have admired thee since the first day we met at Iowa Yearly Meeting. Thee is blessed with a sharp mind and a determined will. Both will be necessary to success-fully carry out the work once I am no longer able. But for now, my dear, we must get to the warehouse and see what needs to be done before the governor's arrival."

Julia could see Elizabeth was determined that it would be work as usual in spite of her protests. Sighing, she went back downstairs to wait for her friend and mentor to dress.

"I am really worried about Lizzy," Maggie Hollingsworth said pointedly as Julia sat at the kitchen table to wait. Maggie was a woman known to say exactly what was on her mind. "She jist ain't herself these days. And that cough. Heavenly days you'd think she was gonna cough up a lung the way she goes on."

Even though she shared her landlady's concerns, Julia laughed at the exaggeration. "She is a tough one, Maggie. She will be better before you know it." Julia only wished she felt as confident as she tried to sound.

"I know she's tough . . . pert near tough as me. But she ain't gonna get over that cough if she don't quit goin' down to that cold barn to work."

Julia was afraid Maggie was right. Although Elizabeth's office had a coal-burning stove for warmth, there was no heat in the warehouse where she spent a good part of her day. Maybe I will just insist she stay in her office today, Julia thought. Yes, just like you insisted she stay home, she chided herself. With the governor coming there was no way Elizabeth would have time to sit and rest for any reason—not even for her health.

"You take care of her, will ya Julie? I don't know what I'd do if anything happened to Lizzy." Maggie's voice broke as the worries for her friend overwhelmed her.

Julia felt a lump in her throat as the crusty Maggie Hollingsworth shared her true feelings. "Please do not worry, Maggie. I am going see to it that Lizzy's here to stay with us for a long time."

Now just how was she going to keep that promise?

"I'm telling you, Elizabeth, we have got to do something about the masses of black folk that continue to pour into this state. You can't care for them all, and neither can I." The governor had arrived in the middle of the afternoon, catching Julia and Elizabeth in the midst of helping a new family needing food and bedding. "I've tried to support your work here, but we have got to do something different. This cannot be allowed to continue," he said, staring at the newly arrived family. The governor's words surprised Julia. She had no idea he was so knowledgeable about the refugees.

"I agree," Elizabeth replied, "but other than putting a wall around this entire state I am not certain how you will stop the flow from the South."

"I do have one idea," the governor replied, looking first to Elizabeth and then Julia. Was he wanting her to take his side in this matter? Julia wondered. Surely he would know her loyalties were with her friend. No governor or any other "important" government official would persuade her to turn against Elizabeth.

"And what might that be?" Elizabeth asked warily.

"It seems to me that if we could convince some of our neighboring states—perhaps Illinois, Wisconsin, Minnesota, and Colorado—to take some of these folks off our hands we could share the burden."

"I believe thy idea has merit," Elizabeth said, "but how would thee ever accomplish such a plan?"

"You, Elizabeth Comstock, are the most persuasive woman I have ever heard speak. I am convinced that if you were to go to the statehouses of each of these neighbors and tell them of our plight, you could convince them to accept the former slaves. Once word of opportunities in other states travels back to the South we should be able to handle those who still choose to settle in our state."

Elizabeth's smile was somewhat concealed by the look of shock she intended the governor to see. "Does thee think a little old woman like me could persuade some high and mighty government officials to open their state's gates to the refugees? I am afraid thee has greatly overestimated my skills, Governor."

"No, I am certain you could do the job," the governor continued emphatically. "In fact, I am so certain of it that I have purchased train tickets to each of the capital cities I mentioned to you. You are scheduled to leave in January and travel for eight weeks. Try to get rid of that cough by then, though, or you'll scare them half to death. They will believe working with black folks makes a person sick!" The governor laughed, but neither Julia nor Elizabeth saw the humor in his words.

"And if I say no?" Elizabeth asked.

"You won't. I have seen how you care for these people. I hear the concern in your voice when you speak of the many needs and few resources. You will do this because you care. It is who you are, Mrs. Comstock," he said.

"I suppose thee thinks that is what makes thee a good governor: the ability to read the hearts of people."

"That, and knowing how to smile and kiss the little ones!" he finished with a grin. "I must be on my way now. Here are the train tickets. I am certain your assistant here can manage the work while you are away."

Julia swallowed hard. Had she heard the governor correctly? He believed she could run the Association in Elizabeth's absence? She was an evangelist, for goodness sake. She knew nothing about overseeing an operation as large as the settlement. Laura or John would be much better suited for the position.

"Well, Julia, what does thee think of our governor's suggestion?" Elizabeth asked after the Kansas leader departed.

"I cannot believe you accepted his proposal," Julia said emphatically.

"Does thee not believe in my powers of persuasion?" Elizabeth asked with twinkling eyes.

"No! Thee is the most powerful speaker I have ever heard. I would not be here otherwise."

"Yes, thee would, because it was not Elizabeth Comstock who brought thee here, but the will of God."

"But I came as an evangelist, not as someone who could take over for thee—not that that is possible, of course. Surely Laura or John would be a better choice."

"Thee will do just fine in my absence," Elizabeth assured her. "I am sending Laura to view the conditions in the southeastern corner of the state where it is reported refugees are swarming in like flies. John has his hands full overseeing the training of the men.

"I will only be gone a few weeks and hopefully my mission will eventually free us of some of the burden we now carry. Thee realizes that what we do at the headquarters is only the beginning of the work. Once the men are trained arrangements must be made for them to purchase a small tract of land and a home they can afford with the small wages they make. Surely thee has heard the refugees speak of Littletown, Redville, and Tennesseetown. All are settlements of former slaves who are now fully employed. One family has a grocery business, one a temperance restaurant and lodging, one is a builder. I tell thee, Julia, given the proper training the Negro can be just as successful as any white man. The problem does not lie with the black man; the problem lies in the minds of white men and women who believe the black race to be inferior. In many eyes even the Indian is seen as superior to the Negro. I tell thee, Julia, the older I get the more disappointed I become with my fellow human beings."

Though Julia heard Elizabeth's words, her mind was still contemplating the news of her upcoming duties.

"What is it, Julia? Does thee not agree with my assessment of human nature where the black man is concerned?"

"Oh, no. I agree with every word you said. I was thinking of other matters . . ."

Elizabeth smiled. "Whenever I hear thee say 'you,' I know thee is deep in thought. Please share what thee is thinking."

"I am just contemplating thy confidence in my abilities. If thee believes I can manage the Association in thy absence, then I will do my best. Most of the refugees know nothing of me save what they see in worship, so there will be many who are surprised when they learn I am in charge. But I have worked by thy side on many occasions, so I do believe I know what must be done to make certain things run smoothly in thy absence."

"Wonderful! We have much work to do before I leave, dear. But for now I believe I have given enough of myself to this day. The aches in my bones tell me it is time to return to the warmth of Maggie's kitchen. Yes, I think I will soak my feet in a nice dishpan of warm water and then retire to do a bit of correspondence. If I am going to be traveling to other statehouses I would like to prepare them for my arrival."

Julia smiled. Elizabeth's confidence in her abilities was contagious. If this older, somewhat weakened woman could plan for her future with confidence, why could she not do the same? I will do my best, she vowed. I will not disappoint Elizabeth.

On his bunk in the barracks Hosea thought about the young woman he could never completely chase from his mind. Every day he saw her in worship. Every day he felt anger within, though he could not understand his feelings. Was he angry for having to accept the white man's way of life—which included worship service—in order to have any hope for a future? Or angry that a white girl had somehow managed to get into his thoughts no matter how hard he tried to forget her.

Maybe he had been rude to her the day she had him taken to the infirmary, but she deserved it, thinkin' she knew what was best for him. Why should he care what Miz Julia thought? She knew nothing about the real world. Some said her daddy was a doctor and she lived in a nice house in some place called Iowa. Iowa was as far away to Hosea as Africa. She had no idea what it meant to fight for your life. She had no idea what had been done to his daddy.

Hosea thought once more of the father who was the focus of all his admiration. Following their emancipation his father and five other former slaves had worked several years to save enough money to rent a plantation in southern Mississippi. The plantation had prospered and Hosea's family had managed to build a new home and he and his brothers and sisters worked on the plantation each day to ensure its success. Then one day, a day that would be forever branded in his mind, white men took everything that had ever meant anything to him. Declaring Hosea's daddy and his partners were getting 'too smart for niggers,' a group of white neighbors rode to the plantation and rounded up the black farmers. They took them back to a cabin and hung them from the rafters. Once the men were dead they were cut down and put on a raft to float down the Mississippi with a note saying any man daring to bury the bodies would share the same fate.

White men. White women. White girls. All deserved the same thing: contempt. Hosea would never respect any white person, and he would never listen to anything anyone might say about God. If God allowed one man to do to another what had happened to his daddy, then that God wasn't worth the spit in his mouth. His mamma had been a believer, went to church every Sunday, she did. And what'd it get her? Dead husband and her goin' insane. Hosea wondered where she was, knowing that nothing he could do for her would help now. She went crazy, that she did. When he left for Kansas she was staying with her sister's family. They were poor, too, and there hadn't been room for a seventeen-year-old boy old enough to support himself. He wondered how his younger brothers and sisters were managing without their big brother. He'd had to send them to live with other relatives. Would he ever see their faces again?

Miz Julia, Miz pure, white, perfect Julia. That girl knew nothin' 'bout life. She could preach 'til her dyin' day; others could listen and think what she told 'em was right, but he would never believe a word that passed from her mouth cuz she'd never suffered a day in her life.

Then why you keep thinkin' 'bout her? he asked himself once again. He hated her! Hated the sight of her. Hated everything she represented. He would finish his blacksmith training and move out of this place with all its rules. Once he became a smithy and got a real job he would never set foot in this place again. Never set foot in another church service, either. Never have to look at a white girl tryin' to tell his people how to have hope. Only hope a man had was in the work of his own two hands. 'Course that's what his daddy thought, too. He'd be smarter. Not trust any man, black or white. He'd made it this far, hadn't he? He'd make a new life, and he'd forget about red-haired girls that wanted to haunt him. He was his own god and that was all he needed.

CHAPTER 4

'A Rockin' ALL Night'

"*M*issy . . . ya gots ta come!" The distraught woman, with rags wrapped around her thin body for a makeshift dress, impulsively took Julia's hand. "It's da little one. I can't get her ta wake up." The strained voice and the force of the grip on her hand convinced Julia something was very definitely in need of her attention. And just when she thought she was finished for the day.

"Don't worry," she began, "we can help whatever is troubling thee. Let me get Mrs. Haviland." Julia had been elated to relinquish her leadership role once Laura had returned from her travels in southern Kansas. Though Julia still helped out in the office and warehouse each day, she no longer carried the responsibilities of the relief work solely on her shoulders.

"Laura!" she called down the hall in the direction of Laura's office. When there was no answer, Julia turned back toward the anxious young woman. "Laura will help thee as soon as she returns." Julia was certain Laura, being considerably older than herself, would be able to handle the situation as soon as she returned from whatever errand she was on.

"No, Missy, Hosea says ta bring the girl with fiery red hair. That be you, and you gots ta come right now!"

Julia was startled at the woman's words. "I do not understand. Hosea? Hosea that lives in the barracks?"

"He be da one. Hosea been lookin' out fer me and da little ones since we got here, and he say you da best at gettin' help when someone gots a need."

"But Laura, Mrs. Haviland, has much more experience working with your people, and I know you will want her to help."

"PLEASE! I ain't got time ta stand here. Ma baby may be dead and we jist standin' here. We gots ta go, and we gots ta go now!"

Julia's thoughts were a jumble. Did she dare go alone with this woman? Elizabeth had always said to be careful and stay close to the compound unless you knew exactly where you were going. But the woman seemed to be speaking from her heart. Where are you, Laura? Julia wondered.

Just then Laura came into the relief office. "What is it, Julia? Did thee call for me? I was in the far corner of the warehouse and I came as soon as I could."

Quickly Julia told her of the woman's request. Grabbing her heavy coat from the peg on the wall, Laura motioned for Julia to do the same. "But, I mean, I think thee could manage without me—" Julia began.

"Nonsense. I may need thy help. Get thy coat and come with us now!"

Julia obeyed, trusting Laura as she did Elizabeth. Unfortunately, Elizabeth was still in Illinois and had wired the headquarters to say she would not return until March at the earliest. Julia felt a great sense of gratitude that Laura had safely returned from viewing the conditions in the southern part of the state. Though Julia and Laura were not close friends, Julia greatly respected the woman who was in many ways Elizabeth's right hand.

Following the two women, Julia pulled her coat tightly around her neck. The north wind that bit at their faces and hands seemed to be saying 'turn around, go back.' How was the woman in the lead managing to stay warm with nothing but a light shawl around her shoulders? Julia shivered at the thought.

"They be right over there," she motioned.

Although they had walked only two blocks, this was another world than the streets Julia normally traveled. Near the tracks, the makeshift camp was the place where some of the refugees climbed off the boxcars and decided to stay. Why had these people not come to the Association for help? Julia's mouth dropped open as she scanned the area indicated by the woman. Not a home, not even a cattle shed. The woman was leading them into a tattered tent that had been somehow attached to the side of an old wooden wagon now missing two wheels. Scattered around in more or less a circle were other similar shelters made of boards, scraps of tin, and various odds and ends. A large fire blazed in the middle of the encampment where several men of various ages struggled to keep warm in their thin, tattered clothing. Upon the arrival of the women several men looked toward them, mostly staring at Julia's hair—or so it seemed to her. Eventually their suspicious eyes turned back to the fire. A lone black kettle hung on a tripod near the edge of the fire pit, but no woman seemed to be tending it. Other than the occasional howl of a dog or two there was an eerie quiet to the scene. Julia shivered once again, wondering about the wisdom of being in such a place.

"Well, come on, y'all!" the impatient woman admonished once again. Cautiously Laura, followed by Julia, bent to enter the makeshift door. A putrid odor greeted them, and Julia felt the bile rise in her throat as she scanned the dark interior of the tent for the object of their journey. A still form was lying against the side of the wagon on a platform of some sort, perhaps what had once been a small door. Sitting on a box in the opposite corner were two young boys so similar in appearance that Julia immediately surmised they were twins, probably two or three years of age. There were blankets spread over corn husks at the end of the tent opposite the opening, and a crate containing a pan and some scraps of cloth at the other end. Julia shivered. This was a home. This was the home of these three small children and their mother. Was there a father? If Hosea were watching over the family there must be no other man.

Gently the mother gathered the motionless body of a child Julia estimated to be four or five years of age, several years older than she had expected from the woman's earlier description. The belly of the child protruded grotesquely through the opening in the front of the blanket that was loosely gathered around her. The arms and legs were mere sticks with skin loosely covering them, with no visible muscles. But it was the child's face that haunted her: skin the color of coffee with cream, eyes almost crystal blue, and a tiny mouth. This child looked nothing like her mother. Nor did she look like the majority of Negroes at the refuge. Julia's eyes were once again drawn to the poor child's stomach where she saw a faint movement, announcing life still existed in the emaciated body.

"She been sickly all her life. I done da best I could fer her, but she jist never eat right and never wanna run an' play like da other chilins. Then today she jist not wake up after her nap. I shook 'er 'n shook 'er." With those words the woman began to cry softly, great tears rolling down her cheeks onto the face of the nearly still form in her arms.

It didn't take long for Laura to assess the situation and take action. "Ma'am, first of all, please tell me thy name and the name of thy child."

"I is Betsy and this here's Julianna." Julia's head turned toward the woman at the mention of the child's name. Had she heard right? Julianna? A name nearly the duplicate of her own? She instantly felt a bond with the suffering child.

"All right, Betsy," Laura continued, "we are going to take Julianna to the infirmary. Thee may go with her, of course, but if thee needs to stay with thy other children, Julia and I will take care of her for thee. I do not believe it will be too difficult to carry her the short distance to the infirmary."

"Oh, bless ya, you is an angel...both a yous. I shore do wants ta go with ya, but I don't know who gonna watch da little ones."

"I gonna watch 'em for ya, Betsy."

Julia twisted to see the form in the entrance that belonged to the voice she would have recognized anywhere. "Hosea," she said quietly to no one in particular.

His voice was quiet and gentle, unlike the previous times she had heard him.

"Oh, Hosea, you be jist too good to me and the youngin's. I don' know what we would do without ya!" Then, turning to the twins who had been sitting still as mice in the corner, "You both mind Uncle Hosea, ya hear? He da boss when mamma be gone. We is gonna take Julianna so she kin get all better."

Hosea moved with an air of importance to where the grinning boys were sitting. It appeared this family had taken the place of the one ripped from him. "I kin stay as long as ya needs me, Betsy. Jist make Julianna get well. That's all dat matters now." He picked up the boys and sat down with one on each knee. "We gonna have us some fun tonight, Isaiah and Jeremiah. Now say bye to yer mamma."

Both boys waved goodbye as the women left the tent and quickly headed for the Association headquarters. Taking turns carrying the nearly weightless child, they reached the infirmary in a matter of minutes.

"Julia," Laura began as she carefully laid the child on a bed, "see if Doctor Samuels might still be in the building. I do not see him in this area, but perhaps he is somewhere nearby."

Julia quickly went in search of the compassionate doctor. Calling his name as she walked, she finally found him near the barracks talking to one of the older men who, from his gestures, seemed to be asking the doctor about his arthritis. Julia quickly explained the situation and in no time at all Doc

Samuels was gently examining the child who lay motionless on the bed.

"Ma'am," he asked Betsy, "has this child been eating regularly?"

"Well, it be like I done tol' these here ladies. She never did eat much, and she never wanna run and play."

"Does she cough at night?"

"No sir, not 'less she gots 'namonia."

"And how often does she get pneumonia?"

"Oh, bouts ever' other month er so."

"How about her stomach? Does she complain about pain in her belly?"

"Well, sir, she do complain a lot 'bout dat belly of hers. I jist tell her ta pay no 'tention to it."

"Laura, is there a place on the grounds for this child's mother?"

"Yes, Doctor, I think there is room in the fourth barrack. She also has twin sons back at the, uh, wagon," she said, for lack of a better term to describe their dwelling. "They can stay with Betsy, too, if we need to treat Julianna for more than a day or so."

"All right, mamma," Doc said, turning to Betsy. "you can go back and get your other children and their belongings. I imagine you will all be here for a spell, so you might as well bring whatever valuables you brought with you. What part of the South are you from?"

"Miss'ssippi, sir," she said quietly. "Hosea, he be my neighber there. He already live here at da barracks."

Doc's eyebrows rose at the mention of Hosea and he looked curiously at Julia.

"*Our* Hosea, Julia?"

"Yes," she said, an embarrassed look on her face.

"So am I to presume the young man healed nicely from his previous injuries?" he asked, not willing to let Julia forget her insistence that the doctor check Hosea.

"Yes, as a mater of fact I believe he will soon be finished with his blacksmith training, and then he will have a job and home away from here."

Doctor Samuels looked as though there were more he would like to say, though he simply closed his bag and looked back at the child. Shaking his head he motioned for Laura and Julia to follow him back to the offices.

"She is starving, ladies, plain and simple. That child has been malnourished for at least a year. Whether it has been intentional or not, I can't say. But I can find nothing wrong with her save the lack of nourishment. It seems strange that the mother appears to be in such good health. Has she ever come to the shelter in the past to ask for food for her children?"

"Not that I remember, Doctor," Laura answered. "But there are days when several dozen men and women come to the warehouse for supplies. Most likely I would not remember whether I had seen her or not. Some of the refugees feel it is a disgrace to accept food and goods from us so they live in the kind of poverty this woman shares with the others by the tracks."

"And it is the children who suffer most." Doc just shook his head and looked back at Julianna. "It is my belief that given proper food and rest the child's body will respond. It has nearly shut down in order to preserve what little life is still present. You will have to begin with weak broth from a dropper. When she will take the broth and keep it in the stomach we will move to milk. Is there enough dry milk in the supply room?"

"I believe Elizabeth made a large milk purchase before she left in order to assure we would not run short for the children in the barracks," Laura replied.

"Good. Then do as I say and I will check on her each day until she is strong enough to move to the barracks. I would get those other two children in here too, because their condition is no doubt similar to their sister's."

Julia thought about the two little boys she had seen sitting on Hosea's knees. Even in the dim light of the tent dwelling the boys had not seemed to be suffering like their sister. In fact, they had seemed quite healthy.

"We will do our best," Laura said quietly.

"I know you will." There was a softer quality to Doc Samuel's next words. "You do a really fine work here, Laura, and I know Elizabeth feels comfortable leaving you in charge."

"Actually, before she left she asked Julia to care for the work." Laura's smile was kind though Julia would have preferred she not reveal her former position to the doctor.

Doc Samuels turned to look more closely at Julia. "Elizabeth left you in charge?" He might as well have added 'what ever possessed her to do such a thing?' because Doc's expression revealed his disbelief.

Julia decided her best answer was a simple, "Yes."

"My, my. I never will understand you women. It is some-times a burden for me to give an hour or two each evening to these people. But I can't fault the work you do here. Who knows what would have happened to hundreds of these poor souls if Elizabeth hadn't stepped in and taken over. Julia, I apologize if my words were unkind. You just seem so young to me. Why, I have granddaughters your age. But I suppose one's age is not as important as one's desire to serve."

"Now that Laura is back from her travels in the south of Kansas, she is the one in charge. I merely try to help where the need is greatest."

"Now Julia," Laura protested, "if anything we are partners in this work, thee and I. Together we try to make everything run smoothly."

Julia smiled at the woman nearly twenty years her senior. She never acted that old, Julia thought. I hope I will have as much energy when I am her age.

"I'll see you both tomorrow if you are here when I make my rounds. I'll be anxious for a report on our little patient. And good luck. I don't believe she's eaten for some time and she may need a bit of coaxing to take the broth and swallow it."

Getting Julianna to accept the nourishment was more of a challenge than Julia would have dreamed. For whatever rea-sons, the child seemed to rally her strength and would not allow her mother to squeeze the dropper of broth into her mouth. With jaws clenched tightly the liquid ran down her chin but not in her mouth. Laura tried with similar results. Julia wondered if she might be more successful, remembering a few months earlier when she had played games with her little sister when she had not wanted to eat following an illness.

"May I try?" she finally asked.

Betsy looked at Julia; Laura looked at Julia; and Julianna looked at Julia. Without speaking Betsy handed the frail child to Julia. Talking very quietly, Julia tried to make some kind of connection with the young child who felt as light as a feather in her arms. She talked; she sang; she hummed; she talked some more. Then, when Julia thought she could feel the child relax in her arms, she touched the broth in the bowl and then put her finger to Julianna's lips. Over and over she repeated the action until the child was sucking on her finger. Eventually she was able to feed her with the dropper.

There was a strange look in Betsy's eyes; not admiration, nor gratitude, but unhappiness. Her face did not speak of the relief Julia thought she should have felt. Julia was puzzled. She thought most mothers would have been jumping for joy.

When Betsy did not return to the campsite, Hosea brought the twins to the infirmary where he told Betsy he would take the boys to the barracks to spend the night with him. Once everyone was settled in their respective places for the night, Laura and Julia headed for Maggie's. The wind was even sharper than it had been earlier in the evening, and Julia shuddered as she thought of the encampment by the tracks. At least Hosea had brought the little boys to stay with him in the barracks. His behavior that evening had been so different than their previous meetings. Had something happened? Had he become more tolerant of her and those trying to help him? She truly hoped so.

"Julia," Laura interrupted her thoughts. "Did thee think it strange Betsy was not filled with joy at the news her daughter would recover with proper nourishment?"

"A bit," Julia admitted. "And another thing that seems strange to me is that the twins seem to be rather healthy." She paused a moment, then continued. "Even so, I suppose it has been a difficult time for her and the family. She must have managed to get them all this far, but that tent is no place for children or adults."

"Thee is right about that. I have never seen such living conditions, not even fit for cattle, let alone human beings."

"Laura, thee has been here almost from the beginning of the work. Does thee think the Negroes will continue to move north to free states like Kansas? And if they do, who will care for them? Will Friends see this as important as the Indian work?"

"Julia, that question is one that weighs heavily on my heart. Friends have long recognized the need to evangelize and provide for the Indians. At the Kansas Yearly Meeting in November we spent nearly an entire day hearing reports from the various Indian Affairs committees. But when Elizabeth asked to speak on behalf of the freedmen she was offered a few minutes and then Friends did what Friends always seem to do: appointed a committee to study the issue. Studying is not what is needed; action is needed. I am not certain how to convince Friends of the expediency of committing funds and collecting supplies for these needy souls. If we could somehow capture a picture of what we saw tonight and engrave it in the minds of

Friends everywhere then perhaps their compassion would be kindled and we could do so much more than we are doing."

As they reached their destination Julia turned and embraced this woman so filled with love and compassion. "Thee is the perfect woman for this work, Laura. I wish I had as much care and concern as thee has. Maybe worship services would have real meaning for these people if thee were to lead them."

"But thee does care, Julia," Laura said gently, "thee does. I see it in thy eyes; I see it in thy hands as thee cares for the sick and needy; I see it in the gentle way thee held Julianna and loved her tonight. Thee is young, Julia, and thee has many years to do God's work. I only wish I had begun to feel as thee does at thy age."

As Julia collapsed into bed Laura's words came to mind, giving her a warm feeling. Perhaps she was doing what God expected. Perhaps she was not a failure after all. Perhaps she would finally go to Hosea and ask about the Negro spirituals. Drifting off to sleep Julia felt a peace she had not known for many weeks.

CHAPTER 5

'Rise Up, Shepherd, AND Follow'

*J*ulianna continued to improve each day under the constant watch of Julia. Much to Julia's surprise, only a week after their arrival Betsy and the twins came into the office with the announcement of their departure.

"But, Betsy, thee cannot take Julianna yet, she is too small!" Julia cried.

"You alls kin take better care o' her here and I's needed back at da camp grounds."

Julia was speechless. What mother would abandon a child who had been on death's door only days before? Julianna would be frightened without her mother, would she not? But as Julia thought of the past week she realized that Betsy rarely held the child, seldom talked to her, and always left the feeding to Julia. Julia tried to recall the day Betsy had come seeking their help. She had seemed concerned then. It was a strange situation with more questions than answers.

"If da child gits well, den I reckon yous can bring her back to ma place. Come on, Isaiah and Jeremiah, we gots to get back home."

Julia shuddered at the word "home," remembering the scene of a week earlier. How could anyone call a tattered tent nailed to a broken wagon a home? Julia thought of her home in Salem. It was not fancy by many standards because of the Friends belief in simplicity, but compared to where this family lived it was heaven on earth. No one she knew in Salem had ever experienced such poverty. She remembered how the families of the community always pulled together when a tragedy struck. There had been a ravaging fire that left a family with nothing but the clothes on their backs. Another time a flood had filled the homes along the Skunk River with murky water, covering everything with a slick coat of smelly, slimy mud. And who could forget the drought several years before that resulted in farm families having no crops to sell to provide for their families. In each case Julia remembered how members of the Salem Meeting had brought food and clothing as well as offered their labor to rebuild what had been destroyed.

Where was the help for these black people? There was no Friends meeting in Topeka; the closest Friends meetinghouse took nearly a day to reach. Why were the Baptists and Lutherans not helping out? It was almost as if the so-called believers were deaf and blind to the suffering in places like the area Betsy called home. Why was there no compassion?

Where is thy compassion, Julia? Does thee think preaching is the answer to every man's needs? It is not enough to merely pity the people. Thee must understand how they live. Until thee can identify with their needs thy compassion is as dry bones.

Julia shook her head. Where had that message come from? Was she imagining things? Was her conscience trying to tell her something? Could it be the Holy Spirit speaking?

"Juwea? I is firsty."

"Okay, honey," Julia called to Julianna. "I will get thee some cool water and be right back."

Julia looked across the office and through the door where the child lay just inside the infirmary. Julia had moved the bed so she could keep a close eye on her young patient while she worked in the office. Taking the empty pail she shivered at the thought of going out in the cold to pump water for Julianna. But she would do anything for the precious child she had come to love. Was that compassion? Feeling so much love for a person that one is willing to put aside personal discomfort to see that the other's needs are met? But how am I to love a whole group of people in that manner?

Seek the answers. Get to know these people as my children who need a Savior. A Savior who can only minister to them through your hands and feet.

That is what I thought I had been doing.

No, you have been playing evangelist. And you wonder why no one is moved by your words. They need your hands and feet to move them, not your lips.

Who was this voice in her head? Could it truly be the Holy Spirit? Whatever the source, Julia was not certain she liked what she was hearing. Did it matter whether the voice was from the Spirit or just her own conscience? It was the message that was important, and the message seemed to be: you, Julia Jones, do not really know these people you are trying to reach with your ministry.

How could she learn more about the refugees? Could Hosea help her understand? He was a Negro who had surely lived through tragedies. But Hosea barely spoke to her. I have got to try, she thought. There will never be any peace in my soul until I find the answers to these questions.

Though the temperatures were mild for the first of March, Julia shivered as she worked the pump handle to fill the pail. Even the thought of seeking answers from Hosea was chilling. Hosea hated her. No, that could not be true or he would not have told Betsy to seek her help. He may not hate me, but he will not want to talk to me, either, she thought. But I will have no peace until I do my best to persuade him to share his feelings with me. I will go tonight.

When Julia's work was finished for the day she told Julianna she would be gone for a while but would be back to tell her a story before bedtime. Although there were no words from Julianna's mouth, the look in her eyes was one of fear. Fear of being abandoned? Fear of being harmed? Probably both. Hugging her as tightly as she dared, Julia's arms spoke of her love and care for the four-year-old. For the first time since coming to the infirmary, Julianna's arms reached out to return the embrace. Julia felt her eyes fill with tears. Is this how it feels to be a mother? she wondered. And then the familiar questions of her own future stirred in her mind. Would she have a husband and children some day? Why could she not be content with this call to minister? Was it her own selfish desires that were getting in the way of doing all God asked her to do? Having no answers, she left quickly to search for Hosea.

Unlike earlier in the day, the cool temperatures of evening had no effect on Julia. Her cheeks were flushed as she tried to form in her mind the conversation they might have once she found Hosea. No words seemed appropriate. How will he know what I am seeking, she wondered.

Julia walked quickly toward the barracks, passing the nearly completed school building. She smiled as she thought of the days of persuasion it had taken to convince Elizabeth of the need for a school.

"But Julia," Elizabeth had said at first, "there are so many other pressing needs. We must build more barracks, we need buildings for job training, and we are nearly out of storage space."

"But Elizabeth," Julia had said time and again, "education is what will make the biggest difference in the lives of these people." Education was never far from Julia's mind. Her mother, Rebecca, had been a teacher when she first came to Iowa, and her uncle, Levi, taught Julia and her friends for two years at the Pleasant Plain Academy. Levi was now a professor at William Penn College in Oskaloosa where Iowa Yearly Meeting was held each year. Her father and brother had both trained for the medical profession in Chicago. If a person were not educated there was little hope of providing for themselves and a family, of that Julia was convinced.

Finally Elizabeth had agreed to authorize the construction of a school for the Negro refugee children, though Julia was not certain whether she was truly convinced of the importance of a good education or just tired of hearing Julia expound on the subject day and night. The school was scheduled to be finished in a few weeks. Maybe even Hosea could go to school, Julia thought, then quickly realized a man of his age would no doubt feel too embarrassed to be learning with younger children. Then I can teach him to read and write myself, she thought determinedly. Perhaps then I can understand what his life has been like.

Hosea does not need you to educate him out of pity. He needs to know you care and accept him as he is. That is all.

"But how do I do that?" Julia asked out loud, shaking her head.

As she passed the school she crossed an open area where the children often played. The ground was still hard from the winter's freeze but the small footprints that were once a common winter sight had disappeared with the melting snow. Soon it will be mud prints, Julia thought, knowing how the children liked to play in that area no matter what the weather was like.

Continuing on the well-worn path, Julia came to the first barrack. She knew that older men with no families stayed there. These men were very protective of the others living in their community.

"Evnin', Miz Julia," said the man she had confronted the night Hosea had been hurt. He was standing outside the cabin with two other men.

"Good evening, Moses. It is nice to see thee again."

Moses chuckled. "I don't 'spect that be quite da truth, Miz Julia. Why is you down here dis evenin'?

Wanting to be on her way, but not knowing where to find Hosea presented a problem. If she admitted she were looking for him, would the men try to keep her from him? Finally she swallowed her pride and asked for help.

"I would like to speak with Hosea if thee could tell me where I might find him. I am not certain which cabins are for the families and which one is for young men."

The look on Moses' face was a mixture of disbelief and anger. "You ain'ts got no bizness stickin' your nose in dat youngin's life. He gots 'nough troubles without you tryin' ta talk ta him 'bout dat fancy religion you spouts ever' day."

"But you do not understand! I have to . . . I need to . . . " How did a young girl explain to an old black Negro the need to understand a different way of life in order to have compassion?

Evidently the look on her face said more than the words she could not express because a gentler expression replaced the angry one, and he wordlessly pointed to the far barrack. "But ya might not find him in. Young Hosea be jist 'bout da most independent soul on this here earth!"

"I thank thee, Moses," Julia said kindly as she turned toward the barrack he'd indicated.

Walking quickly before she could lose her nerve, Julia marched to the door and knocked sharply. When there was no answer she knocked even louder.

"He most likely won't come out."

Julia jumped at Moses's voice. Somehow in her anxiety she had not noticed him following her. "Then what will I do? I must talk to him!"

Moses looked again at the beautiful young woman. Of course her hair was her most outstanding feature, but her eyes were clear green pools that seemed to shimmer in the evening's dim light. Her facial features were small, perfectly matching the thin body beneath the light coat she had hurriedly thrown on her shoulders. But it was more than her physical beauty that one was attracted to. There was pride, and spirit, and energy to tackle whatever problems came her way. That had been evident the night Hosea was hurt in the fight and Julia insisted he be cared for.

Even to an old man like Moses, everything about Miz Julia was perfect, and that was the problem. Hosea, like any young man, would be blind not to notice her beauty, both inward and outward. Moses shook his head. No good could come from the young white girl associatin' with Hosea—if that was what she was aimin' to do. No good ever came from black folk mixin' with white. But Hosea knew that, didn't he? Be best he jist let the young man tell Julia hisself that she don' belong here at da barracks.

Opening the heavy wooden door to the cabin, Moses looked inside. Moving through the door Julia could hear his feet shuffle to the far cabin wall. Shaking a figure on a lower bunk, Moses roused the young man. "Hosea. Wake up. You bein' da only one in here sleepin' oughts ta tell ya its too early ta be callin' it a day. There's somebody here ta see ya."

"Let me be, ol' man," was the uncooperative response.

"No, ya needs ta come with me, boy. It's somethin' ya needs ta do."

After several minutes had passed the two black figures emerged from the cabin. Still half asleep, Hosea shook his head as if to clear away a bad dream. Looking again at Julia he muttered something to the old man.

"Ain't gonna hurt nothin', son, jist ta talk ta her a bit. Then ya can go back ta sleep—ifin ya can," he seemed to add as an afterthought.

'"Whats you want?" Hosea asked curtly.

"Just a chance to understand." Julia had no way of knowing how to word her request.

Hosea's eyebrow raised at her strange reply. "Well, what's you tryin' ta understand?"

"Could we talk in my office?" she asked, feeling uncomfortable in the presence of the older man.

"Jist say what be on yer mind," Hosea said coldly.

She could not do it. Not here, not standing out in the middle of the circle of barracks with Grandpa Moses listening to every word. "I am sorry. This was a mistake." Julia was fighting the tears that caused her voice to quiver and threatened to spill down her cheeks if she did not leave immediately. Turning to go she felt the steel grip of Hosea's hand on her arm.

"I go."

Afraid to look up, Julia kept walking back toward the offices. Though it was only a short distance, it seemed like a hundred miles. She could not see him, but she knew by his soft footsteps that Hosea was behind her. How did such a large man walk so quietly? And why such a sudden change of heart? Would she ever understand this complex man?

"In here," Julia pointed to her office as they entered the headquarters. Her first task was to check on Julianna. Seeing the child sleeping, she gently closed the door to the infirmary, but made certain the door to her office remained opened. Julia did not want anyone to think there was something improper happening when she talked to Hosea. She took longer than necessary to complete the simple task of taking off her coat. Her thoughts were a whirlwind: what should she say? How could she make Hosea understand her need to know everything about his life?

Pointing for him to sit on one of the two wooden chairs in front of the desk, Julia chose to sit behind the security her desk provided.

"I do not exactly know what to say," she began. "We seem to have gotten off to a bad start. I have been praying for thee—all of the refugees, that is—and the Spirit has been speaking to my heart."

Hosea's eyebrows rose. "Da Spirit speaks to your heart?"

Although there was a touch of sarcasm in his voice, Julia was certain there might also be a trace of admiration. "I would like to know some of the songs thee sang when thee was a slave. I thought it might help with the worship,"

"Oh, I gits it. You wants me ta help ya with that gawd-awful thing ya all call wership. Well, I ain't gonna do it. Like I says to ya before—I don't believe in no God cuz there's no God that's gonna let them white men do what they did ta ma daddy 'n momma."

Julia sensed an instant change in Hosea. Whereas before he had been agreeable to go with her, now he could not get away fast enough; whereas before his face held little emotion, now it was filled with hatred toward her. His hatred seemed to include all white people and their God.

"No, wait!" Julia cried, impulsively grabbing his shirt as he rose to leave. She felt sick as she heard the material rip. "I am sorry! I am so sorry! I will get thee another shirt from the warehouse! Immediately!"

"Jist like always, you white folk thinks you kin put a piece a cloth on da body 'n' change it, magic-like, to be jist like you. It ain't gonna happen, lily-white, I tells ya it jist ain't never gonna happen!"

"But that is what I need to know!" Julia cried out. "What is it like to be a Negro? What thoughts do you think? What feelings do you feel? What makes you sad? What makes you happy?"

"What's it matter ta you? I's black, you's lily-white. Ain't nothing on this earth gonna change that. No talkin', no fancy clothes, no white man job. I's still gonna be black and that's what yous white folk gots ta get figur'd out."

"What harm would it do to tell me about your life as a slave? How can I ever understand if you refuse to talk to me? How can I relate to your people if I do not know what you have suffered?" she pleaded.

Hosea looked skeptical, but this time he did not say no. "What yous think if I tells you my daddy got hung by da rafters of our cabin cuz' he make too much money on da plantation? Hows you feel if I tells you that my mammy went crazy and had to go live with her sister and her po' family? Then there be ma bruders and sisters . . . ain't never gonna see 'em again, that for sure. Wishin' I could save that forty-seven dollars it take ta git 'em moved here. Don't even have a job yet. They probly be married and have youngins by da time I has a real job. That what you wants ta know?" Hosea's voice was calmer now, but the pain was still fresh in his memory.

"Yes. Please tell me more."

Hosea proceeded to tell Julia of the atrocities that had happened to him and others following the war. He told her of the regulators, local white men who took the government in their own hands to make sure Negroes were kept in their places.

"They come ever night ta black folks' cabins. Sometimes they jist try ta put a scare in folks; other times they rape da women 'n torture da men.

He shook his head sadly. "When our neighbor didn't know where her husband be one night, they took her out of da cabin and hung her." He told of another Negro who refused to sell his vote to a regulator and was taken to the nearby woods and hung—along with his three sons.

Story after story poured from Hosea's memory. Stories of Negroes unable to recover debts owed them by white men. Former slaves working for a small pittance and then swindled in their attempts to trade with the cheating white men. The sanctity of the Negro's homes was in no way respected, nor their attempts to educate their children. He told of schoolhouses that were burned to the ground and black teachers treated brutally by their white neighbors.

The most heart-wrenching story, however, was saved for last. Joshua had been an older friend of Hosea's and the two of them had talked many times of moving to the North to escape the fear they lived with each and every day. Joshua, who had a wife and three small children, finally decided to head for the promised land in Kansas to see if there might be a future there for all of them. Hosea promised to watch over his family while he was gone. Several months later Joshua returned with enough money for his family and Hosea to make the trip back to Kansas. He told stories of opportunities for those with ambition.

I gots ambition, ain't I? Hosea had asked himself, and the decision was quickly made: he would go with Joshua and his family.

Hosea was harvesting a field next to Joshua's cabin the next morning when he heard the pounding of horses' hooves approaching the cabin. Staying out of sight, he watched and listened as the men called Joshua out of the cabin.

"We hear you been busy these last few months, Joshua," he heard them say. "Why, those hands of yours must be mighty industrious. You think you can go up north and tell stories about how terrible we white men are? Well, let's show Joshua here what happens when niggers get to thinkin' they're just a little bit better than us white folks." And then they cut off Joshua's hands and put them in the lap of his hysterical wife. "Now go to Kansas," they mocked him as he lay bleeding to death in front of his wife and children.

"I knew where Joshua hid da money he make in Kansas, 'n I waits till da middle of da night." Hosea continued the story. "I sneaks in da cabin and gits da money and Betsy and da chilins and we runs fast as our legs take us, me carryin' da twins 'n Betsy wif da girl. And we never looks back. I be like a uncle to da chillins, and I do my best ta watch after them."

Julia was weeping softly as Hosea finished.

"That enough fer ya today? You still thinks ya wants to know what it be like ta be a black man?" he asked, rising to leave.

"Yes," Julia said quietly. "I do. "

Hosea just shook his head. "No, missy, ya don't. It be a ugly world and da white man is da ugliest of all da creatures on this earth. I is sorry to say that to ya, but it be da truth."

Yes, Julia thought, it probably is the truth. How could one man do those awful things to another? How could it happen when slaves had been granted their freedom? Even more importantly, how could she reach out to this young man and the hundreds like him who had suffered such atrocities at the hands of her race?

"Hosea . . . "

"Yessum?"

"Would thee come back tomorrow night and teach me one of the songs thy people sang when they sat around the campfires at night?"

"When we was slaves, ya mean?"

"Yes, I want to be able to use your people's spirituals in worship."

Hosea shook his head. "Won't do no good," he said, "but I guess ifin' ya wants me to, I could do it. Ain't got nuthin' else ta do of an evenin' cept visit Betsy and her kin."

Julia wanted to ask him the questions she had about Betsy and her treatment of Julianna, but was afraid to say any more this first night. Hosea had revealed so much of who he was. No wonder he seems so bitter, she thought. But there was hope, of that she was certain. Under the tough exterior was a gentle, loving heart, and Julia would be the one to open that heart. It would be her mission.

CHAPTER 6

Jacob's Ladder

*E*lizabeth's return the first week in May was as welcome as the newly blooming prairie flowers. She was a breath of fresh air, with tales of places and Friends she had visited.

"I was delighted, of course, to actually speak with John Whittier," Elizabeth began late one First Day afternoon as she, Julia, Laura, and Maggie sat on Maggie's front porch enjoying the fresh-smelling spring air. The faithful women had left for home early as First Days were normally quiet at the Association and this was no exception. Maggie was more like a family member than a landlady, and she often enjoyed times of conversation with her boarders.

"John Greenleaf Whittier, the poet?" Laura asked with surprise in her voice.

"Yes, John Greenleaf Whittier, the Friends poet."

"Did thee know he once taught at the Friends Academy in Salem?" Julia asked excitedly.

"No, but I am not surprised. That man has lived in so many places it would make one's head swim," she said with a laugh. "He is as compassionate a man as I have known, next to my dear husband, of course, who cheerfully runs our household in my absence and allows me to be off on these missions!" she said, still chuckling.

"It simply amazes me to think Friend Whittier has written a letter to every influential man and woman he knows—and he knows many, I dare say. He just asks them to send whatever money they can and to give from their abundance. He compels them to feed and clothe the naked, give a bed to a family that has none, or give the price of a pair of boots or shoes. He even asks them to give garden tools, implements, seeds . . . I tell you the man is a powerful writer! That letter made me want to come right back here and get to work, it did."

Julia stared at Elizabeth with admiration, just as she had done many other times since their first encounter. Had Elizabeth heard the horrible stories Hosea told her, she wondered? Was that the source of her passion to carry on this work?

"Tell us about the places thee visited, please?" Julia begged.

"Oh, let me see. First, I visited the state legislature in Illinois to enlighten those gentlemen as to their need to help Kansas shelter and provide for some of the refugees."

"Were they receptive?" Laura asked.

"Yes, at least I believe they will follow through with their promise to accept several thousand of the Negroes. One can never be certain with government officials, however." Elizabeth's tone spoke of her frustrations with the law-making bodies she had tried to work with in the past.

"From Illinois I traveled by train to our nation's capital where once again I spoke with legislators of our problems here. I repeatedly told them of our inability to get the goods shipped by our English Friends into our country duty-free. I tried to explain how these were charitable goods donated by religious men and women desiring to help the refugees. I also told them how the shipping companies were waiving the charges on the goods brought across the ocean, and how the rail companies were willing to ship the items from the ocean dock to Kansas free of charge. The only fly in the ointment is with the bureaucracy in our federal government! It is imperative that a bill be drafted in Washington to waive the duty on these goods. I spoke with every influential man I could find who would listen to me, and I wrote at least fifty letters to others with whom I could not get an interview. It is such a burden to me to think that our government can spend thousands of dollars sending relief to the needy in Ireland while failing to support such a simple bill as this. It does not require our government to spend one penny from our treasury, merely to set aside the charges it would normally levy."

"What is the status of the bill?" Julia asked.

"It is scheduled for a vote any day now, but I have little hope it will pass. For some reason there is distrust of any work with the freedmen. Not a single congressman has visited our work. No one will listen to the stories Negroes tell us, stories of black men, women, and children suffering at the hands of whites in the South. Not a soul seems to care whether these people have food or clothing or shelter." She shook her head sadly. "It is most discouraging."

"But what about that cough of yours?" Maggie interrupted. "I don't s'pose ya took very good care of yourself while you was gone."

"Maggie, Maggie . . . I do believe thee has a heart of gold underneath thy tough old skin. I am pleased to tell thee my cough is nearly gone and I have more energy than I have had in some time."

"Well, that is a blessin', I must admit. I was powerful worried 'bout ya traipsin' round the countryside like ya did."

Elizabeth reached over and squeezed the elderly woman's hand. "I do thank thee for caring about my health, Maggie. I will do my best to ease thy worries."

Elizabeth paused, thinking back over her travels of the past weeks. "I did have one interesting meeting in our own state capitol building."

"Tell us about it," Julia encouraged.

"There were agents from the Sandwich Islands and Hawaii who wanted me to help persuade some of the refugees to relocate on their islands. It seems there are many plantations in need of labor to harvest their sugar cane. Oh, they were not talking slave labor, but were offering paying jobs to men and women who would move there. They would pay for all the expenses to relocate as well. I asked them why they wanted my help and they explained they could not get one refugee to take them up on their offer. It seems when the Negroes hear the word 'plantation' they are frightened that once they get there they will be forced into slavery. Having heard the Negroes respected us because of our work here, the agents begged me to try and convince some of the refugees to make the move."

"Has thee tried?" Julia asked. She had seen Elizabeth visiting with many of the men outside the barracks in the evenings since her return.

"I believe I did my best. I am not convinced those with families would be happy so far away from loved ones, but I did ask a number of them to consider the offer. Most just shook their heads, not willing to risk what they have here for the unknown. Perhaps it would be good for the right families, but who am I to know which ones to choose?"

Julia thought of Hosea, and Betsy and her children. Would a tropical island be good for them? Surely not. They were settled here now, were they not? For some reason the thought of Hosea leaving the country left Julia with an empty feeling inside. That is ridiculous, she thought firmly. I have no interest in where Hosea chooses to settle down. In her heart, however, she knew that was not quite the truth.

Elizabeth continued to share details of the cities, Friends meetings, and government officials she visited. It was her last comment that surprised Julia.

"I just wish our Friends papers would quit disputing 'nonessentials' like the second baptism, holiness, and the Inner Light, and unite all our forces and strength to aid poor, suffering humanity. The time and talent and money would be much better spent caring for the refugees. I told them so, too, when I visited the publishers of *Friends' Review*."

Julia's face reflected her surprise at Elizabeth's criticism of the periodicals her father so passionately read when time allowed. Charles had been so enthused with the papers that he had often pointed out articles for her to read when she was living at home. Elizabeth's words, however, certainly made a great deal of sense. What good was it to debate spiritual issues when there was such physical need? She thought again of Hosea. She could not keep his disgust with her God from her mind. What would he think of her father delighting in the persuasive articles of powerful writers? Not much. Hosea would scoff at those papers just as he scoffed at every other part of her life.

"I believe I will go to my room," Laura said rising. "My headache has gotten worse as the day has progressed and I need to lie down."

"An' my old arthritis is actin' up again," Maggie added, "an' these cool evnin's set my joints afire."

"And thee, my dear," Elizabeth inquired when she and Julia were alone, "what about thy life? Laura told me thee did an admirable job in my absence, but what else has been happening?"

How did Elizabeth always seem to know when there was something on her mind? Julia wondered. "I have continued to lead worship each day," she began, "and although I wish it were more meaningful for the refugees, I do feel the presence of the Holy Spirit most days."

"And what is the Spirit saying to thee?" Elizabeth asked gently.

Julia found herself pouring out the story of the Spirit prompting her to learn about compassion and caring for the Negro people. She even told her of Hosea, for to leave him out would have made her story less than truthful.

Elizabeth's eyes searched the face of the beautiful young woman who sat before her, so eager to do what God had asked yet so innocent in her knowledge of the world of the refugees. And what of this young man Hosea? Surely Julia would not be so foolish as to allow feelings to develop for a black man. What words of experience could she offer?

"How does thee feel about Hosea's spiritual progress?" Elizabeth asked cautiously.

Julia's head dropped in defeat. "He does not believe in a God who could allow men to torture and kill other men, often in the presence of their families."

"And what has thee told him about God's love for him?"

"Nothing. I do not know where to begin, Elizabeth. Perhaps thee can tell me what to say to convince him of the Truth as we believe."

Elizabeth shook her head. "It is not for me to say, Julia. Remember the scripture verse that says the Spirit will intercede when we know not what words to speak? Thee must be led of the Spirit, the Inner Light, Julia. Then the words will not be thy own but the exact words Hosea needs to hear."

"But what if I say the wrong things? Hosea will hardly speak to me, though he did teach me one song from the time he was a slave."

"What was that?"

"Something about Jacob and a ladder."

"Ah, yes. 'Jacob's Ladder'."

"Thee knows that song?" Julia asked in astonishment.

"Yes, I know many of the Negro spirituals."

"But—but—when I asked thee about trying to learn some of the spirituals thee told me it was a good idea to ask the refugees."

"Yes, I did. It was not to make extra work for thee, Julia, it was to enable thee to have a way to reach out to these people that only see thee in worship each morning."

Julia's face felt flushed. She had asked no one but Hosea, and he had been reluctant to give her the words to even one song, let alone many. Why had she not gone to some of the women who sat around the fire in the middle of the barracks preparing the meals each night? Surely they would have been more cooperative than Hosea.

Because thee wanted a reason to talk to him.

Julia knew the accusatory voice spoke the truth.

"I am sorry, Elizabeth. I feel like I have let thee down. I suppose I wanted a chance to talk to Hosea again," she admitted.

"And how does thee truly feel about Hosea?" Elizabeth asked quietly.

"He needs a Savior!" she said emphatically.

"And would that be thee?"

"No! I mean, he needs to know that Jesus died a death every bit as terrible as those he has seen, and the reason He died was so Hosea could have his sins forgiven. He will never be free from the bitterness he carries unless he can receive the forgiveness of our Lord."

"Thee is right, Julia, and if some day Hosea becomes a believer, then how will thee feel?"

Why was Elizabeth asking her all these questions? Did she think Julia felt something other than compassion for Hosea? Surely not! Even the thought made Julia uncomfortable. Why would Elizabeth believe such a thing?

"If Hosea accepts the promise of forgiveness from God and becomes a changed man then I shall be happy for him. That is all." Julia hoped the firmness of her voice would put the issue to rest once and for all.

Elizabeth just smiled.

Was she finished speaking? Julia wondered.

"I believe I have had enough for one day," Elizabeth finally said. "I hope thee sleeps well tonight. It is good to be back with my faithful partners who have done a valiant work in my absence. It is a relief to know that if I were to return to my husband in Michigan the work here would continue to run smoothly."

"Oh no! Please do not say that," Julia implored. "We need thee! Of course I am certain thy husband would be happy for thy return, but thee must stay until the work is complete."

Elizabeth smiled again. "God needs each of us to do His work, Julia, and when one leaves He equips another to carry on." And with that she rose and left.

Julia sat for a long time pondering the work Elizabeth always seemed to accomplish. What was it that made her such an effective instrument of God? Would she, Julia Jones, ever feel so confident of her own abilities? She was not even successful convincing Hosea of his need for God. I must try harder, she resolved. I will speak to him as soon as the opportunity arises. God, please provide that opportunity, she prayed as she went in to prepare for the night.

"Julia, there is someone here who would like to speak with thee," Laura called from just outside the main entrance to the offices several days later. Julia had been helping Julianna eat her lunch, amazed that her young charge had made such re-markable progress and would soon be able to return to her family.

Maybe it is Hosea, Julia thought, her heart beating a bit faster. She had been praying earnestly that God would bring Hosea to her, or that their paths would cross in such a way as to open the door for her to speak with him about salvation.

"Julia!"

Julia blinked to make certain her eyes were not playing tricks on her.

"David?"

"Julia!" he said again, moving quickly to embrace the sister he had not seen in almost a year.

"What . . . what is thee doing here?" she stammered.

"I came for a visit," he said rather triumphantly.

"But, how did thee, I mean, why did thee, when did thee . . ."

David laughed. "Oh Julia, thee has not changed one bit!"

Julia frowned. Surely something about her had changed in the time she had been away. She knew she had changed.

"Thee is just as pretty as ever."

"Oh," Julia giggled, "and thee is just as great a flatterer! Where is Hannah? Did she accompany thee? Did thee come together on the train?"

"No, Hannah was not able to make the trip. She is due to deliver our first child in two months and we did not feel she should make the trip at this time. I took the Atchison and Sante Fe and arrived here an hour ago."

"Oh David, I am so happy for thee," Julia said, giving this brother she had sorely missed another hug. "Thee is lucky to have Hannah, and lucky to be starting a family. I know that is what thee both wanted."

"Yes, it is. Hannah is such a wonderful wife, and she will be an even more wonderful mother," he said, admiration filling his voice. "But what about thee? I want to know all about thy work. We —Hannah and I—have often wondered exactly what it is that thee does on this barren prairie. Barely a tree in sight, and acres and acres of flat land!"

"There is so much to tell. How long will you be staying?"

"Ah, that's my little sister," David smirked. "Never could remember to use 'thee' and 'thou' all the time. Tell the truth, Julia. All those years when we were growing up, did thee forget to use the plain language of Friends or did thee choose not to use it when it suited thy purposes?"

"That is something thee will never know, dear brother." Julia smiled as she thought of the times David chided her for her improper language, though never in anger or in a superior tone of voice. Though she would never tell him, the truth was simple: sometimes she forgot and sometimes she deliberately chose the more natural 'you'. To Julia, the issue of language was one of those things Elizabeth referred to as 'non-essentials,' not worthy of all the fuss.

"How is mother? And Rachel?" Julia asked. Seldom a day passed that she did not wonder what her mother and little sister were doing. Their letters had been few and far between, and Julia felt a pang of guilt for not being more faithful with her correspondence. She wanted to ask about Father, but his anger over her departure kept her from inquiring.

"Mother is doing so well, Julia. Thee would be proud of her. She is leading the women's group at Salem and they have sent two large crates of supplies with me for the refugees. She is very supportive of thy work, Julia. She tells everyone who stops by of her beautiful daughter who had been so brave to leave her family and move to Kansas to assist the refugees."

Julia smiled as she imagined her mother boasting of her accomplishments—in a humble way, of course. "And Rachel?"

"What a little stem-winder! That girl is never still unless she is sound asleep. Rather reminds me of thee as a child."

"You are only two years older than I, David Jones, so do not tell me you would know what I was like as a two-year-old!"

"There thee goes again, forgetting the 'thee'."

"Perhaps it was time you gave up on that 'non-essential,' David," Julia shot back, becoming a bit irritated with his reprimands.

"Okay, please do not be angry," he grinned, giving her a playful punch on the arm, just like when they were children. He always could calm her faster than anyone.

"Would thee like to know about Father?" he asked curiously. When Julia did not answer, he continued. "He is thinking of laying down his practice this fall. He would like to spend more time with Mother and Rachel, and he is training a new assistant to join me in the partnership."

Julia was speechless. Her father giving up medicine? Whatever for? He was not nearly old enough to give up the one thing he loved more than anything else.

"Why, David?"

David looked puzzled. "I told thee, Julia, he wants to spend more time with Mother and Rachel."

"I know what thee said, but why would he do such a thing? He is a young man—well, perhaps not young—but he has many years of service ahead of him. What is the true story, David? There is something thee is not telling me."

David hesitated. Did he dare tell her the truth? What if it upset her so that she could not do the job she felt called to do? No, this was not the time. Perhaps later, but not now.

"We can talk later, Julia. Right now I would appreciate thee taking me to the hotel so I might make arrangements for the nights I will be here."

Julia's heart felt lighter. David was going to stay for a few days. She could not wait to hear all about the Salem Meeting and Will and his hotel and the other friends she had not seen for nearly a year.

Taking David's arm Julia said good-bye to Julianna and Laura, who were working in her office, and set off with her brother and a dozen questions in tow.

CHAPTER 7

'LITTLE David, Play ON YOUR Harp'

David and Julia spent the next five days catching each other up on the events of their separate lives. Julia was more than pleased when David accompanied her to worship each morning. She hoped her brother might have insights on making their worship at the Association more meaningful. She had followed Elizabeth's suggestion to have silent worship after her message, but it seemed to make little difference.

It was the third day of their worship together that Julia would never forget. Much of the night before she had spent mulling over the idea of how to include "Jacob's Ladder" in the service. She was not blessed with a beautiful voice, and had never minded the Friends practice of frowning on everyone in the Meeting singing the same songs. But time and again during her meditation and prayers she had felt the Spirit moving her to include this important part of the Negro's worship experience.

"David," she began that morning after her brother arrived at the Association, "what would thee think of helping me lead the gathering in singing "Jacob's Ladder" in worship this morning?" She paused, then rushed on. "The black people who fill the room each morning have made singing one of their main forms of worship. It seems almost a travesty not to allow them to worship in the way they are accustomed."

David was silent for a few moments, then finally spoke. "From the passion in thy voice I can see this is something thee has considered for some time. I am not familiar with the spiritual thee would like me to help with, but if thee can teach it to me in the next few minutes, I am willing to do my best to help thee."

Julia impulsively threw her arms around her brother. "You are the most wonderful brother in the world," she exclaimed. "How shall I ever thank you enough?"

"By remembering to use 'thee' in stead of 'you'." Then he smiled. "But more importantly, by continuing to be the most wonderful, sensitive, caring, stubborn sister a brother could ever hope for."

There were tears in Julia's eyes as she and David held each other for a moment, each feeling great love for the other.

As Julia began teaching David the song Hosea had taught her, there was a knock on the door. Rather annoyed at having been interrupted, Julia reluctantly went to the door.

"Good morning, Miss Jones."

Though she did not know for certain the reason, Julia was more than a little peeved to see John Stanley on the doorstep.

"May I come in?" he finally asked when Julia did not extend a greeting.

"I am sorry," she finally said, "please come in."

"David, this is John Stanley. He occasionally volunteers his services here and it appears this is one of those times. John, this is my brother, David, from Salem, Iowa."

"Pleased to meet thee," David said, extending his hand to the man Julia did not seem happy to see.

"I hope thee does not mind, John, but David and I are preparing for worship and we do not have a great deal of time to spare."

"Oh, please excuse me," John stepped back. "I had no intent of intruding."

"Thee is not intruding," David's tone of voice was much softer than her sister's. "Julia is wanting to try a new addition to worship, and somehow she talked me into helping. I hope thee will have time to join us in worship in a few minutes."

Julia looked at David. Why had he invited John Stanley, a man who never smiled and probably never had a good time doing anything? She was certain this man would have nothing but criticism for what she was trying to do.

"I have a lot of work to do in the warehouse," John said coolly. "I doubt I will have time for worship this morning. I thought perhaps Elizabeth might be in her office this morning and I would inquire as to what she would have me do today. I can see that she is not here, so I will look elsewhere." With that he turned and left.

"Sour apple," Julia said with distaste.

"Julia, kindness is more becoming than anger."

"I am not angry," she protested. "I just do not understand how one can profess to be a child of God but never have a smile cross their face."

"Perhaps he has good reason."

"Then he should get over it and look for the blessings in life."

"Is that what thee is doing?"

Julia looked intently at her brother. What was he asking? "David, we have little time for discussing such things. Please. We must go over the song one more time."

"All right, honey," David grinned. "'Jacob's Ladder' one more time."

When it was time for David to help lead the spiritual during worship, Julia introduced him to those gathered for worship. She deliberately kept her eyes from seeking Hosea, not wanting his bitterness to spoil her own spirit of worship.

As David began singing the familiar Negro spiritual, Julia could sense a change in the worshipers. At first it was the smiles that began to appear on the black faces. By the second stanza many were beginning to move their bodies in rhythm to the music. A few began to clap their hands and before Julia knew what was happening, one by one, young and old, the Negroes began to rise and sing with their whole bodies, moving in a circle around the room.

What have I begun? she wondered, as the song began to take on a life of its own. David was no longer leading the chorus but merely following the swell of the song. Around and around the room they moved, clapping and singing the song in beautiful harmony. Then, almost as though being orchestrated, the song ended amid a number of "hallelujahs" and "amens" and each returned to their previous place on the benches. Feeling moved by the Spirit, Julia remained seated. She fervently hoped the Negroes would understand they were moving into silent worship. After a short time of silence, an older lady rose to speak of her God in a reverent and respectful voice. She was followed by several others, both men and women, who spoke of both their blessings and burdens. Julia felt David's arm around her shoulder as tears fell down her cheeks. God had spoken to hearts and true worship was being experienced. There was no spoken message needed from Julia that morning as the various ministers of God brought messages meant for the those present in the meeting house.

Julia hoped it was the beginning of a new way of worship for the Negro people, though she did not believe everything would be perfect from then on. She would have to learn more spirituals, and do her best to get to know the refugees as people with a different set of experiences than her own. She vowed to do her best to learn as much as possible from these wonderful friends.

During the course of his visit, David and Julia had many opportunities to catch up on each other's lives. They both delighted in hearing of the other's joys and trials. David loved practicing medicine, and from what Julia could gather from stories of the patients he treated, she knew he must have the same healing touch as their father. Although she asked once or twice why their Father would give up something he loved so dearly, David stuck with his same answer: Father wanted to spend more time with his family. Julia was certain there was more to the story, but David seemed resolved not to talk about it.

David was delighted to hear of the things Julia had done at the Association, particularly when she had been left in charge in the absence of both Elizabeth and Laura. "Thee would be a natural leader, Julia," he praised, "just like the rest of our family. We do not sit around waiting to be useful; God has a purpose for each of us and we have sought to do His will."

"Then why is Father giving up that purpose?" Julia asked one last time.

David's look was one of torn allegiance, and had Julia not been so concerned for her father she would have dropped the subject. "Please, David, thee can tell me the truth. Is he ill? Is that the real reason? Thee must help me understand!"

"Oh, Julia. I wanted my visit to be one of pleasure for thee, not a cause of sorrow."

"Thee is frightening me, David. Father is ill, is that it?"

"Well, no—not the way thee means, at least."

"Then what?"

"Father has not been the same since thee left, Julia. It is as if . . . I do not know the exact words to describe it, but he seems to have lost his desire to practice medicine. When thee left, Julia, a part of Father left, too. He was so angry when he came home that day last seventh month and found thee gone. Mother used every ounce of strength she had to persuade him not to ride after thee and remove thee from the train." David chuckled. "I do believe he would have ridden until he caught up with the train and forced thee to come back home with him."

Julia's face paled at the thought. "How on earth did Mother ever persuade him?" she asked, knowing the stubbornness of her father once he determined to do something.

"I was still in Chicago, of course, but Mother shared the entire story with me when I returned. It seems that the minute thee left with Luke and Betty Johnson, mother took Rachel and rode to the Clark homestead. She and Will's mother spent most of the day in prayer, both for thee and for Father. Mother says it was their prayers that prepared Father's heart for the news of thy departure, though there were also many words spoken by her on your behalf."

An overwhelming love for her mother rose within Julia as she thought of the strength it must have taken for her to take her daughter's side against her husband. "And Father was persuaded it was God's will?" she asked hopefully.

David was silent for a moment. Deciding it best to speak the truth in all things, as taught by Friends, he told her the rest of the story.

"No, the reason Father did not try to bring thee back was because Mother reminded him that thy strong will was very much like the will he possessed and that thee would find a way to go—if not this time then some other. The two of you are very much alike, Julia, thee knows that."

Had she known that? Surely she was not as stubborn as her father. "But why is he giving up the practice of medicine? It still does not make sense to me."

"He feels that he failed thee, Julia. He believes that if he had been a better father—perhaps spent more time at home when we were young—that thee would have made a better choice for thy life."

"How does thee feel, David? Does thee think I am foolish for coming to Kansas to minister to the Negroes?"

"I must admit when I first heard thee had left, I felt thy decision a bit foolish. To leave thy family and move to a foreign place teeming with desperate refugees seemed too risky for a beautiful young woman. But now I believe thee has done what God called thee to do."

"What changed thy mind?"

David grinned. "I must admit it was Elizabeth who first helped me see the light, though having just shared in thy ministry during the worship service I am even more firmly convinced thee is following God's will for thy life."

"But how was Elizabeth a part of thy acceptance?"

"Elizabeth came to Salem on her way back from Washington D.C."

"I do not understand. Salem is not anywhere close to where she was traveling."

"She said the Lord led her to visit our family as she knew how much thee missed everyone and how thee hated leaving Father without his blessing. She thought she might share of the work in Kansas with us and help Father gain insights into what it was thee did here. She also spoke to the Quarterly Meeting one evening, so she was able to reach more than just our family."

"Father would not listen, would he?"

"Oh he listened, and very politely. But nothing she said seemed to break through the wall he has built around himself. It is really sad, Julia, and I feel so helpless at times. I want Father to continue his practice. He has wonderful gifts of healing and he knows just what to prescribe for whatever ails a person. But I cannot seem to convince him that he is needed. He just says Matthew, the new intern, and I, can handle the practice without him. But we cannot, Julia, because he is the one with years of experience. Matthew and I have the head knowledge, but we have not had the opportunities to practice it as he has."

Julia heard the frustration in his voice.

"But David, if thee told him what thee has just told me, would he not see the wisdom of thy words?"

"I have tried, Julia, I have tried so many times. It just seems to make no difference."

Julia was overwhelmed with sadness. Sadness for her father wanting to quit his livelihood because of her, sadness for her brother who would have to bear the weight of their practice on his shoulders, and sadness that she had not tried to find a way to heal the rift between her father and herself before she left. "I am sorry, David. Truly I am. Is there anything I can do to help thee?"

"No, it is something we will have to deal with as time passes, but thee could certainly remember me—and Father—in thy prayers.

"Oh, I will, David. I am so grateful thee has shared this with me." Now she knew the real reason for his visit: he had needed to talk about their father.

"But tell me about thy social life, my Fiery One," he said, wishing to lighten the conversation.

Julia laughed. "My social life? Let me see. Oh yes, I go to worship each morning and bring a message to the people, but thee has seen that. And there are First Day afternoons with Elizabeth, Laura, and Maggie."

"What about that young man who stopped by the office looking for Elizabeth the other day? He seemed like a young man worth getting to know better."

Julia wrinkled her nose. "John Stanley is an old married man, David. Well, at least he used to be. He lost his wife several months ago and I believe the only reason he comes here to volunteer is because it takes his mind off his troubles."

"But has thee ever visited with him? Offered sympathy and perhaps shown him life can be fulfilling in spite of our adversities?"

"No, and I do not intend to," Julia said firmly. "And no more talk of John Stanley. He is an old man, anyway!"

David laughed. From his observations John Stanley could be no more than a few years older than Julia. From the look on Julia's face, however, he decided it would be best to keep his thought to himself.

Julia wished she could tell her brother about the evenings she had been spending with Hosea recently, but she thought better of it. For the past several weeks Hosea had been coming to the offices each evening near the time Julia would be telling Julianna a bedtime story. Once in a while he would tell a story from his past, often a folk tale about a poor child who some-how became rich. But mostly he just listened. When Julianna fell asleep the two of them would quietly walk to her office where Hosea would sometimes tell her the words to another spiritual, or occasionally another story of pain and suffering of his people. But she knew she could not share this with David. If David had been concerned about her safety just working here, there were certainly no words that would explain her meeting with a black man to hear about his past. The things David had shared about Father, the closeness she felt, no, she could not risk his disapproval. She had hoped perhaps Hosea would stop by while David was still visiting so she could at least introduce them, but it was almost as if he had disappeared these past few days. Why had he stopped coming to see her and Julianna? She had been so busy entertaining David she had not been concerned about his absence until now. I will make it a point to find him as soon as David leaves, she vowed.

"Thee needs to be with people thy age, Julia," David said as he noticed her gazing off in the distance. "Surely there is a Friends meeting nearby where thee might enjoy the fellowship of other young men and women. Of course, I am certain thee enjoys the company of the older ladies here at the Association, but that is the problem—they are old!"

"David," she said playfully, "they are not old. Perhaps they have a few years on me, but they are not old."

"Seriously, Julia, thee needs to find people thy age. Surely thee must want to find someone suitable for marriage some day."

"Perhaps some day, but for now I am happy with what I am doing."

Was she happy? Truly happy? The same question was in the minds of both, though neither spoke their thoughts. Julia thought of the evenings she had spent with Hosea. She felt happy then. And most of the time it made her feel satisfied, if not happy, when she was bringing a message in worship. And now with the success of the spirituals she was excited just thinking about the possibilities for meaningful worship.

Working with Elizabeth and Laura was rewarding, too. If she was doing God's work, that was happiness in itself, was it not? It was not the same as the excitement of going to the Pleasant Plain Academy and planning occasions like the Snow Fest that first winter. Nor was it the joy of helping bring her new sister into the world. She missed her family and friends, but that was to be expected. It was not a question of happiness or unhappiness. It was simply being in the place you were called to be.

"I have enjoyed visiting thee, Julia," David said, interrupting her thoughts. "The work here is truly amazing. I am hopeful that when I tell Father of the magnitude of aid thee is offering here he will see the good in what thee is doing."

A loud knock on the office door put an end to their conversation. "Julia, I hates ta interrupt ya, but theres a problem with Julianna."

It was Hosea. Julia felt the excitement rise within her at the sound of his voice. "Come in, Hosea, I would like for thee to meet my brother, David."

"Didn't ya hear me? I says Julianna needs ya." Impatience etched his features as he stepped into the office.

"I heard thee, Hosea, but surely it is not that urgent. This is my brother, David. David, this is my friend, Hosea."

David looked curiously at the large, handsome black man shifting from one foot to the other. Eyes guarded, distrustful. Friend? Since when did his sister associate with young black men? David shuddered as he acknowledged the spark of excitement he'd seen in Julia when she had heard the young man's voice. Even now she could not conceal the warm smile he provoked. What was their relationship? Surely Julia would not think it appropriate to become friends with a young Negro man. Finally David extended his hand, with no acknowledgement from Hosea, only a piercing stare.

"David is a doctor in Salem, the town where I grew up," Julia said hastily, sensing the chill between the two men. "He has been visiting here for a few days and will leave on the afternoon train."

"I seen him with you. You say this your brother?"

"Yes, my older brother from Salem."

A look of relief seemed to replace the sullen expression on Hosea's face.

"Oh."

Then it occurred to Julia that Hosea must have thought David was a friend who had come to visit. A special friend, perhaps? Could it be that Hosea was jealous of David? Julia felt a flush in her cheeks. Was that why he had not come to the infirmary these last few evenings? She would have to assure him there were no 'special young men' in her life—here, or back home in Salem.

"Julianna say she need ya, Julia." Hosea finally said, re-membering his mission.

"I will see what she needs. Please excuse me, David. I will return as soon as possible." Julia left, fervently hoping the two men might get to know one another a bit in her absence.

"Please tell me about thyself, Hosea," David began.

"Ain't nothin' ta tell."

David tried to push away the displeasure he felt with Hosea's responses. He was certainly a striking figure: tall, broad shoul-ders, handsome facial features. But his unwillingness to enter the conversation was disappointing.

"I am sorry if I was too forward. I just supposed thee was someone important to Julia, and as her big brother I have al-ways been a bit protective of her."

"She ain't needin' no pertection, mister. She be one fine lady who not be afraid of anything."

David sensed the pride in Hosea's voice. Just what was the relationship between these two? he wondered again. Why did I not learn of this when I first arrived? Is this something to be concerned about? Julia was stubborn, but she was not foolish. Surely he had misread the situation. Nevertheless, it would need to be a matter of prayer. Julia might live hundreds of miles away, but he was still her big brother, and if at all possible he would protect her from the hurt and pain this young man might some day cause her.

Hosea watched David leave from the window by his bed in the barrack. Now that Julia's brother was gone he would be free to once again seek her company in the evenings. He had sure been fooled by her brother. The way he'd seen them hugging each other that first day had convinced him the young man was a suitor come to see his love. Hosea remembered the relief he had felt when she'd introduced him as her brother.

What's you thinkin' bout, fool? You ain't gots no business settin' your sights on no white girl. White women ain't allowed to associate with black men. She ain't gots no use for ya anyways, she jist wants ya ta get that religion o' hers.

That ain't so, he argued with himself. She like me jist fine. I see the pain in her eyes when I telled her 'bout da killin's 'n shootins' 'fore I comes here. She ain't like the other white men and women I knowed. She be different. She care about me—don't she?

Julia's brother had not liked him, of that he was certain. But big brother was gone now, and Hosea quickly changed into clean clothes and headed for the offices where he was sure Julia would still be working. Hosea's heart began to pound as he neared the Association headquarters. After stopping a moment to calm himself, he finally walked the last few steps and knocked gently on the door.

"Hosea!" Julia's voice was warm with a touch of excitement. How Hosea wished she would give him one of those hugs she was always giving her brother when he was here. Something in his gaze must have conveyed his feelings because before he knew what had happened she had come toward him and lightly touched his arm. It was brief and reminded him of the way his mother used to run her hand up and down his arm.

"What has thee been doing this past week?" she asked curiously.

Hosea frowned. What did she think he had been doing? Same thing as always: goin' to the blacksmith shop and workin' in the fire with metal so hot it would burn a hole clear through ya; sittin' out on the grass in the evenings listenin' to tall tales Moses liked to tell; and feelin' sorry for himself. None of this would interest Julia, of that he was sure. She had been too busy with her brother to even notice his absence.

"Jist been doin' da same as always, Julia. Workin' and sittin'. I did go out ta see Betsy and da boys one night this week. An' I gots some bad news about that."

"What is it?" Julia had been worried about Betsy, too. She never came to see her daughter now that Julianna was healthy again. And those living conditions . . . it was easy to be concerned about someone living in a situation like Betsy and her family.

Hosea shook his head. "She say she don't want Julianna no more. She say you alls kin keep her for all she care."

"Oh no, Hosea, why would she say that? Julianna is the most precious child on this earth! She is so loving and so eager to learn. Can I tell thee a secret about her?"

"Shore, Julia." You can tell me anything, he thought happily.

"I have been teaching her the letters of the alphabet and how they make words. She is so quick, Hosea. She will be reading before you know it." Julia felt proud of the way Julianna had responded to her teaching. The ability to teach others must truly run in my family, she thought.

Hosea's eyes narrowed. "That not be smart, no, not smart at all." He seemed to be talking to himself.

"And what harm will it do?" Julia demanded.

"She ain't never gonna wanna go back to da family ifin' she think she too good for us poor black folk."

"But you just said Betsy—"

"I knows what I said, but she ain't gots no choice. She gots ta go back to her momma cuz thats all she gots."

"But what if someone wanted to adopt her?" Julie posed.

"Who gonna wanna adopt a mulatto that ain't white an' ain't black?"

Julia considered his words. Of course she knew Julianna's skin was much lighter than Hosea's, but most of the Negroes were lighter than Hosea. Why would anyone not want to adopt such an adorable child?

"She is a beautiful child, Hosea. I should think there would be a family that would want her."

Hosea just shook his head. "Like I tells ya, ain't no white folk gonna wants a baby that's got black blood in da veins. "An' no black that knows about her gonna want her neither."

"What do you mean?"

Hosea paused as if deciding whether or not to reveal the child's past. Julia be so almighty sure she know what best for everbody, it jist might teach her a lesson, he decided.

"Julianna's daddy be a white bastard. Betsy, she be a house slave on one of da biggest plantations in Miss'ssippi. Her massa think he like to have her for his own pleasure and he sneak in her room 'bout ever' night. She not like it, but what nigger slave gots any chance 'gainst da massa? Then one day his seed starts ta grow in her belly and when he see she gonna have da child he sells her to da meanest Massa dey ever was. That

Massa beat her an' when she have Julianna he knowd who da daddy musta been an' he say he never wanna see dat child again. That be when Betsy find Joshua. Dey marries 'n Julianna have a daddy. Joshua, he luv dat chil' like she be his own." Hosea shook his head at the memory. "Joshua, he be da best man I ever know'd."

Julia thought she detected tears in the eyes of her tough young friend.

"I still do not understand why Betsy does not want Julianna now."

"She never did take to da child. I guess it be all da trouble da child cause her with both da massas."

"But it was not Julianna's fault!" Julia cried.

"I knows that, 'n you knows that, but sometimes things happen in da brain and it make a mamma not think right."

Was Hosea thinking of his own mother now? Julia's heart nearly broke as she thought of the horrors Hosea had witnessed in his life.

"What will we do?" Julia asked, thinking of the precious child she had grown to love.

"I is workin' on it, but right now I jist don' know. There's a woman in da barracks that has a mulatto 'n she say maybe she take Julianna. But she already gots six chilin' of her own."

"I could adopt her," Julia said more to herself than Hosea. The thought of raising Julianna had been on her mind nearly every time she worked with the young child, even though she believed some day Betsy would come for her daughter. But if Betsy did not want her, would she not be the best choice for

Julianna's mother? She had been like a mother to the little girl all these weeks. She loved Julianna and Julianna loved her, of that she was certain.

Hosea's laughter was bitter, tainted with the hatred he held for the white race.

"That child best be with her own folk," he said firmly. "She ain't gonna have no easy life anyhows, and tryin' to be white jist won't work."

"But I love her! I would make it work," Julia insisted.

Hosea shook his head again. "Jist put it outta your mind, Julia. You's gots a big heart, but ya don't know much about dis world."

His words stung. She knew plenty about this world. She knew love was stronger than hate and surely if she loved Julianna enough it would be better than putting her with a family that already had six mouths to feed. She would talk it over with Elizabeth first thing in the morning. Surely Elizabeth would be in favor of Julianna living with someone who could be a real mother to her, the real mother she never had. It would be worth the fight. She could raise the child as her own; she did not need a husband. She was a strong woman and when she set her mind on something it was as good as done.

CHAPTER 8

'ALL Night, ALL Day'

*J*ulia's desire to adopt Julianna grew stronger with each passing day. The bubbly little girl with the big blue eyes pulled at her heartstrings. Every day Julia spent several hours with the child, reading to her, teaching her about letters and words, exploring numbers and counting, and drawing pictures on the wall of the infirmary. Julia smiled as she thought of Elizabeth's reaction when she had first asked permission to use the space behind Julianna's bed as a mural where the little girl might learn to express her feelings.

"Julia, I do not believe marking a wall will teach a child respect for her surroundings," Elizabeth had begun.

"But Elizabeth, please give this some thought before saying no. The only ones who will see the wall are Julianna and patients who are usually too sick to care. And when they do get better the wall will be a source of hope and cheer. I want her to use bright colors—red, green, yellow and blue. I want her to see the beauty of nature and recreate the things that make her happy."

Elizabeth had finally consented and Julia and Julianna were rapidly becoming inseparable. Julianna was allowed to sit in Julia's office while she worked—if she were quiet. Julia was amazed at how still the child sat, looking at books borrowed from Doc Samuel's children who were now grown, or simply sitting watching Julia. The two 'Julies' were as attached to each other as any child and mother.

Why could Elizabeth not see the importance of keeping the child in a loving, nurturing environment? Elizabeth's reaction to her adoption proposal was nearly identical to Hosea's. It would not work, she said, because the child would never feel like she belonged in either world. Whites and blacks alike would ridicule Julia for trying to raise a mulatto child. She was not even married, for goodness sake. Criticism would abound.

But I would not let that bother me, Julia had insisted. Elizabeth remained firm in her opposition, however, and nothing more had been said about the matter. She had allowed Julianna to continue to live in the infirmary, though the child was now completely recovered. Julia knew it was only a matter of time, though, before some other arrangement would have to be made. The child deserved to be in a loving home, and there simply was not one available. Except mine, Julia thought. Maggie would have a fit at first, but she would get used to having a child in the house, especially one as quiet and polite as Julianna. It might even brighten the elderly woman's life to hear the sweet sounds of laughter and see the smiles on Julianna's innocent face. Julia would have to find a way to change Elizabeth's mind.

"Julia, we have a problem," Elizabeth said one morning several weeks after David's visit and Julia's first proposal to adopt Julianna. It was hard to believe it was the eighth month and had been nearly a year since Julia's arrival.

"We have a lot of problems, Elizabeth," Julia joked, trying to lighten the conversation.

"This is serious, Julia. We are missing nearly three hundred dollars from the cash box."

Julia was silent for a moment. "Why was there so much money in the box?" she asked, knowing normally less than twenty dollars was kept on hand for emergencies.

"Remember me telling thee about a gift from a gentleman in Iowa Yearly Meeting? He wished to purchase desks, books, and supplies for the school. Yesterday he made a special trip here to deliver the gift and see our work. The bank was closed by the time he arrived and I felt the money would be safe in the cash box over night."

"Who knew the money was there?" Julia asked.

"I told no one. Only Nathaniel and I knew the money was in the box."

"Is Nathaniel the Friend from Iowa?"

"Yes, and he would certainly not steal his own money!"

"No, of course not," Julia admitted. "Did thee tell anyone else about the gift?"

"Only Laura and thee. Did thee happen to mention it to anyone?" Elizabeth asked cautiously.

Julia's face paled. No. It could not be him.

"Julia? Did thee?"

"I . . . I may have mentioned something about it to Hosea," she admitted.

The look on Elizabeth's face was more sorrowful than angry. "Oh, Julia . . . I wish thee had not mentioned it to anyone."

"Hosea did not take it!" Julia said emphatically. "He would never do such a thing. He likes, I mean, he respects us. He would never take the money for our school. He loves the children here, especially Julianna. He would not do it," she repeated. Then, as an afterthought, "Maybe someone entered thy office during the night and took the money. We never lock the doors."

Elizabeth just shook her head. "No one has ever entered these offices during the night, at least not to my knowledge, and no one would have known the money was there last night. Who would do such a thing?"

"I will make it my job to find out," Julia said.

"Please do not mention this to anyone," Elizabeth implored. "We will wait and see if there is any talk among the refugees. Perhaps thee could keep an ear open when visiting with thy friend Hosea."

Julia blushed. Did Elizabeth know she talked with Hosea nearly every night? Of course she knew they were friends, but Julia always made sure Elizabeth had left for Maggie's before opening the door to the offices as a signal to Hosea that she was alone. She thought of some of their visits and how gentle Hosea had become after sharing the stories from his past. He often talked of the family he longed to have someday and how he would provide his children with love and understanding. Occasionally Julia imagined how it might feel to be married to a man whose compassion ran so deep. She always chided herself for those thoughts, however, knowing it could never happen. No matter how wonderful Hosea seemed to her, he was still a man of a different race, something no one she knew would accept.

"I will be especially watchful," she finally said, putting thoughts of Hosea aside. "We will find the money, I know we will." Her words were spoken with a confidence the circumstances did not warrant.

"I hope thee is right, Julia. And thee might say a prayer, too. Surely God knows how much we need those funds."

When Julia went in search of Hosea that night, he was nowhere to be found. Knowing Moses was aware of the whereabouts of almost everyone living in the barracks, she sought out the old man.

"Moses?" she called, seeing the elder sitting under one of the larger trees near the barracks.

The stoop-shouldered Negro motioned for Julia to come near while sending away the adolescents he had been visiting with. Julia sat on the grass near the patriarch, hoping he might feel more comfortable talking to her if she were sitting. "Moses, does thee know where I might find Hosea?"

Moses sat staring into the distance for several minutes before answering. Julia was beginning to wonder if he had heard her question when he finally spoke.

"Hosea, he be gone since last night, Miz Julia," he said quietly.

Julia's hopes for his innocence crashed like a load of rocks dropped from a wagon. "Gone where?" she finally asked.

"Don't rightly know, Missy. He comes to my bunk in da night 'n says he gots business ta take care of. Don't know when he be back."

"Did thee ask him where he was going?" Julia asked impatiently.

"Yessum, I'se did, but he don't say no more, jist take off runnin'."

He did do it. But how did he know the money was there last night? Why would he take money from the children? I know he loves Julianna, she thought, and he is always playing with the children living in the barracks. She thought of the times Hosea had grabbed Julianna and twirled her in the air, and how he lovingly held her on his lap as he told her about his life as a child in the big house on the plantation. She also remembered the times the three of them had laughed and played tag with each other around the infirmary beds. It made no sense. How could she believe Hosea was a thief?

"I thank thee, Moses." Julia rose to leave. Moses looked at her as if weighing whether or not to say what was on his mind.

"I knows you youngin's don't never want no advice from us ole foks, but I reckin' I can say what's on my mind," he finally said. "I sees da way young Mista Hosea look at you when he see you off in da distance, 'n I knows he goes to your office in da evenin's. It ain't a good thing, Missy, it jist ain't ever gonna be da way you alls wants it ta be. A black man and a white woman cain't be married 'n have a happy life. I sees 'em try it in Alebama after da war. Ain't no freedoms for us black folk down there—

or anywhere else fer that matter—and ain't no way da world gonna let a white woman get hitched to a black man."

"Hosea and I are just friends, Moses," Julia said stiffly. "I do not know what thee thinks thee has seen, but I am merely trying to help him see the Inner Light within his soul that will bring him to God."

Moses chuckled. "That ain't all yous wants him ta see, but you jist go on thinkin' that way. Don't make no diff'ernce to a old man like me. I done said my piece and dat be all I say 'bout it. Oh, by da way. . . ya might find Mister Hosea down at de camp grounds with Betsy and da boys. That be da first place I look if I be you."

Why had he not told her this when she first asked about Hosea's whereabouts? Julia wondered, irritated. What a lot of time I have wasted listening to this old man lecture me about my feelings for Hosea. Is there no one who understands? Hosea needs to see the Light. I am trying to help him. That is all.

Julia quickly headed for the campgrounds. It did not matter to her that she was a beautiful, young, white woman entering a ramshackle Negro settlement. She had to find Hosea and ask him about the money. It would be better if he gave the money back right away. They would not have to turn him in to the authorities if all of it was returned safely. But why would he do it? she asked herself again. She would gladly have loaned him every cent of the money she had saved from the gift her mother had given her when she left for Kansas. All he had to do was ask.

Slowing her pace, Julia quietly entered the camping area. The fire pit that had blazed so brightly the first time she had come was now a black hole. There was no one around the fire pit, and no one sitting outside their makeshift homes. Julia never understood why these men, women and children who lived only a few blocks from the Association had never come to them for supplies and had never been convinced to live in the barracks. Elizabeth said it was about independence and making it on one's own. It seemed like a foolish choice to Julia, but perhaps understanding their need to be independent was yet another thing she needed to learn about the refugees.

Julia's heart sank as she cautiously entered the grounds. Where was everyone? Had Hosea come with the money and left with these people to begin a new life? But where would they go? Julia scanned the area beyond the tents and wagons and board shacks. One path led to an outhouse, one to a barren area by the tracks. She wondered if this was where those stowing away on the north-bound trains jumped from the boxcars to their new lives. On the main path that led from the dirt road to the campgrounds she noticed weeds and grass now peeking through the cracks in the ground. Where had everyone gone?

Julia quietly approached Betsy's home—or at least what she had once called home. With heart pounding and knees shaking Julia called softly to anyone who might be inside. Hearing no response she slowly pulled back the curtain that had served as a door. What would she find? After her eyes adjusted to the dim light, they were drawn to the spot where she had first seen Julianna. An old tarp was still on the ground and there seemed to be something in the corner. It almost appeared as if someone were lying under the end of

107

the wagon box that was still supported by a wheel. Did she dare make her presence known? It might be someone who knew of Hosea's whereabouts. Gathering all the courage she could summon, Julia cleared her throat. As the figure slowly rolled toward her a moan escaped his throat. Hosea! Was he hurt? Her heart began to pound as fear filled her senses.

"Hosea, it is Julia. What has happened to thee?"

"I needs help, Julia . . . ya gots ta git help."

Easing him onto his back, Julia gasped at the sight. A pool of blood had gathered under his body, and from the appearance of his shirt it had come from some sort of wound in his side. Sweat ran from his brow and Julia gently wiped the beads from his forehead. She wanted to gather him in her arms and tell him everything would be all right, that she would take care of him. This man, her friend, with the strong body who always held his head so proudly, lay dying. Knowing it would do no good to give in to her feelings of love and compassion, she resolved to do everything in her power to save his life.

"I must get help for thee, Hosea. Thee has been badly wounded. Please lie still until I can get someone."

"I didn't mean ta cause ya no trouble, Julia, honest I didn't." Hosea's voice was weak as he struggled to rise on one elbow.

"Thee must save thy energy," Julia said, much more calmly than she felt. "Thee can tell me all about it when we get thy wound dressed. Just wait here until I return."

Though pain was etched across the handsome face, a smile turned up the corner of Hosea's mouth. "I aints goin' no wheres, Julia. Jist git help."

"I will," Julia called as she left the tent. Fear clutched at her heart as she ran. Could she make it to Doc Samuel's in time? Please, God, she prayed, please keep Hosea alive. He does not know thee yet but I am certain it is just a matter of time before he feels thy love and seeks forgiveness. Please, God, please.

When the doctor answered the door Julia was so out of breath from running the several blocks to his home that it was hard to explain what had happened to Hosea.

"Now Julia, this wouldn't once again be young Mr. Hosea to whom you have appointed yourself as guardian angel, now would it?" Doc teased.

"Yes, thee knows it is. Please, Doctor Samuels. There is no time to waste. Hosea is dying and you must come immediately!"

"Where did you say the wound was?"

"Here," Julia said, pointing to her lower abdomen.

"Not likely life threatening, unless the wound is through a major artery, in which case he would have been gone by the time you reached him. But we'll go have a look and see what can be done for your young man."

"He is not my young man," Julia said angrily. Why was it everyone thought she had an interest in Hosea? Other than in his soul, of course.

"All right, Julia. Let's get going."

Once the doctor had examined the wound he told Julia it looked to be a clean stab from a small blade, possibly a pocket knife of some sort. It had hit a major vein that left the pool of blood that had scared her so. As he prepared to pour antiseptic to cleanse the wound, he turned to Julia.

"You might want to take his hand, Julia. This is going to be quite painful and Hosea might appreciate having something to clutch."

Julia placed both her hands around the one that was nearly twice as large as hers. The callouses from working with the iron felt rough yet strong against her soft skin. Oh, that she might never have to let go.

Once Doc had cleaned and bandaged the wound he informed Julia it would be best for Hosea to stay in the makeshift tent until he felt strong enough to get up, probably in a day or two. He looked curiously at the young woman who still clutched the hand of the patient, but said nothing.

"Then I will stay with him," Julia said.

A look of disbelief crossed the old doctor's face. "Now why would you want to do that? I just told you he will be fine. He's lost some blood and will be weak for a day or two, but otherwise he'll recover nicely. This is no place for a young woman. I hear tales of nightly raids on these makeshift camps ."

"What kinds of raids?" Julia interrupted, worry once again etching her brow.

"Police raids. Seems they take delight in scaring these poor folks half to death with threats of jail if they don't move on. I imagine that's why there's no one living here now, except your friend here."

"That is awful!" Julia cried. "Why would they treat these people that way?"

"Humans are strange creatures, Julia. I've seen a lot in my day, treated poor folks and rich folks alike with every kind of ailment known to mankind. I'm sorry to say it, but some white folks treat their animals better than they treat these Negroes. As long as I live I swear I'll never understand why folks do what they do. It just seems to be human nature, Julia, to want to think you're superior to some other human being or race. These folks haven't done anything against the law that I know of, but the police act like they're hardened criminals. I don't have the answers for you. I guess we each have to do what we can to stick up for those who are treated unfairly."

"It is not right," Julia said more to herself than to Doc. "What did Hosea do to deserve this? He was almost finished with his training and in another month he planned to be working for himself and finding a home for Betsy and the children. Now Betsy is gone and Hosea's injured. I just do not understand what could have happened."

"Let's go home, Julia," Doc said quietly. "You will have the answers in a day or two—if Hosea decides to talk to you. He can be a bit contrary, as I recall."

"He will talk to me," Julia said confidently as they left Hosea for the night. "I know he will talk to me."

CHAPTER 9

'Nobody KNOWS THE *'Trouble, I've Seen'*

*J*ust as Doc Samuels predicted, two days later Hosea knocked on the door to the offices. Julia recognized the three short raps he always used to announce his arrival and rushed to open the door. Though she thought Hosea's shoulders seemed a little slumped and his usually bright eyes somewhat dull, it would have been difficult for a stranger to notice any remaining ill effects from the stabbing.

"Hello, Julia," he said quietly, not looking at her face. "We needs ta talk, but I don' wanna talk to ya here." He kept looking around the hallway leading to the three women's offices as if someone might be watching for him. Julia read the worried expression on Hosea's face and instantly wondered if he were more ill than he appeared, or if Betsy and the twins were in danger, or if someone might be searching for him. Though Julia felt she knew many things about the young man before her, she realized that in many ways she knew little about him except for the trials he had faced in the South, and his hopes for the future.

Once again her eyes examined his body for signs of pain from the stabbing. Though he shifted from foot to foot, his movements seemed more from nervousness than discomfort. He was still a handsome man: eyes that spoke readily of the emotions he was feeling; a small nose that seemed to be somewhat out of place above the large, sensuous lips. Julia's eyes lingered on his lips a moment before she realized what she was doing. Quickly looking down the hall, she motioned for Hosea to follow. "We can use Elizabeth's office. It has a solid door and she has been gone for a few days trying to raise money for desks and books for the school. We had the money, but now it is gone." Julia looked at Hosea to see if there was any reaction to her news. If the missing money bothered him, he did not show it.

Once in the office, Hosea seemed tongue-tied, reminiscent of the first few times they had talked.

"What is it, Hosea?" Julia asked impatiently. If he was going to confess he might as well do it and get it over with. They would just have to deal with the consequences. Was Hosea really capable of stealing from the Association? She thought of all the times they had shared important parts of their pasts with each other. They even talked about worship and how she was making it more meaningful for the refugees. She had been including one or two spirituals in every service and Hosea had told her the refugees now thought the singing was one of the best parts of worship. The two of them had even talked of their hopes for the future, how they each wanted to some day find someone with whom they could share their lives and raise their children. And . . . she had told him about the money. Did I make a mistake? she agonized. But I know Hosea. I cannot believe he would do such a thing. But the evidence . . .

"You is thinkin' I took da money, ain't ya?" he said accusingly, his bitterness from the past coloring his words, anger flushing his cheeks.

"Did you?"

"I knew you'd think I did it. I jist knew it." Hosea began to pace back and forth in the small office, each step punctuating his anger. "Are you saying you did not take it?" she asked again, failing to understand why he could not just tell her the truth. Lying would simply prolong his—and her—misery.

"Not o' my own free will. Ya gots ta believe me." Now Hosea's voice was quieter, his anger evaporating like late August dew on a hot morning.

"Then you had best explain it to me, Hosea, because you, Elizabeth, Laura, the Friend from Iowa, and I were the only ones who knew about the gift. Neither Elizabeth nor Laura would take the money, nor would the man who made a special trip all the way out here to give it to us. I did not take it, and that only leaves you."

"I know. It's my fault. I is so sorry." Hosea's chin sunk to his chest and he collapsed in the wooden chair in the corner, his hands reaching up to cover his face.

"What happened?" Julia's frustration mounted. Why had he taken the money? None of it made any sense to her. "Please, Hosea, I need thee to tell me exactly what happened."

"I know'd I shouldn't a done it, but one night I went ta see Betsy and da youngins and I gots ta talkin' 'bout da new school. I wants Isaiah and Jeremiah ta get some learnin' so's they can be somethin' when they grow up. I tell Betsy all 'bout da new books 'n desks dat some rich man in Ioway gonna buy. She ask me all kinds a questions 'bout how much money that gonna take, and I tells her it be three hunner' dollars. 'Three hunner' dollars, you say?' She gits a funny look on her face 'n asks when da money gonna come. I tells her I don't know, cause I don't. But she musta told some o' the men at da campgrounds, cuz dat night da Quaker man come with da money, some o' them mens comes an' gets me outta bed. They had a knife 'n I knowed they mean business. I jist didn't wanna git in a fight 'n maybe gits killed."

"But how did the men at the campgrounds know the money would be in the office that night? I did not even know when it was coming."

"They keep watch on da offices 'til they sees da man with da black hat 'n coat come ta visit. They figure he be da one with da money and that's da night they comes and gets me."

"But how did you know where the money was?"

"I didn't know for shore, but I knows it probly be in Missus Comstock's office cuz she be da one in charge. So I takes 'em there. They da ones that find da box, though. I wouldn't' go in da office with 'em."

"But you took them there!" Julia cried out in anguish.

"They had a knife at ma throat, Julia. Yous be happier ifin I dies?"

Julia's chest felt tight. The thought of Hosea being killed was nearly more than she could bear. "No, of course not," she answered emphatically. "I suppose you had no choice but to take them. I just wish you had not said anything to Betsy. Then none of this would have happened. And what about Betsy and the twins? After the men left with the money did everyone at the campgrounds leave?" she asked, remembering the empty encampment.

"Yessum, they did. Even Betsy and da boys. They say they gonna move on ta Colorada and have themselves a better life. I shore gonna miss 'em," he said sadly.

"What about Julianna?" Julia suddenly remembered the child who had begun to call her 'mammy.'

"I's done told you, Julia. Betsy don't want that chil'. I don't know what gonna happen to her. I 'spose she gonna have ta live with that family with all da chilins in da barracks."

Though Julia was angry with a mother who would abandon her child, she also felt relieved that Betsy would not arrive some future morning demanding her daughter be returned.

"This could have been avoided if you had kept the things I told you to yourself," Julia reminded Hosea. Though she was still disappointed in his inability to keep her secret, she was also relieved to know he had not been a part of the actual robbery.

"I say I's sorry. I don't know what else ta say. You think I's guilty anyway, so what it matter?" Hosea shook his head as he slowly rose from the chair where he had been sitting and moved toward the door.

Julia's face softened. "I do not want you to go to jail for this, Hosea. That would not be fair, either. Unfortunately, many here at the Association will blame you when they find out you were the one who knew about the money."

"They don't have ta know, Julia. I be leavin' town this mornin' soon as we done talkin'. Don't no one know I's leavin' and they don't have ta know. Yous don't have ta tell 'Lizabeth. Jist go on like I ain't never talk to ya."

"But I cannot do that. You simply must not leave," she said, desperation evident in her voice. "If they ever find the men that took the money, you will need to identify them and clear your name."

"My name don't mean nuthin'. I jist poor ol' Hosea who don't got no famly, no home. I knows how ta do most o' da blacksmithin' now, 'n I figures I can find work some place down south o' here. They is lots of black folk round Columbus in da' southwest corner o' da state."

"No. Please, I am begging thee. Do not go." Julia's pleading eyes spoke more than her words. They spoke of the fear of losing someone you care for deeply and the need to hang on to the things most important in life. "We will find a way to make them see your innocence—I promise."

"Ya shouldn't make promises ya can't keep," Hosea said gently. "I is a Negro. They gonna throw me in jail 'n never let me go. There ain't no help for me here."

Julia refused to listen. In desperation she threw her arms around him and drew his head to hers as she blocked his exit to another life. The kiss she gave him was one filled with passion and despair. And she realized it was something she had longed to do for weeks.

Hosea started to push away the beautiful girl he knew he could never have, but then gave in to the weeks of longing for just such passion. Her lips were softer and sweeter than he could have imagined. But it was wrong; how strongly he felt the inappropriateness of their actions. But why should it be wrong? They were two people, man and woman, who cared about one another. Her kiss told him their feelings were mutual.

But yous don' even believe in her God, he reminded himself. That and da fact that she be white. Finally he broke away from Julia, pushing back the one person in the world who seemed to understand him.

"What is wrong?" Julia asked, perplexed.

"It ain't right, Julia, 'n you knows it."

"But you have to know how I feel. You have to understand that I do not want you to leave. I care about you and what happens to you."

"What I does know is that you is da preacher here at da mission 'n I don' even believe in that God o' yours. What they all gonna think if they hears that you 'n me gots feelin's fer one another? They ain't gonna believe a word you says."

Julia had already thought of that. She knew everything Hosea said was true. She shuddered as she thought of what the U.S.F.W. women in Salem would think if they had witnessed her just now, crossing the boundaries between black and white, right and wrong. She thought of her parents and the betrayal they would feel if they knew what she had done. Though a part of her wanted to scream at the injustice of whites refusing to see each man and woman as a part of the larger world of humanity regardless of their color, she knew the reality of the real world. She could think of no one who would sanction a relationship between a black man and white woman.

But was it wrong to feel compassion for another's soul? she asked in desperation. Surely no believer could fault her for wanting Hosea to affirm the Light within himself and become a child of God. She would put aside her personal feelings for Hosea and think only of his soul. If Hosea were to confess his sins and become a believer, her ministry would have real meaning. It would be a sign to the other refugees that even the most stubborn disbeliever could receive forgiveness from a loving God.

"Then perhaps it is time you came to know my God," Julia said quietly.

"Shore 'nough, that be da answer ta all my problems. I says I believe in that God o' yours n' then everbody say there's no problem with da money. You knows it ain't gonna happen' that way, Julia. I ain't gots no choice but ta get outta here, fast."

Hosea seemed resigned to leaving. Julia was frantic. What could she do to stop him? Leaving was not the solution, of that she was certain. If he stayed and told the authorities what really happened, surely they would believe his story, especially if she stood up for him.

"Wait, please." Julia reached out to Hosea as he opened the door to leave. "Will you do one thing for me? I am begging you. If I have meant one thing to you these past months, will you please talk to Elizabeth before you leave? I know you can tell her what happened and have no fear she will go to the authorities. If she hears your story and then tells you it would be best for you to leave, I will not try to stop you."

Hosea looked at Julia for a long time. This beautiful woman, so full of passion. His lips still remembered the heat of her kiss. Would he cause her more pain by staying? But if Mrs. Comstock wouldn't turn him in, couldn't he at least hear what she had to say? The look on his face showed his indecision and gave Julia hope.

"You see I am right, do you not?" she said.

"You forgets ta use them 'thees' 'n 'thous' when you gets excited," Hosea said, smiling for the first time since his arrival. After more consideration of her proposal, he finally agreed. "If ya gets Missus Comstock ta promise she won't turn me in, then I reckon I can talk to her. But you say she not be here now?"

"No, she is not, but I am expecting her back from Indiana late tomorrow. Thee can surely stay that long. No one knows the money is missing except Elizabeth, Laura, and I. If you just go back to the barracks and pretend like everything is the same, no one will be suspicious."

"But ol' Moses knows somethin' happened. He be watchin' da night da men comes fer me, 'n he knows I ain't been at da barracks fer two days."

"Moses will not say anything, thee knows that. He would never betray one of his own. All of you young men at the barracks are like sons to him."

Hosea seemed to consider whether or not it might be possible to go on as if nothing had happened. If what Julia had said were true, that no one knew the money was stolen, then maybe it would work. "I guess there ain't much choice if I's gonna stay."

Julia's heart suddenly felt lighter. Everything was going to work out. It had to. Though she wanted to reach out and embrace Hosea, she refrained. His soul would have to be her focus. She could not give in to the emotions she felt for Hosea or her entire work might be in jeopardy.

"Please be careful," she called to Hosea as he walked toward the barracks. Hosea turned back and the look in his eyes was one of hope and despair, confusion and helplessness at what had happened between them. Julia sat for a long time watching the solitary figure fade into the distance.

Where are you, God? she implored. Why will you not answer my prayer for Hosea's soul? As she prayed another prayer formed in her heart.

What have I done? she asked. Please forgive me, Father, if my actions have been displeasing to thee. I want to be your servant here in this place to these people.

The next morning during worship Julia anxiously watched for Hosea's arrival. If he came to worship, she would know for certain he had kept his word about staying to talk with Elizabeth. As the hour approached with no sign of him, Julia's fears grew. All night she had worried: worried that Hosea would panic and leave, worried that if he stayed Elizabeth would convince him to go to the authorities.

As they began with the first song, one of the spirituals Hosea had taught her, he slipped into the back row of seats. The relief Julia felt radiated through her body. She must have been smiling, for many in the congregation began smiling back at her. There was nothing wrong with smiling in worship, she reminded herself, even if it was not necessarily in response to the presence of God.

Robust singing had become the mainstay of daily worship in the meetinghouse. The service was punctuated with many vocal expressions of praise and thanksgiving. Even silent worship was filled with messages from the Holy Spirit as tongues were loosened by the revival of the active worship the Negroes were accustomed to.

As the morning's service progressed Julia noticed Hosea looking intently at her. What was going on in his mind? Was he thinking of the robbery? The talk with Elizabeth? Her message? Or perhaps the intimacy they had shared the day before? It was difficult for Julia to keep her mind on the thoughts she had prepared about the Prodigal Son.

Not long into the message Julia became engrossed in the story of the man who had two sons and his elder son's desire to have his inheritance in order to enjoy life. He was tired of working on the farm for nothing and desired to have his inheritance so that he might live life to the fullest. Julia told about the father's willingness to give the son what he wanted, even though he knew it was not in the young man's best interest. Then she described the disaster the son made of his life, how he squandered all his money and had to eat from pigs' troughs to keep from starving. Heads nodded in recognition of such dire conditions.

"But a wonderful thing happened," she continued. "The son decided he would be better off returning home as a slave than eating with the swine." Julia noticed several looks of amazement that anyone could believe being a servant was better than having your freedom.

"But when the son begged forgiveness for his foolishness and asked to be taken back as a servant, his father killed a fatted calf, invited the neighbors for a feast, and gave the son his place back in the family."

This time there were looks of astonishment on the faces of many of the refugees present that morning. "I saved the best news for last, however," Julia continued. "God is our heavenly Father. There are times when we decide we can run our lives better by ourselves. We do not ask Him for help; we do not want to work for His kingdom. But just like the son, when we ask for forgiveness He takes us back and gives us all the privileges of a son or daughter. We are once again in His family and will someday sit at his feet in heaven where the streets are paved with gold and there are no tears or sorrows."

"Amen, sister," came a voice from the back.

"I know some of you are just trying to get through this life in order to have a better one in heaven. I also know some of you have suffered greatly at the hands of massas. You have seen family members killed before your very eyes, homes burned, and jobs taken. I cannot promise you will never again have problems on earth. But I can promise you God is the only One who can give you peace. The Bible tells us we all have sinned: you, me, those who have done you wrong, all of us have broken God's laws. But like the father in the story Jesus told, God is always ready to welcome us back into His family. God loves us more than we can imagine. More than our mothers and fathers. More than you love your children. All He asks is that we recognize our sin and ask His forgiveness. Then, and only then, can we find peace and happiness. God is the only one who will never let us down."

Julia looked at Hosea as she finished. Had he heard the message? Did he understand that everyone, not just him, had sinned and that God offered forgiveness to anyone who asked? She prayed fervently that he would experience God's love and know that the gift of eternal life was given to all by the death of His son. Oh that Hosea could know the love and joy found in accepting that gift.

Hosea's head was bowed, the way it always was in worship. Julia asked for those who wished to pray for forgiveness and receive God's love to come to the front and kneel at the wooden benches. Though many sat with heads bowed in prayer, and several women and one older man came forward, Julia's heart nearly broke when Hosea was the first one out the door—as always.

"God, I am a failure," she prayed when everyone had left the room. "All I want is for Hosea to know your love and forgiveness."

Is it? Are you not fooling yourself? You want Hosea to come to Me in order to justify the feelings you have for him. Hosea is mine, Julia. I have a great work for him, but you must let him go that he might find me on his own.

Julia shook her head. God would surely not ask her to give up on a man's soul because of any feelings she might have for him. No, that sounds more like something my father would say, she thought with relief. "God, please speak to Hosea's heart," she prayed aloud. "Help him feel your love and know the great sacrifice you made when you gave your son to die on a cross to bear our sins that we might come to you and receive eternal life."

As Julia rose, an idea began to form in her mind. Jesus had been falsely accused, just as Hosea felt he would be. Could she help him understand that Jesus knew exactly how he felt because he had been in the same position?

Excitedly Julia rose to leave the building for worship. This would be the way to reach Hosea. Soon he would become a child of God and what rejoicing they would have. Her step was light and a tune was on her lips: Nobody Knows Da Trouble I've Seen. Jesus knows, Hosea, she thought, and soon you will understand just what it means to have someone who knows your troubles and can give you hope.

CHAPTER 10

'Ain't GONNA Grieve MY Lord NO MORE'

*E*lizabeth sat and listened as Hosea poured out his story of the happenings the night of the robbery. There was something different about the young man. She remembered him being angry and arrogant, but this evening he seemed genuinely remorseful. And Julia . . . what was her part in all of this? Sitting beside Hosea, listening intently to every word, nodding in agreement. There was something else Elizabeth noticed about her capable assistant, something quite disturbing. It was the look of admiration—or could it be even something more—in her eyes. She quickly dismissed the thought. Julia is an intelligent young woman from an upstanding family. She would never allow herself to develop emotional feelings for Hosea. But still, there was an unmistakable spark in her eyes as she sat gazing at the young man by her side.

"What would thee have me do, Hosea?" Elizabeth asked when he finished giving his account of the robbery. "Thee brought the men to my office. Could thee not have said thee did not know where the money might be? If the men had been watching these headquarters that night, as you say, certainly they would have known you were never anywhere near Nathaniel and me the entire time he was here."

"I knowd you'd never believe me," Hosea said bitterly. All the anger, hurt, and hopelessness of a lifetime seemed to be epitomized in Elizabeth's words, and Hosea rose to leave.

"Please sit down, Hosea." Elizabeth's voice was now laced with kindness as she sought to do what was best for the young man before her. "I did not say I did not believe thee. I merely asked thee why thee took the men to my office. I am still not certain I understand the reason, but I would like for thee to tell me what thee was thinking that night."

"Like I done already told ya, ma'am, they had a knife 'n I didn't wanna be in a fight where da odds was four ta one."

"But you ended up being wounded anyway."

"I plans ta get even for that someday," Hosea said angrily. "I hears 'em talkin' and they say they ain't takin' no chances I gonna tell somebody what they do. I jist lucky they sees all da blood 'n they thinks they kill me."

"But you recovered so quickly. Surely they would have been more certain thee were dead if that were their intent."

Julia rose to his defense. "If thee had seen the pool of blood, Elizabeth, thee would have known why they thought he was dead. It was dreadful."

"And how was it that *thee* saw the blood, Julia?" Elizabeth queried.

Julia shared everything that had happened that night, including her trip to the makeshift settlement. Elizabeth shook her head at the risks this young woman had taken to find her troubled friend. She could not understand why Julia had not known the dangers she might have encountered.

"And what would thee propose I do, Hosea? While I can understand thy desire to protect thyself, the fact remains thee played a part in the robbery."

"He was forced, Elizabeth!" Julia burst out. "Surely thee can see that he had no choice."

"What I see is a young man who seemed fairly willing to bring these thieves into my office with no regard for the loss to the school children. How do I replace the funds so that our school may open on time? Did thee think of what it would mean to the children, Hosea?"

"I is sorry, ma'am. That's all I can say. Ifin' I made a mistake, I is sorry. I didn't think I had a choice. But maybe you is right. I shoulda jist said I didn' know nothin' bout where da money might be."

"And they would have killed you on the spot," Julia interjected.

"They try to anyways, so what it matter?"

"It matters to me!"

"Julia, would thee please leave the office now?" Elizabeth asked quietly. "I would like to speak with Hosea alone."

"But—"

"Please, Julia. I believe thee said a new shipment of supplies came in on this afternoon's train, and it would be best if thee began unpacking and sorting the items."

Julia saw the resolute look on Elizabeth's face and knew she would not take no for an answer. "I will be in the warehouse when you finish, Hosea. Please stop by before you return to the barracks."

When they were alone, Elizabeth began to share her thoughts with the somewhat humbled young man. "I am not as concerned about the money as thee may believe, Hosea, although I still wish thee had simply said thee did not know where the thieves might find it. I know the need to protect one's life is strong, particularly when one has seen death as thee has seen it. The money is gone, and I must take some of the responsibility for not securing it that night. I should have kept it with me and then this would not have happened. I cannot see how we can find these men, unless, of course, thee knows them by name."

"No, ma'am, I don't know who they be, 'n they has their faces covered that night. I reconize some of da voices from when I visits Betsy, but I ain't got da names."

"Then I suppose we will have to try and raise the money again. Because I do not wish to see thee mistreated at the hands of some of the lawmen in this city, and because thee seems repentant for what happened, I do not intend to report this to the authorities. In exchange for my silence, however, I will require thee to accompany me on some of my visits to Friends meetings to explain the needs we have at the school. If thee is willing to do this, I believe the matter is finished."

Hosea looked confused. "Ya wants me ta go with ya to these meetin's, but what am I 'spose ta do? I ain't had no learnin', 'n I cain't talks ta people that don't know me."

"Thee will do well, Hosea," Elizabeth reassured him. "I will simply ask thee to tell about thy training as a blacksmith and how the Association has helped thee. And then thee can tell them about the school and how the money given for desks, books, and supplies was stolen and how badly we need to re-place it. Thee can do that, Hosea, I know thee can."

Hosea thought about what this woman was offering him. A chance to be free from the crime he supposed he really had been a part of. All he had to do was go with her and talk about his life. He didn't understand her willingness to help him, but what choice did he have? He shuddered to think of what might happen if she were to report the robbery.

"All right, Miz Comstock. I is willin' ta do it fer you."

"You are doing it for the school, Hosea, and to make resti-tution for your part in the crime."

"Yessum, I speck you is right."

"Now," Elizabeth continued, not quite ready to dismiss her new helper. "I would like to know if what I saw between you and Julia means what I suspect it might."

"I don't know what you be talkin' about." Hosea's proud head dropped and he gazed at the floor.

"I think thee does, Hosea. Please tell me how thee feels about Julia."

Hosea did not speak for what seemed like hours but was only a few seconds. Finally, lifting his head and looking di-rectly at Elizabeth, he resolved to tell her the truth.

"Miz Julia, she be da most beautiful, powerful woman I know. When I first come here she seem so high and mighty, like some rich spoiled girl. Then she help Julianna 'n me and lots a other black folks. She begs me ta teach her some of da songs we sing when we be slaves so she kin make wership bet-ter fer us all, and she even joins in da singin'. I don't know 'xactly what I feel 'bout her 'cept she make me feel warm inside 'n she be a good friend to me."

"Hosea, I am going to tell thee something I hope thee will think long and hard about. I believe Julia has been called by God to work in this mission. She had two young men in Iowa who would have asked for her hand in marriage if she had not put her work here ahead of settling down and having a family. If thee has any notion of being more than simply her friend, thee had best put it out of thy mind. I prayed to God for over a year that He would send someone here to preach His word, and both Julia and I were convinced she was the woman God intended to be my assistant in ministry. I do not want to sound unkind, but thee would be interfering in God's work if thee were to do something foolish like try to persuade Julia the two of you might someday have a life together."

A look of anger crossed Hosea's face. "What make you think I do such a thing?"

"I saw the look of adoration on her face this morning," Elizabeth said quietly, "and I see the look in your eyes when I mention her name. If I am not mistaken, the two of you have strong feelings for one another. It is far better to recognize those feelings now and address them than wait until thee has ruined her ministry."

Hosea thought about Elizabeth's words. Then he thought about the kiss he and Julia had shared; the way he loved to look at her and talk with her; the feelings of joy that rose within him whenever they were together. Elizabeth was right. There were strong feelings. But Julia had those feelings, too, he knew she did. Why was it wrong? Just because he was black and she was white? The Emancipation Proclamation said all men were equal, regardless of the color of their skin. Obviously this woman did not believe that. But if their feelings for one another would interfere with Julia's work at the mission, that would not be right either.

"Whys can't we both work here?" he asked defensively. "I be helpin' you with raisin' da money, 'n she be helpin' in da meetin' fer worship. Why can'ts we do it tagether?"

Elizabeth shook her head. "Hosea, thee knows as well as I that there are no refugees who would approve of a black man marrying a white woman. Not to mention all the white people who support our work here who would never understand how this could happen. Thee must think of Julia's future, not just the love thee might think thee has for her. The apostle Paul said if our actions cause our brothers to stumble, then we must cease from doing them."

"There you goes again, spoutin' that religious stuff," Hosea's anger over her words now focused on the issue of religion.

"There is that of God within each of us, Hosea, whether or not thee wishes to seek it. The Inner Light, Friends call it. Thee has chosen to reject that Light, Hosea, but I am praying that some day thee will accept God's love for thee and then thee will be seeking to do *God's* will, and not thy own."

"Like I says before, ma'am, ain't no God in me, ain't no God on this here earth cuz if there was there wouldn't be no fightin' and hate and killin' folks for no reason 'cept da color of their skin."

"Yes, Hosea, there is a God, although thee is right about the sins men do to one another. But that is the consequence of man having the freedom to make his own choices. Once Adam and Eve sinned in the Garden of Eden, we each carry that seed of sin within us. Only by believing and accepting God's sacrifice, the gift of his Son to us, can we be forgiven of that sin and led by the Inner Light. Does thee know about that gift, Hosea? Jesus was God's perfect son who walked on earth teaching about His Father and the need to love God and one another. The people did not like to hear they were sinners so they hung him on a wooden cross, pounded spikes in his hands and feet, and killed him."

"Shorely he done somethin' wrong," Hosea's voice was less defensive than before.

"How did thee feel when thee thought no one would believe thy story of the robbery?" she asked.

"Like it ain't fair."

"Precisely. And it was not fair to Jesus because he never did a single wrong thing. He was God's son, perfect in every way. Yet he let them kill him so he might pay the price for our sins. Would you have accepted payment for your freedom when you were a slave in Alabama?" she asked patiently.

"Ever body wanna be free," he said quietly.

"In the same way we can be free of our own sins, those things we do that separate us from God. All we have to do is accept this gift of payment Jesus already made for us. Then we can know God within and He will be in control of our lives and lead us where He would use us." Elizabeth paused, giving Hosea time to think of everything she had said.

"God did not kill your family, Hosea, sin did. God wept for your family, just as God weeps for you when you deny God's existence. God wants to offer you a wonderful life here on earth, and even more—eternal life with Him in heaven."

Hosea rested his head in his hands. Why was she telling him all these things? She knew how he felt about God, he'd said it often enough. But what if she was right? What if there really was a God, and he, Hosea, could have this Inner Light she talked about? Moved by something he didn't understand, Hosea began to cry, softly at first, then with great gasping sobs. Sobbing for the losses he had seen in his life, sobbing for the truth that he now believed he heard, sobbing to release the pain of a lifetime.

Elizabeth knelt beside the distraught young man and began to pray for him. The words were simple but Hosea felt more love at that moment than ever before in his life.

"Just tell God you are sorry, Hosea, and that you accept the payment he made for your sins. An innocent man died that you might have true freedom, Hosea. All you have to do is accept that payment."

Hosea began to pray softly, believing for the first time in a God who loved him and wanted to be in his life. It felt like a heavy weight had been lifted from his shoulders, a weight of guilt and pain he had carried for too long.

"Thank ya, Missus Comstock, fer helpin' me see da Light. I is gonna try ta do what God wants me ta do."

"Just spend time sitting in the quiet each day listening for God's voice, Hosea. He will lead thee in the way thee should go."

"I gots ta go tell Julia. She be so pleased."

"Just remember what I said about her future, Hosea. I know you will want do the right thing."

"Yessum, I is gonna try. I 'preciate ya not goin' to da police about da money."

"We have a deal, Hosea. Thee will pay me back when thee tells others how God has changed thy life."

Hosea quickly left Elizabeth's office in search of Julia. He found her unpacking dishes from Friends in London, shaking her head with each uncovered item. "I do not understand why these Friends continue to send tea pots, sugar basins, and cup handles. What refugee has tea?" she asked incredulously.

"Has you ever told 'em we aint gots no tea?" Hosea wondered.

"Numerous times. Elizabeth, Laura, and I have each spent hours writing correspondence to these meetings, telling them exactly what we can and cannot use. Look at this teapot. . . what refugee family do you know that could use it?" she said, irritated.

"Ain't they doin' what they think be helpin' ya?"

"I suppose."

"Then be thankful an save 'em till us refugees get rich 'n kin use 'em."

Was he joking? Julia looked more closely at Hosea's face. Somehow he seemed different than when she had left him in Elizabeth's office, and there was definitely a smile on his face.

"What has happened to thee?" she asked curiously. "What did Elizabeth say?"

Hosea proceeded to tell Julia everything that happened after she left, excluding Elizabeth's admonition to forget his feelings for her.

"I am happy for thee." Her expression, however, did not speak of the joy he expected her to feel. She almost looked angry at his announcement.

"What is it, Julia? Why ain't you happy 'bout this? You's been tryin' to git me ta believe in your God since you came here. Now I tells ya I find Him and you don't even look happy."

Why don't I feel excited, she wondered. It was what she had been praying for since the two of them met so many months ago.

Because you wanted to be the one who helped him see the Light. Can you not be happy that a soul was lost and now is found? You planted the seed and continued to water it. Now it has blossomed and you should be rejoicing.

Julia knew the voice was right. She had so wanted to be the one who led Hosea to the Lord. What good was it for her to be preaching every day if she could not lead people to their Savior?

Pride, Julia. Pride is the source of thy unhappiness. Your work is important or I would not have called you here. Trust me to know what is best.

"I really am happy thee has accepted God's gift, Hosea." This time her words were warm and expressed the joy she was beginning to feel. As she moved toward him she was surprised at the arms that held her at length.

"What is it, Hosea? What is wrong?"

"We cain't do this, Julia. God gots a job fer you, and he gots one fer me. But we has ta stop."

"Stop what, Hosea? Stop caring for thee? Is that what thee wants? I certainly hope not, because I cannot bury my feelings for thee."

"No, Julia. It ain't ever gonna work fer me 'n you ta be seein' one another. I likes you better 'n I eve'r liked another human, but there ain't never gonna be a life we can share, you 'n me."

"Why not? Surely you do not believe it is a sin for one human being to care for another."

"Jist leave it be, Julia. I cares fer you more din I wants ta say. But it ain't God's plan." He then shared with her everything Elizabeth had said about their lives and futures.

Julia was furious. She was nearly twenty years old and did not need a sixty-five-year-old woman telling her how to live her life. She would have to talk to Elizabeth and make her understand how she felt about Hosea. Elizabeth had a husband who must love her a great deal to allow her to be gone for months at a time. Surely she knew how it felt to care for someone in a special way.

"Please do not cast me aside like this, Hosea. I will talk to Elizabeth. I know I can make her understand. The two of us can minister together, Hosea, I know we can. We will show people that their prejudices can be overcome, that blacks and whites, Indians, all God's children are the same on the inside. Please, Hosea, please say you believe me."

Hosea's look told her he did not want them to go their separate ways any more than she did. "But I—"

"Please do not say another word. Leave it to me."

Though he had doubts that Elizabeth could be persuaded differently, Hosea smiled, remembering why it was he liked Julia so much: her strength of purpose and her desire to get what she wanted. The question was, would it be enough this time.

CHAPTER 11

Lonesome Valley'

Nearly every waking moment, whether drawing a picture with Julianna, sorting clothing in the warehouse, or preparing the message for worship, Julia thought of what she might say to persuade Elizabeth that she and Hosea should not be forced to end their relationship. Though she had asked Hosea not to come to the offices until she had talked with Elizabeth, it had been a week since she had seen him and she sorely missed his presence in her life. She longed to look at him, talk to him, and yes, imagine a life with him. She still could not understand why Elizabeth was unable to accept their ministry together.

When I talk to her, the words must be just right, she reminded herself. What I say must center on the possible ministries Hosea and I might have. I must convince her this could be God's will for our lives. But how? That was the dilemma. Though she had tried to sound optimistic when she announced her intent to persuade Elizabeth, she knew deep inside it would be a daunting task. Though Elizabeth was as compassionate a person as Julia had ever met, she was also one of the most stubborn when she believed she was right.

The matter was taken from Julia's hands with unexpected news delivered a week after Hosea's acceptance of God and His love.

"Julia, we must talk," Elizabeth said as she marched into her protege's office second day morning.

Julia looked up from the book she was using to record the shipment of clothing that had arrived the previous day from North Carolina. Before she could answer, Elizabeth began talking once again.

"I have decided I must travel and visit as many Friends meetings as possible in the next two months before winter sets in. My destination will be the East Coast, hopefully including the White House. I have high hopes I might be granted an audience with the new president."

Julia remembered the conversations she and Elizabeth had had on the train trip from Iowa. She had been particularly impressed with the woman's tenacity which had gained her an audience with President Garfield nearly two years earlier. To think that a common, ordinary woman could persuade those surrounding the president to permit her to speak with the leader of their country seemed almost miraculous to Julia. But then, Elizabeth was truly no ordinary woman, she reminded herself.

"But that was President Garfield. Does thee think President Arthur will be as receptive?"

"I am not certain what his response will be, but I must try. The government is still placing a duty on our shipments from abroad, and it is a travesty to the people here. When we must spend money on duties that could be spent building more barracks and schools for the refugees, something must be done. How does a God-fearing Congress offer thousands of dollars of relief to a foreign country like Ireland, yet neglect those here at home? All it takes is a bill passed in Congress and signed by the president to stop this injustice." Elizabeth had expounded on this subject more than once, and Julia was more than familiar with her desire to see this law passed.

"I am hopeful Hosea's first-hand experience with the suffering of his people will help convince the president we need this bill."

Hosea? Had she said Hosea? What was the meaning of her words?

"Thee said 'Hosea'?" She felt a tightness in her throat at the prospect of his leaving—even if for a short time.

"Yes, Julia, I said Hosea. He will be a great help to me when we visit the meetings in the East. When he tells of the tortures he has experienced it will shed new light on the condition of the refugees we are trying to help. Friends must understand why it is so important they share what they can with these refugees, and Hosea is the key to their understanding."

"But—"

"Now Julia," Elizabeth interrupted before Julia could protest. "This is important for thy work, too. We must not only replace the money that was stolen, but also generate enough to continue to be able to help meet the needs of those still coming from the South. Surely thee understands how beneficial it will be to have Hosea with me on this trip."

What could she say? Everything Elizabeth had said was true. Hosea would be a wonderful asset in gaining support for their work. But what would she do for two months without him?

"And," Elizabeth interrupted her thoughts, "I have decided thee should attend the Yearly Meetings in Indiana, Iowa and here in Kansas to continue to ask for their support for our work."

"Me? Surely Laura would be a better choice, and I know I can manage the Association again on my own. Laura is much better at speaking to large audiences than I." For some reason the thought of returning to Iowa was more than a little frightening.

Elizabeth chuckled. "That sounds a bit strange coming from someone who rises to speak in Meeting for Worship each morning."

"Thee knows what I mean, Elizabeth. I know these people here, but there are large crowds at the yearly meetings. Surely they will not want to listen to me."

"Quite the contrary, my dear. Thee is young and ambitious and has been following God's leading. What better testimonial of the importance of this work could there be?"

"But what about Julianna? I could not possibly leave her here alone."

Elizabeth looked away for a moment, then back at Julia with a sorrowful expression. Fear clutched Julia's heart. What was going to happen to her beloved Julianna? "What is thee going to do with Julianna?" she demanded.

"Several months ago, when I was nearly certain Betsy did not want the child, I talked to Doc Samuels about her. Doc has been arranging adoptions for families who have no children for many years."

That was not a surprise to Julia. Occasionally her own father had delivered a child of an unmarried young woman and then arranged for a childless couple to adopt it. Surely Elizabeth did not mean . . .

"Doc knows a man and wife that have been hoping to have a child for several years with no success. They came to the offices one day a few weeks ago and visited Julianna. Even though she is a mulatto, they are willing to adopt her and make a real, loving home for her." Not allowing Julia a moment to protest, Elizabeth continued. "I know thee loves the child, Julia, but thee must think of what is best for her. If thee were married and had a husband, it would be a different matter. This couple yearns for a child and I believe I am doing what is best for both them and Julianna."

"I will not let them take her!" Julia cried.

"They are coming for her this afternoon," Elizabeth said quietly. "I am telling thee now so the two of thee may have lunch together and thee may say good-bye to her."

"But *I* wanted to adopt her," she sobbed.

Elizabeth walked over to Julia and took her in her arms, much the way her mother would have done had she been there. "I know thee loves the child, Julia. But sometimes love must do the most difficult things, and this is one of those times. Julianna's new parents will provide a wonderful home for her and they have assured me thee may visit her any time thee wishes."

"But Julianna loves me and I love her! She needs me. How can this possibly be what is best for her?"

"Thee will be leaving soon, and that would also be difficult for Julianna. Children soon adjust to a new environment and I am certain Julianna will accept her new family in no time at all. I will let thee tell her the news over thy lunch. If thee can think of what is best for Julianna, I believe thee will be able to tell her in such a way as to help her accept her new life.

"As for your journey, I shall not take no for an answer, Julia. In fact, here are thy train tickets. First thee will attend sessions in Richmond, then thee will spend a few days with thy family in Salem before attending Iowa Yearly Meeting sessions in Oskaloosa. The last leg of thy journey will be in Lawrence for the sessions here in Kansas. Here is a copy of thy destinations and the dates thee will arrive and depart. I have sent minutes to each of the yearly meetings informing them of thy visit. Each will provide lodging and meals for thee during thy visits. Of course thy family will see to thy needs when thee is in Iowa."

What was happening to her world? First the news of Julianna, and now this visit with her family. How long had Elizabeth been planning this trip? Since the day she determined to interfere in Julia's life with Hosea? Julia grew angry thinking of Elizabeth's meddling. She did not care to see her family, she did not want to speak to large sessions of yearly meeting Friends, and she did not want to be separated from Hosea.

"And if I do not agree to go?" she asked softly.

"Julia," Elizabeth said gently, "thee has been called to this work. Our needs are not always the same. Thee has been here over a year and I have not asked thee once to travel and speak. Normally I would have asked Laura to attend these sessions, but she has not felt well the past few months and I fear the travel would be too much for her. I am hoping she will be able to carry the load here in our absence. I spoke with John Stanley the last time he was here and he has agreed to check with Laura each week to make certain there are no pressing needs. If a problem arises, he will handle the details, relieving her of the burden of carrying the load alone. Each piece of the puzzle has fallen into place in God's own timing, Julia. I, for one, am excited there will be two places visited for every one I would have been able to reach on my own."

"How does Hosea feel about thy plans?" Julia asked. "Surely he does not feel at ease speaking before a large crowd." And surely he does not want to be away from me, she wanted to add.

"Of course he was a bit reluctant at first. But Hosea must have told thee of our agreement, Julia, that he would speak in meetings in exchange for my silence regarding the robbery."

"Yes, he told me. But does thee think it is fair to ask him to accompany thee to see the president?" she asked, grasping at anything to prevent the inevitable. "Perhaps he might travel with me instead of thee. Surely there would be much more support from the yearly meetings were they to hear his story."

Elizabeth stared at her in disbelief. "I certainly hope thee is not serious, Julia. What servant of God's would send two children, male and female, black and white, on a two-month trip? With no chaperone?"

"But what about me?" she countered. "Thee would send me, a young woman, alone on a train to travel across three states?"

"God will be with thee, Julia, and I do not foresee any dangers. I believe the train stations in the cities you will travel to and from are safe, and there is certainly little danger once thee is greeted by the various Friends. I should think thee would be excited at the prospect of traveling and seeing thy family and friends in Salem."

Julia knew Elizabeth's mind was made up and there would be no alternate plan. She would spend two months traveling alone. She would speak to large groups of men and women. Even that, however, did not frighten her as much as the thought of being home in Salem and having to face her father. Of course it would be wonderful to see Rachel again . . . what would her little sister look like by now? Julia imagined she was never still a minute. And her mother . . . how wonderful to once again feel the love and acceptance her mother never failed to give. David and Hannah . . . her heart quickened as she thought of their baby due to arrive sometime within the next month. Hannah often wrote long, newsy letters, even though Julia seldom responded in kind. Perhaps she would be there to welcome the newest member of the family. Yes, she would love to see each of them.

But Father. What would the two of them say to one another? More important, would her father even speak to her? Julia shivered as she remembered David telling how determined Father had been to chase her down and bring her home. Would he now insist she remain in Salem and end her work in Kansas? Had Elizabeth thought of that possibility?

"I know thee is concerned about being with thy father again," Elizabeth said, seeming to read Julia's thoughts. "I have been in correspondence with thy family since thee came here, Julia, and I believe this will be an opportunity for thee to mend fences with thy father."

Julia stared once again at this woman who always seemed to be one step ahead of her. "Has thee spoken with my father?" she asked curiously.

"I visited thy family last spring, remember? And yes, thy father and I talked of thy work. I believe he was quite surprised at thy success here—and thy willingness to continue on with the work."

"That does not surprise me," Julia said bitterly. "From the beginning he refused to believe this could be God's call for me."

"But I believe time heals all wounds, Julia, and perhaps thy father may now be more willing to see thee as a young woman rather than his little girl."

Julia was doubtful. Her father was the most stubborn man she knew. But also compassionate, she reminded herself, remembering all the times he had given from his own pocket to those in need. Would that compassion extend to a daughter who had sorely disappointed him? That remained to be seen.

Julia's thoughts returned to Hosea. She longed to see him, to talk to him about their upcoming separation. Would he miss her as much as she knew she was going to miss him? Or would he forget the way they felt about each other, the ministry they might have together?

I called thee here to do my work, Julia. Thee need not be concerned about Hosea. He, too, is my child now, and he must be faithful to my call.

What call? Julia thought. Her main concern had been for his salvation; she had not thought of God having a specific call for him. Perhaps this was God's way of preparing Hosea for a ministry the two of them might have together. Julia's heart suddenly felt lighter. A plan. God must surely have a plan for the two of them, and this was the first step. She could accept that. She would go to the yearly meetings and do her best to represent the work they did. And when they all returned to Topeka perhaps the picture would be clearer, God's plan revealed to Hosea and her.

"All right, Elizabeth, I will go to the yearly meetings for thee."

"For God," Elizabeth reminded her.

"Of course. For God." And also for Hosea and me, she thought.

Saying good-bye to Julianna aroused the same emotions Julia had felt when she had left home for Kansas. It was an overwhelming sense of loss, of a separation that would never be repaired. Yet she did not want to cause Julianna the pain she herself was feeling.

"I have some good news for thee, Julianna," she began, using every bit of resolve she could muster to keep her sorrow hidden from this dear child.

"What, Juwea? Is thee going to play a game wif me? Or help me draw a new picture on the wall?"

"No, this is a better surprise than that! How would thee like to have a real mommy and daddy, and a real house and a room of thy own?"

"Am I going to move, Juwea? Am I going to live wif you now?" Excitement laced her voice.

"No," Julia said slowly, "thee is going to have a new mommy and daddy. They live in a nice house and they want a little girl just like thee for their very own. And they are coming this afternoon to take thee to thy new home."

A frown appeared on Julianna's face. "But you is my mammy, Juwea."

"No," Julia said gently, "I am your very good friend, and I love you very, very, much, and I will come to visit you very often. But your new mommy and daddy will love you even more and you will be very happy with them."

Julia wished she believed what she was telling the wide-eyed five-year-old before her. How could anyone love this child more than she did? How could they make her happier?

"Ok, Juwea, if you will visit me I will go there. But I will miss you."

Julia grabbed Julianna and held her tightly so the little girl could not see the tears she could contain no longer. "I love you," she whispered.

"I wuv you, too, Juwea. Don't cry."

"I will come and see you very soon, Julianna. Remember to practice your letters and sounds. And your new mommy will have lots of books for your to read. When I come to visit you I want to hear you read me a story."

"I will. I promise."

Julia was nearly overwhelmed with sadness. Her Julianna, her child, had been taken from her. When would life get easier?

There was only a week before the three workers were scheduled to depart for their respective destinations. Hosea was determined to finish his blacksmith training before leaving, and Julia was working feverishly to unpack and sort all the boxes currently piled in the warehouse in order to ease Laura's burden once they were gone. Still, Julia and Hosea found stolen moments in the evenings to at least catch up on each other's lives. Hosea was able to comfort Julia after the loss of Julianna, while Julia shared some of her favorite scriptures with Hosea in an effort to help him prepare for the speaking he must do with Elizabeth.

The night before her train was to leave for Indiana, Julia and Hosea had one last chance to be alone. Elizabeth had a speaking engagement in Spring Grove Friends Meeting that evening which necessitated leaving in the middle of the afternoon. Julia opened the door to the offices as soon as Elizabeth left, her sign to Hosea of an opportunity to be alone. As soon as Hosea returned from the blacksmith's that evening he noticed the open door, and his excitement was evident in the giant strides he made toward the offices. Cautiously, still careful not to tread where he was not welcomed, Hosea peeked into the hallway and looked toward Julia's office. Seeing her door was open, he softly called her name.

"Hosea!" she said warmly, running from her office to welcome the soot-and-ash-covered worker.

"Whoa, Julia," he laughed, backing away from her. "I's ain't had no chance ta wash ma self 'n you is so clean and perty." He grinned, absorbing the sight of her once again. How he would miss not seeing her every day. Some days the only time he saw her was in worship, but it had been enough to sustain him until the next time they could be with each other. But now it would be two months before he could gaze at her beauty. Was he doing the right thing, leaving Julia for so long, allowing her to go off by herself to these places he knew nothing about? He had no choice, he reminded himself. This was part of his agreement with Elizabeth.

"Hosea? Did thee hear what I said?" Julia asked, wondering what Hosea was thinking.

"Whats you say?" he asked, focusing again on her green eyes that, at times, seemed to shoot sparks of fire.

"I asked if thee had enough clothing for the trip. We just received a box of nice clothes from the Lawrence Meeting, and there were several dress shirts and pants that I thought might fit thee."

Hosea felt embarrassed. His clothes must not be good enough to wear when speaking to Friends in other places. "You think da clothes I has ain't proper fer talkin' ta folks about dis place? I figures if'n I looks like I ain't got no fancy clothes, then da peoples gonna wanna give more money."

Julia laughed. "That might work, but I believe Friends will be more impressed with a changed man—including his clothes—than with someone who looks like he is poor and destitute."

"I *is* poor 'n desteetute, as you calls it," he reminded her, suddenly feeling very inadequate for the job he was being asked to do.

Julia blushed. "I did not mean to insult thee, Hosea. I am sorry. I just meant thee has made many changes in thy life and it is important for Friends to see what this mission can accomplish. Would thee like to take some of the clothes to the barracks and try them on? Thee could bring them back after thee has had a chance to wash."

Hosea's heart felt light again. He would do anything for Julia, anything at all. And she asked him to come back. Perhaps things might work out after all.

Hosea's step was light as he ran to the barracks after selecting a few pairs of pants and shirts to try. He wanted Julia to be proud of him; he wanted her to see him as her equal, not a poor black man with no family, no money, no education. Maybe that was why Elizabeth had said he must not entertain thoughts of any type of future with Julia: he had nothing to offer her.

He continued to think about their differences as he tried on the new clothing. It was so much more than the color of their skin. Her daddy was a doctor, his a murdered slave. Her momma sent letters to her and wanted her to be happy; his had gone insane. She had store-bought clothes that enhanced her beauty; he wore cast-offs from white folks. She had been a believer her entire life and knew all about the Bible; he had hated God until a few weeks ago. What was he thinking? They had nothing in common. Her professed feelings for him must be more pity than the kind of love a woman felt for a man she wished to spend her life with. It was impossible for her to love him when he had nothing to offer. That was the only thing that really mattered. He had nothing. He had been a fool to ever have entertained thoughts of the two of them sharing a home and raising a family. Julia had never even said that was what she wanted anyway. It was probably all his imagination. Fool, he thought. You are nothing but a big fool. Feeling the hopelessness of the situation, Hosea collapsed on his cot.

Julia grew concerned when Hosea did not return to the offices. Had that not been the plan? He would wash up and try on the new clothes and then return? When an hour passed with no signs of him, she was certain something terrible had happened. She had to find him.

Hurrying to the barracks and seeing no one outside, Julia boldly marched to the door of Hosea's cabin and pounded. Moses, not Hosea, greeted her.

"Moses, I must speak to Hosea. Is he here?"

"Yessum, he be over there on da bed." Moses looked over his shoulder at Hosea whose back was toward them.

"Did he say anything to thee? About me, I mean?" Julia whispered to the elder member of the group.

"Nah, he jist say he nothin' buts a po' black boy wif nothin' ta offer no one 'cept he be a hard worker. What's you think that mean, Miz Julia?" Though he seemed puzzled, Julia was certain Moses understood more than he was telling her.

"Please leave us for a few minutes, Moses," Julia asked, knowing it was going to be a hard request for the old man to grant.

"That not be proper, Miz Julia, fer me ta leaves ya both in this buildin' with nobody here."

"Please, Moses, please." Something about her expression convinced him the situation was quite serious, and finally he agreed.

"Jist fer a minute er two, that's all," he warned. "There be trouble from da others that lives here iffin' they knows I 'llowed this ta happen."

"I will not be long," she assured him.

Moses shuffled out of the barrack and Julia knelt beside the bed where Hosea was lying. "Please look at me," she said quietly. "If I have ever meant anything at all to you, please look at me," she repeated when there was no response to her first request. Slowly Hosea turned toward her. She saw the telltale tear streaks and began to panic.

"What is it, Hosea? What has happened? Is thee ill? When thee left the offices thee looked so happy. I was so worried when thee did not return. Did thee not understand I wanted thee to come back so we might have our last night at the Association together?"

Hosea shook his head. With a voice that broke often—and nearly broke her heart—he told her all the reasons why they could never share a life. He said she needed to really think about the many ways they were different: the differences in their families and the way they had been raised, the things they had seen and done that made them who they were now, even the difference in their speech.

"Why should that be of importance?" she asked, unwilling to accept his sudden change of heart, in spite of her own doubts.

"Tell me, Julia. Does you really think you 'n me could ever have a life together? Or was you jist interested in getting me

153

saved? Sometimes when I sees your smile I thinks you really likes me. You even kissed me once. But I ain't sure how you feels. Mostly I jist think you feels sorry for me 'n my life as a slave. You know da white folks ain't ever gonna 'cept you 'n me havin' feelin's fer one another. My people ain't gonna 'cept us, neither, 'n they shore ain't gonna listen to what you gots ta say in wership ifin they thinks you 'n me wants ta be together. Ya see, it jist ain't ever gonna work, Julia. People don' like ta change da way they sees da worl'. They don't wanna think that a white girl could love a black boy. They don't want us black folk being like them 'cause they truly believes they is superior to us."

"I do not feel superior to thee," Julia said defensively.

"But it ain't you that's got ta do da acceptin', Julia. It's da peoples of this world. They da ones that ain't gonna accept da differences."

"But we cannot give up, Hosea. How will they change if we do not help them see the error in their thinking?"

"That's another thing, Julia. Yous always usin' them big words I never heared before. I ain't had no learnin' like you. Yous been ta that fancy 'cademy 'n alls I's done is sit 'n listen to da massa's boy git his lessons."

"But I could teach thee, Hosea, I know I could," she countered.

"It ain't no use. Jist gonna have ta 'cept da way things is, Julia. I's gonna go with Miz Comstock and then I be done with my payment fer da robbery. Then I's gonna come back 'n start me a blacksmith shop down south in Cherokee county. Plenty o' black folk down there, and I be able ta find me a wife so's I kin have a famly." He paused, then added softly, "She won't be as purty as you is, Julia, but ifin' she love me, that won't matter."

"But *I* love you, Hosea!"

"No, you don'ts love me. You *helpt* me, Julia. That be all. You help me find God and I always be happy 'bout dat. But there ain't no hope fer us, Julia, and you jist needs ta ferget about me."

Julia didn't care that she was crying. Deep in her heart she knew what Hosea said was the truth. Perhaps her feelings were not the love she thought she was feeling. But the thought of never talking with Hosea, of him going off to find a wife and raise a family and never seeing him again were not acceptable, either.

"Please, Hosea," she begged. "Please wait until we both return before making thy decision about our lives. What if God planned for the two of us to work together? Would thee go against God's plan?"

Hosea seemed to think about her words for a moment. Knowing he had hurt her gnawed at his peace of mind. What harm would it do to agree to think about it? Perhaps after they had been apart she would see he was right.

"All right, Julia. I's gonna think 'n pray about what you say. If God have a plan fer us, then I be willin' to listen. But I think da answer be da same."

"Just wait, Hosea, that is all I am asking of thee."

"Okay, Julia. I waits till we gits back." But it won't make any differ'nce, he thought. No differ'nce at all.

CHAPTER 12

'THE Gospel Train'

Although Julia, Elizabeth, and Hosea rode the same train for the first half of their destinations, there was little conversation the first day. Elizabeth was catching up on some of the latest news in the Society of Friends via the periodicals *Friends' Review*, *Western Friend*, and *Christian Worker*, and she expected Julia to read the editorials so she might gain an understanding of the opinions of some of the leaders in the various yearly meetings. For Hosea, the sight of the two women who sat across the aisle from him reading the papers was just another thorn that seemed to continually poke at his inadequacies. You cain't even read, he chided himself, not even a child's book, let alone adult books and magazines.

Occasionally Julia glanced Hosea's way, wondering what he was thinking. Hosea, however, sat motionless, staring out the window. Maybe he has never seen this part of the country and does not want to miss anything, she reasoned, as corn fields ready for harvest continually passed by their windows. Elizabeth sat directly across the aisle from Hosea, occasionally pointing to a landmark she thought might interest him. His general response was barely a nod. If only the two of us could sit together, Julia lamented. I am certain I could coax a smile or two. At that thought, however, she was reminded of their last conversation and his announcement that their differences were too great an obstacle for any future together. If only he might somehow believe in himself and his ability to move others with the story of his life. Perhaps Elizabeth was the perfect one to lead him in this new venture. Surely after he saw the effect of his words on those listening he would feel better about his God-given gifts and abilities. And he did have gifts, of that she was certain, the main one being his compassion for others.

The entire five-day trip from Kansas to Indiana was as monotonous as the never-ending prairies of Kansas. Every time the train stopped to board passengers, Julia got off to walk around. She had never been one to enjoy sitting for any length of time. As a child, her inability to sit still had led to numerous reprimands from her mother during silent worship. I am lucky Father was on the men's side for worship, she thought with a grin, or my chastisements would have been considerably more severe! The thought of her father once again brought waves of anxiety as she wondered how he would receive his prodigal daughter. I will not worry about it until the time comes, she told herself for the fiftieth time.

When the train pulled into Richmond the reality of her mission settled in. She, Julia Jones, was about to be separated from everything that was familiar to enter a foreign land. At least it seemed that way. Indiana, of course, looked very much like Iowa and she would never have known she were not in her home state were it not for the signs greeting them as they entered the city. It was not knowing a soul in Indiana Yearly Meeting, however, that was causing the nervousness in her stomach.

When it was time to leave the train, Julia was excited to see Hosea following Elizabeth down the steps of the car. He had gotten off only twice since they left Kansas and Julia was afraid he would not want to say good-bye.

"God bless thee, Julia," Elizabeth said with a hug. "I know Thee will represent our work well. Remember the children, Julia, and how needy they are when they come to us. That will be help thee stay focused on thy mission."

"I will do my best, Elizabeth, although I am still not certain I am equal to the task."

Elizabeth's smile hinted at the teasing tone of her next words. "When I first met thee, Julia, thee seemed confident of accomplishing anything God might ask of thee. Surely living with me has not caused thee to become weaker instead of stronger."

Julia laughed, lightened for the moment by Elizabeth's comment. It was true. She had been certain of God's call on her life, and certain she could do whatever He asked of her.

"Thee is right, Elizabeth. This is God's work and I have no reason to worry. I will persuade those Friends to give the very socks off their feet!"

Even Hosea smiled at the idea of all the Friends in the Yearly Meeting taking off their socks and giving them to Julia to take back to Kansas.

"That is the Julia I love," Elizabeth said warmly. "Oh—I nearly forgot. Please give my regards to David Updegraff if thee should see him at one of the joint sessions of men and women. If thee is fortunate, he will be asked to bring a message to the gathering. He is a powerful revivalist and I am certain thee will enjoy his ministry."

The word revivalist brought a flurry of memories. Julia remembered her only experience at a revival meeting when she and her Academy friends had traveled to Richland to hear Lawrie Tatum. It had been her first experience with group singing and a preacher who pointed at various worshipers in the gathering and asked them to come forward and kneel in prayer. No, she had not enjoyed the evening. But even her mother had written about David Updegraff and the wonderful messages he brought to the Salem Meeting.

"I will give him thy regards, Elizabeth," she said, vowing to listen with an open heart and mind to what he might have to say.

Just then the train whistled, signaling its pending departure. "I do not see the Friends who are to meet thee, Julia, but I am confident they will soon arrive. If not, thee has the address of the Yearly Meeting office and thee can walk the few blocks and wait there. Good-bye, my dear," Elizabeth said with a quick hug, turning toward the train and motioning Hosea to follow.

Hosea paused, his eyes expressing all the confusion he felt at that moment. "I will miss thee, Hosea," Julia said boldly. "I hope thee will at least think of me now and then."

"I always be thinkin' of you, Julia. Even though I knows they ain't much hope fer us, I is gonna try real hard ta be da best speaker I can, and maybe I gets better at bein' da kind a man you kin be proud of."

Julia's heart nearly broke. "I am proud of you, Hosea. So proud of all you have done with your life. I do not want you to ever forget that." Not caring who might be watching or what they might think, Julia quickly squeezed Hosea's hand as the train began to pull away from the station. Hosea had no trouble catching the slowly moving passenger car and in no time he was aboard and the train was out of sight. Would she ever see him again? That is a poor way to think, she chided herself. Of course I will see him again. If God has a plan for us, neither Hosea's insecurities nor my doubts can keep us apart.

"Miss Jones?"

Julia turned toward the voice and instantly recognized the Quaker gray and black of the man and woman who had come up behind her. "Yes, I am Julia, and thee must be from the Yearly Meeting," she said warmly, wanting to make a good impression.

"My name is Joel Clark, and this is my wife, Rebecca. Thee will be staying in our home during the sessions."

"Rebecca is my mother's name," Julia replied, turning to the small woman with the traditional bonnet that nearly hid her face.

"Then we shall get along famously," she said gathering Julia's arm in her own. "Our horse and carriage are right over there. Joel, please gather Julia's belongings. I am certain she would like an opportunity to rest a bit before tonight's opening session."

Julia smiled. She liked Rebecca's take-charge manner, much the same as her own mother's. She was certain she would enjoy this visit.

The opening session of Indiana Yearly Meeting was a combined meeting with men and women joining together for worship. Although her mother had tried on several occasions to explain the importance of men and women being separate for worship, Julia never understood the reasoning. Why would the men be distracted by the women and vice-versa? Surely when one's head was bowed and eyes closed there would be little opportunity for distraction.

A feeling of sadness came over her as she thought of the questions Julianna had begun asking her the weeks before she went to live with her new family. 'Why do you wear dose clothes?' and 'Where do your God live, Juwea?' She never grew tired of Julianna's inquisitive mind. She certainly hoped the couple that adopted her would be able to provide the spiritual nurturing a young child needed.

The yearly meeting business sessions were just as Julia remembered: long and dry. Why could Friends not omit the long numerical reports of children in First Day School, and the number of members using tobacco and strong drink? Whose business was it if a person used tobacco? If believers were seeking God in the silence, then the matter should be between the two of them and not the entire Yearly Meeting.

It was during one of the joint business sessions that Julia was asked to tell about her work with the refugees. "They already know some things about our work, Julia," Elizabeth had coached, "and thee will need to tell them stories of the things thee has seen and heard that will move them to once again give from the generosity of their hearts."

Julia began by telling them of the morning Betsy had come and demanded she and Laura go with her to help Julianna. Though she told most of the story, she did not tell them of her attachment to the little girl who had become so much a part of her life. She also told them about Hosea and the way his family was tortured and killed. She then outlined their immediate needs, particularly the need for cash to buy desks and supplies for the school. She asked each one present to prayerfully consider what they might be able to give to the work. She felt truly humbled by the response as the recording clerk wrote furiously to keep track of all the donations being offered by Friends present. "Thank you, God," she prayed quietly. "Thank you for giving me the right words." For the first time she began to believe Elizabeth had not been mistaken when choosing her to travel to the Yearly Meetings.

Julia spent the next few days listening to reports from the various Yearly Meeting committees, discussions of the different mission fields being supported, and messages from various evangelists. She also enjoyed informal times of sharing with groups of four or five Friends. It was the final day's worship service that proved to be the most interesting, however.

Though she had heard David Updegraff's name mentioned by one or two Friends, he was not in attendance at any of the sessions. It was another revivalist by the name of Dugan Clark Jr.—Joel and Rebecca's nephew—who was scheduled to speak in worship the last day. Julia was impressed by the appearance of the man: fifty-ish, tall and slender, standing straight with head held high. Confidence radiated from his body. But there was something else. Whereas Lawrie Tatum had paced, preaching and singing and exhorting believers to come forward to receive all God had to offer, Dugan Clark seemed calm, though there was a hint of excitement in his voice. Julia subconsciously sat up straighter and did her best to center on the worship service.

The message was simple. Dugan Clark was David Updegraff's right hand man, a theologian by trade. Whereas Julia's first experience with holiness had left a bitter taste in her mouth, this time she found herself yearning to know more.

Clark told of growing up in a family where both mother and father were ministers. As a young man he had valued his education, studying medicine and eventually becoming a professor at Earlham College. He identified with the revival movement, believing that changed hearts would change the world.

Then came a time of questioning his spiritual training, and it was David Updegraff who helped him see the power of the holiness experience.

"Oh, it filled me," he said, his voice becoming more animated. "When I publicly laid claim to God's promise of holiness, all my being was filled with this wonderful peace . . . dead to self and sin, alive to Christ, and filled with the Holy Ghost! I became a changed man. I did more for God in the three weeks following my sanctification than in all the years prior to that day."

Clark's words had a powerful effect on Julia, and she began to wonder if, indeed, a person could become holy by merely asking it of God. She knew salvation was by grace—God's gift to mankind that could never be earned—but what about holiness? It did not seem reasonable that a person might become sinless by merely asking. Did not one need to crucify daily the sinful desires of the body, constantly denying those things that were not pleasing to God?

When the service was finished, she sought to have a word with Dugan Clark, much the same way she had sought Elizabeth two years earlier in Iowa. Evidently she was not the only one in the meeting with questions, for there was quite a crowd gathered outside the meeting house to hear more about holiness to be had for the asking.

When Julia was finally able to gain the man's attention, she asked the question that had continued to rise in her mind: was it possible to be free from sin once and for all?

"Of course I do not profess to know all there is to be said on the subject," he began, "but I do know of that which I have experienced. I know that my former nature was bent on sinning and my sanctified nature desires to do that which will benefit those in my world. Does it mean I never commit a sin?

Of course not, because I am human and have the seed of Adam within me. It is my attitude toward sin that has changed, Julia, and it has had a powerful effect on my life."

His words made sense to Julia, but something still bothered her. "Does thee know Lawrie Tatum?" she asked, determined to find out once and for all if Tatum were a true evangelist or a man who enjoyed manipulating people.

"Yes, we have met, though I have never heard him preach. Others have told me of his effectiveness, however, and I have no doubt he has been sanctified and is sincere in his desire to preach the kingdom of God as he sees best. Why do you ask?"

Julia noticed the absence of "thee" and "thou" in his speech and instantly felt a bit closer to him.

"What is it?" he asked, noticing the smile that turned up the corners of her mouth.

"I was just noticing thy speech," she said simply.

"Ah yes, the 'thees' and 'thous' we Friends are so proud of. I have found that in talking with the average person on the street it is best if I speak in the same manner as they. It seems to put them more at ease. I do understand the original justification for the plain language, but it does not seem appropriate for this modern day and age. Am I to presume you feel the same way?"

"Yes."

"And what do you think about sanctification? Is it something you would like to experience?"

"I am not certain I completely understand it, but it would certainly be wonderful not to have to worry about sinning any more."

Dugan laughed. "That does not mean you can go out and rob a bank or murder your enemy, you realize."

Julia liked his sense of humor. "I shall be on guard lest my greedy nature causes me to stumble and fall," she teased back.

They continued visiting for a few more minutes and then Dugan became serious again. "Holiness is a wonderful thing, Julia. Please examine your heart and see if you would not benefit from the gift of sanctification from the Holy Spirit. It was nice meeting you," he added, "and I wish you the best in your work with the refugees."

"But—"

"My aunt and uncle have been telling me all about your work. It seems they are quite enamored with you! Seriously, it is a wonderful thing you are doing in Kansas. Almost makes me wish I could visit there sometime."

"Oh please do. Thee—I mean, you—would be most welcome any time."

"I just might take thee up on it!" he said, his eyes twinkling.

As Julia left for the Clark home later that day, she thought again of Dugan's words. He had said nearly the same things that Lawrie Tatum had said, only in a different manner. Truth should be truth, should it not? Could both men be saying the same thing only in a different way?

Everyone likes to judge, Julia. For some reason it makes them feel better to be critical of others. If only my children would realize that I make them all different, yet each is pleasing in his or her way. Lawrie and Dugan speak the same message. The question is, what will you do with this message of holiness?

The answer was clear. Tonight when she knelt for prayer she would ask God for a second gift, a gift of sanctification through the Holy Spirit. She would ask Him to give her the desire to be pure, that her actions might be pleasing to Him. Perhaps then she would know how to address her father and how to talk to Hosea. Hosea . . . what was he doing right now? Had he and Elizabeth arrived safely in Washington D.C.? Had he gotten to meet the president? And most importantly, was he thinking of her and the future they might one day have together, a life of service to God?

Her thoughts returned to her father. Tomorrow she would leave for Iowa and within a few days the two of them would once again be under the same roof. Would he speak to her after the way she left a year ago? How would she respond to his criticisms? This would certainly be a test of the power of holiness in her life, she thought as she slowly walked back to the Clark home.

CHAPTER 13

ON THE *Go Tell It on the Mountain*

"Come now, Rachel," Rebecca coaxed the timid two-year-old hiding behind her apron. "You remember Julia, she is thy big sister—the one who used to chase thee all around the house."

Julia stood amazed. She was unable to believe her baby sister had grown so much in the year she had been gone. It was also hard to accept the fact that the little girl did not remember her. "Hello, Rachel," she said with a soft, encouraging voice. When there was no response she looked hopelessly at Rebecca.

"She is quite shy, Julia, not at all like thee as a child. She will come to thee when she feels safe."

"Safe? My own sister does not feel safe with me?" she asked incredulously.

Rebecca seemed flustered. "I am sorry, Julia, but thee must trust me when I tell thee she will warm to thee in a short time."

Julia smiled at the chunky, blue-eyed girl with the long dark curls. She truly was as cute as any doll Julia had ever seen.

She wondered if Rachel still liked to get into the cupboards and closets like she had a year ago, or if her interests were totally different now. Then she remembered something that might bring recognition to the child.

"Rachel, does thee remember Polly-Wog, the little frog we found down at the pond? It jumped right out of my hand into thine. Does thee remember?"

Rachel finally smiled, her first positive response to her big sister.

"Pawy Fwogy?" she asked.

"Yes, thee remembers. I knew thee would."

"Icky Pawy Fwogy!" Rachel's face grimaced as she recalled picking up the slimy frog that promptly slipped through her tiny hand.

"And the doggie? Where's Wolfie?" Wolfie had been Julia's dog, the stray German Shepherd her father brought home one day when Julia was twelve. She still remembered the joy the dog brought into her life and the times she, David, her father, and the dog had romped through the woods. She also remembered the happiness she felt just being with the father she looked up to and wanted to be like. What caused the estrangement she now felt?

"Woofie," Rachel pointed to the fast approaching canine.

"Wolfie!" Julie knelt to receive the warm licks from the animal who obviously remembered who she was. "What a fat dog you are!"

"No doubt from all the scraps thy young sister slips her way each meal."

Julia froze at the sound of her father's voice as he came through the front door onto the porch where the three sat. His tone of voice gave little clue as to the reception she might receive.

"Hello, Father," she said cautiously, turning to face the one who had been so bitter at her departure.

"Hello, Julia. How was thy journey?"

Julia had spent nearly the entire train ride from Indiana imagining the things her father might say to her and how she would respond. She had also considered that he might not even speak to her. Since the closing night of Indiana Yearly Meeting when she had prayed for holiness, she had earnestly asked God morning and night for wisdom and understanding when speaking with her father. It would take holiness to respect the man God had chosen as her father, and holiness to enable her to speak calmly and kindly. She hoped he would recognize a more mature daughter than the one who left a year ago, a woman with the ability to oversee the work of others, and one who had developed a compassion for those in need. She fervently hoped he would consider her an adult and not the little girl he had wanted to rescue and bring back to Salem.

"The passenger car was a bit warmer than the one on the journey from Kansas to Indiana," she finally answered, "but the travelers on either side of me were congenial and we had a good visit. One of them was a fellow nearly my age traveling to Colorado to work in the mines, and the other was an elderly woman who had been visiting her grandchildren in the East. She talked nearly nonstop and I believe I could recite the names and ages of each of her grandchildren, as well as their interests. I finally pretended to sleep when I needed a few moments to myself."

Rebecca laughed at the picture of Julia pretending sleep. Julia was seldom still, even as a young woman. Since arriving she had sat and stood several times. Rebecca was certain it was due to nervousness, as she still recognized the emotions her children were experiencing, even in their silence.

"What about Indiana? Did thee find it different from Iowa? Or Kansas?" Rebecca added as an afterthought.

"Indiana and Iowa are so similar I doubt anyone living in either place could tell which state they were in if they were suddenly dropped from the sky into one of the green fields of corn. Kansas, however, is a different story. I rarely see a tree save for the young ones planted since the area was settled, and the horizon seems to go on forever with acres and acres of prairie."

"I should think one would grow tired of the monotony," Charles said coolly.

Remember your vow to be kind, Julia reminded herself before speaking. "God's creation is never monotonous to me," she said quietly. "The farming is certainly simpler in Kansas than here in Iowa or Indiana, but each has its own unique beauty."

"I suppose it would be easier to farm with no trees to cut or stumps to pull," Rebecca said, looking hopefully at Charles for his affirmation. When he remained silent, she continued. "We are so glad to have thee home, Julia. I hope the rolling fields and tall trees are as pleasing to thee as the miles of prairie. Please . . . let us go in and make ourselves comfortable. It is time for Rachel to prepare for bed, and once she is taken care of we can have a good visit." She looked at Charles, her expression challenging him to disagree.

"Could I put Rachel to bed?" Julia asked, hoping to avoid being alone with her father.

"Would thee like for thy big sister to help thee prepare for bed?" Rebecca asked the toddler.

"Juwea," she said simply, jumping off her mother's lap and taking Julia's hand.

"It seems she remembers thee now," Rebecca said happily. "Thee may have the honor, Julia. Perhaps thee will do a better job preparing her to sleep than your father or I. Oh, I should tell thee. She has taken thy old room. I hope thee will not be too disappointed."

"Why should she be?" Charles said more to himself than to the others. "Runs off without telling a soul where she's going; never sends word she's arrived; why would we expect her to ever return?"

Julia felt the hurt and anger contained in his voice. Did she dare try to explain the events of her departure?

"Juwea, come on!" The little hand pulled on the bigger one.

"All right, sweetie. Time to get you to bed."

"Thee, Julia, thee," Rebecca reminded with a laugh.

Some things never change, Julia thought with a smile, beginning to feel more at ease than any time since she had arrived that afternoon. She would try and do a better job of remembering the little things that seemed so important to her parents. Holiness. It had sounded so easy when Dugan Clark talked of its power. Work was what it seemed to Julia. But it had felt good to be able to reply to her father in a respectful manner.

Several days passed with nothing said to harm the fragile truce that seemed to abide in the Jones' home. Rebecca was delighted to have her elder daughter home, even if it was for only a week, and she constantly sought Julia's thoughts on everything from what the mission was like to how she should rearrange the furniture in the living room. Charles remained civil, asking few questions and reserving his comments. Julia delighted in the exploratory questions asked by the youngest member of the family, so reminiscent of her conversations with Julianna. It was hard to understand why she could not seem to forget the little mulatto who had been such a part of her life those few months. Julia told Rachel of the special girl who had lived with her—at least in every way that counted—and how she had gone to live with a new mommy and daddy.

"Will I have to go live wif a new mommy and daddy?" Rachel asked sadly.

"No, no, honey," Julia hugged her close. "Thee will always live with our mommy and daddy. Thee is a lucky girl."

That seemed to satisfy her and soon she was leading Julia to yet another set of toys to play with.

First day arrived with the usual preparations to attend Meeting for Worship at Salem Friends. Julia dressed with extra care, wishing to present herself in a manner as similar to those of the Meeting as possible. While still in Kansas she had purchased a few articles of clothing for her trip and although most of them were the somber colors of Friends' tradition, Julia had purchased a piece of purple cloth to make a cape to drape over the black and gray dresses she would be expected to wear. With the help of Maggie she had completed the cape the day before they departed and it had become her favorite thing to wear, largely due to the rich purple color. Today, however, was probably not the time to announce her independence from the old ways. No, Quaker gray was definitely the dress for worship this morning.

The first thing that surprised Julia that morning was being greeted by Hannah and David as her family stepped down from their carriage. Though she had been home for two days, she had not yet seen her busy brother and his pregnant wife. Charles had reported on the activities of the office each day, shaking his head over the large numbers of patients passing through the doors. If, indeed, there were so many patients to care for, why did he return home each day in the early afternoon, leaving David and Matthew to "handle the duties"? Her father's behavior was more of a puzzle than ever.

Hannah ran as fast as her condition would allow and embraced the young woman she felt so close to, in spite of the fact they had never been childhood friends. "Julia! I cannot tell thee how happy I was when thy mother told us the news of thy visit. I have so many questions to ask thee about thy work. Thee must come for supper tomorrow evening."

By this time David had joined them and his hug was wonderful as always: strong, yet warm and accepting. "Yes, thee must come to supper, although it might be helpful if thee came early in the afternoon. That would allow thee and Hannah a chance to visit, and thee might also lend her a hand in the kitchen. I have tried to keep Hannah off her feet the past two weeks, but she will have none of it. It seems to matter little to her that she is married to a physician who might know what was best for her condition."

Though Julia knew he was teasing, she also sensed real concern in his voice. "I shall ride my old horse to thy home right after I put Rachel down for her nap tomorrow afternoon. It seems she believes I need to tell her a story before she can go to sleep."

"That will be wonderful," Hannah said again. Though her voice was cheerful, Julia thought she saw a momentary flicker of pain in her eyes. Was there a real reason for David's concern? She would be sure to ask Hannah tomorrow.

After greeting several other members Julia knew well, she, her mother, Rachel, and Hannah walked together to the front of the Meeting House. Julia had always liked the term 'Meeting House' rather than church. As Elizabeth always said, we, the believers, are the church; we meet in a building or house, thus the term Meeting House. Julia also liked the phrases 'Meeting for Worship,' and 'Meeting for Business,' as Friends believed each time they entered into the Meeting House God was present.

As they passed through the women's door, the Friends practice of separating men and women for worship perplexed Julia once again. She had never read in scripture where Jesus asked the women to sit somewhere else while he talked to the men, or vice-versa. It seemed to her that if a person's mind were going to wander to thoughts of men it might be even more likely to happen in the absence of the other sex. There were also times when the women could hear the booming voices of some of the men as they rose to speak in Meeting. Now that was truly a distraction when one was trying to listen for the Holy Spirit to speak. She was hopeful that someday women— and men—would speak up and ask for the walls to come down. Men and women were worshiping together whenever an evangelist traveled to their Meetings, so perhaps the revival movement sweeping through Friends in the Midwest would hasten the end of segregation during Sabbath worship.

No revival meeting was being held this morning, of that Julia was certain. She had never known the Salem Meeting to accept the words of a traveling evangelist—at least not before the time she left for Kansas. Silent worship was the standard for Salem Friends. Perhaps someone would receive a word from the Lord and with the prompting of the Holy Spirit speak to the group. The time always went faster when several women felt moved to speak. Three hours was an eternity when sitting in total silence.

The second thing that surprised Julia that morning was the number of women who rose to sing a song of praise. She remembered the revival service in Richland and how everyone had sung the songs of worship together. She also recalled the admonition of the Salem elders, condemning group singing as the devil's instrument. The singing of those in Richland that night several years ago seemed to be honest and sincere—a real moving of the Spirit through song—not merely singing the words from memory. Another Friends' practice she secretly hoped would soon end.

One woman's song, in particular, moved Julia.

Holy, Holy, Holy, Lord God Almighty.
Early in the morning our song shall rise to thee.
Holy, Holy, Holy, Merciful and Almighty.
God in three persons, blessed Trinity.

Holiness.

Julia thought of her experience in Indiana, how she had prayed for God to sanctify and make her holy.

Thee might tell of My Holiness. There are some here this morning that need to hear the words I will give thee.

Julia quickly put the thought from her mind. She was just a visitor this morning. These were Friends who had watched her grow up. They knew she was far from perfect, and a few of them had been the recipient of her temper on an occasion or two.

This is not about thee, Julia, this is about Me and what I wish for My children. How will they know I want to bless them with my Spirit if thee never tells them?

Once again Julia sat tight. A few more minutes and the elders were certain to rise, signaling the closing of the service. It had only been a few days since she had prayed for God's gift of sanctification. Surely she needed more time to make certain God had truly answered her prayer before telling others of her experience.

This is the time, Julia. I am asking thee to speak now.

Julia was torn between doing what the Spirit seemed to be nudging her to do, and not wanting to appear more righteous than the women she was so fond of in this Meeting. She waited several more minutes, hoping the elders would feel moved to close the Meeting for Worship, thus freeing her of speaking. Finally, after many more minutes passed, Julia felt more and more certain the Spirit was asking her to share her holiness experience. Slowly she rose to speak to the group.

"I know many of you remember me as a feisty child and a somewhat rebellious teenager. Through the nurturing of my wonderful mother I have always believed in God and prayed for salvation at an early age. Most of you know I felt God calling me into ministry and I have been working in Kansas with the Negro refugees this past year. But that is not what I want to share with you this morning." She paused, trying to formulate the exact words the Spirit would have her say.

"What the Spirit seems to be asking me to share with you this morning is an experience I had while attending Indiana Yearly Meeting a week ago. No doubt some of you have heard of the term 'sanctification' and perhaps have even experienced this second act of God. Through simple faith, much like the prayer for salvation, we can ask God for the gift of sanctification that we might be holy. The atoning blood of Christ makes it possible for us to achieve a state in which we no longer desire to sin. Every vile affliction can be nailed to the cross and the fire of the Holy Ghost will melt and refine our very beings. I am no longer the same woman who was plagued by doubts and failures. Today I speak to thee as a purified woman, seeking only to follow God's will for my life."

Not knowing what else to say, Julia sat down. Though she kept her head bowed and eyes closed, it seemed as though everyone in the room was staring at her. Was I truly following the leadership of the Spirit, she asked herself? This time there seemed to be no answer from the Holy Spirit. What did it matter now? Her words had been spoken in obedience to the prompting of the Spirit. God would have to work in the hearts of those present if they were to receive her words.

In a matter of minutes the elders rose and left the room, followed by the other women and children. No one spoke until they exited the building. Hannah was the first to reach Julia.

"Thy message was wonderful," she said with tears in her eyes. "Did thee really experience sanctification?"

"Yes, I believe the Holy Spirit cleansed me within. It was a feeling I have never experienced before . . . of warmth, and healing and power."

"Will thee tell me how I, too, might have this experience?"

Hannah was so open, so honest, so pure already. Why had she never wanted to become friends with her before?

"Julia, thy father is ready to leave," Rebecca interrupted the young women. "And if thee knows best thee will come now." Turning toward her mother, Julia was shocked at the expression on her face. What had happened to cause the look of panic?

"We will talk tomorrow," Julia assured Hannah.

"All right, Julia," Hannah said excitedly. "I shall think of nothing but thy visit from now until the moment I see thee riding up the lane."

Julia laughed. "Perhaps thee might want to think about thy husband just a bit. My brother might not appreciate thee ignoring him the rest of the day."

Hannah smiled, tenderness filling her eyes as she looked toward David.

Such a perfect woman for my brother, Julia thought with a twinge of regret. Would she ever experience the love of a husband? Would God's call on her life be such that she must remain single to do His work? The thought saddened her, though she was determined to be led by the Spirit. Thoughts of Hosea were strangely absent from her mind as she headed for the carriage and a ride home she would never forget.

CHAPTER 14

'WHAT *You* GONNA *Call Your* PRETTY LITTLE *Baby?*'

"*W*hatever was thee thinking?!" Charles's angry voice boomed out before Julia was even seated in the carriage.

"Charles, please, thy voice," Rebecca admonished.

"The problem is not my voice, Rebecca, the problem is thy daughter! Whatever possessed thee to rise in Meeting for Worship and speak of things thee knows nothing of? Sanctification, holiness, these are not matters to be bringing before the women—or men, for that matter. There is little agreement among Friends regarding these acts, and for one who left the Meeting with nary a word to suddenly return and begin telling the good women of Salem how to believe is an embarrassment to me and this family."

How had father heard of her message so quickly? Surely Mother had not spoken to him. Some other woman, then? But who?

Vowing to remain calm, Julia decided to wait until asked a direct question before speaking—which did not take long.

"Answer me, Julia, why did thee embarrass us by rising to speak in worship?"

"I felt led of the Spirit."

"Which spirit is leading thee, Julia? The spirit of pride? Or self-righteousness? A year ago thee left this meeting without a word of farewell and went off to work in a foreign place—with Negroes, no less. Thee comes back and steps in as if nothing has happened. I am not surprised the women were shocked at thy behavior this morning."

"I am sorry, Father, but I do not understand why anyone would be shocked by the words of the Spirit sincerely spoken." Julia was proud of the way she was able to keep the anger she felt from coloring her words.

"Perhaps the two of thee can talk after Rachel goes down for her nap this afternoon," Rebecca said quietly, her face showing the anxiety she felt at being caught between the man she loved and the daughter who had brought a truly inspired message to their worship service. "I do not believe Rachel needs to be a part of this conversation." Rachel sat on Rebecca's lap, arms tightly around her neck.

"She might as well learn from her older sister so as not to make the same mistakes," Charles said gruffly.

"Please, Charles, please wait," Rebecca pleaded.

Charles said no more, though resentment and anger were still evident in the scowl on his face.

Julia turned away from her father, tears spilling from her eyes. Why was he being so unreasonable? He had never been able to understand the call of God on her life, never been able to accept her work in Kansas. Perhaps they did, indeed, need to talk about the feelings that ran so deeply within him. She would make certain they had the opportunity to speak privately that afternoon. Having resolved to try and get to the bottom of her father's resentment, Julia felt a sense of calm sweep over her.

Once Rachel was down for her nap Rebecca excused herself to the bedroom, mumbling something about a bad headache. Julia went over to the couch where her father was reading a medical journal and sat beside him.

"We need to talk about thy feelings, Father," she said as quietly as possible, despite the pounding of her heart. "Thee has never accepted the work I have been called to do, and now thee is critical of my speaking in Meeting when I felt the clear leading of the Holy Spirit. Please talk to me. What has happened between us? There must be more than my leaving to work with Elizabeth that is causing thy deep resentment."

Charles was silent for many minutes, staring at his newspaper. Finally, after agonizing moments, he began to speak.

"Dost thou remember when I told thee the story of losing my first wife?"

"Yes, I remember thee had to leave in a blizzard to help a young woman who was unable to deliver her child. Then while thee was gone thy wife went into labor and passed away before thee could return."

"Yes, that part of the story is correct. But there is something I have never told anyone until now. You see, the man who sought me in the night was a Negro. He should never have been in a white neighborhood, but somehow he had seen my shingle and knocked on my door. He was quite distraught, and I suppose his wife and baby were all he could think about.

"There were many white doctors in Chicago who refused to treat Negroes, but I had never been faced with that decision as no black person had ever sought my services. Of course I was young and idealistic, believing I could conquer any condition if given enough time. And so when the young Negro pounded on my door that night, I went with him."

"How could thee do anything else?" Julia wondered, thinking of Doc Samuels and his hours of volunteer work at the Association.

"I put some other man's wife and child ahead of my own," he anguished, reliving the events of that night as he had done so many times in the past.

"But thee did not know that thy wife would go into labor, did thee?"

"No, but I should have somehow been able to surmise she was close to delivery."

"Thee did what thee thought best at the time, Father," she said quietly and with admiration.

"But it was my decision to help a Negro man that cost me my wife and child."

Julia did not know what to say. Did her father resent the entire Negro race because of this one incident? How could a rational and intelligent man let this event color his thinking for so many years?

"Is that the reason thee so opposed my leaving to work with Elizabeth? Because thee resented the Negro man who came to thee for help?" Julia had to know what he was thinking.

"I know it is difficult for thee to understand, Julia. But how could I forgive myself for letting this happen? Negroes should never have been allowed to settle in the North in the first place!"

Julia was shocked by his attitude. "Would the Negro race have even been here were it not for white men kidnapping them and shipping them to the colonies? Then we enslaved them and treated them like chattel and now we are angry when they simply want to live like white people. Do you know what has happened to the Negroes in the South now that they have been given their so-called independence?"

When there was no response, she continued, relaying story after story she had heard from the refugees. "Surely thee cannot feel anger toward an entire race because of one incident in thy life, Father. The young man was merely seeking to save the life of his wife and baby. Thee, of all people, should know that the only differences between any of the races on this earth is the color of their skin and the experiences they have lived."

"But I lost my wife and child! Thee has not even been married. How would thee know what it feels like to undergo such tragedy?" Charles cried out, obviously still haunted by the incident from his past.

"Thee must forgive the young Negro, Father, for whatever it is thee feels he has done, and thee must forgive thyself for the choice thee made that night. Only when thee can forgive can thee know God's forgiveness and peace."

Charles looked intently at the young woman before him. The woman he saw today was so unlike the girl he had lived with for nearly eighteen years. None of the rebelliousness or disrespect he had often been faced with was now present. Perhaps she was right, perhaps he had blamed the young man for the death of his wife and child. Forgiving him had never entered his mind. If what Julia had told him about the Negroes in the South was true—and he was certain it must be—should he not be feeling compassion rather than bitterness and anger? If it were possible to forgive both the young man and himself he might be able to put the past completely behind him. His heart suddenly felt lighter.

"Thee has given me much to think about, Julia. But what about the sanctification thee spoke of in Meeting? Does thee truly believe God can take away one's desire to sin?"

Julia was careful to answer, wanting to be as honest as possible. "It is something I experienced, Father, that is all I can say. Thee knows of David Updegraff, does thee not?"

"Certainly. I have read his editorials in Friends papers for years."

"Then I will tell thee his assistant, Dugan Clark, is the one who convinced me of the availability of sanctification for all believers. I believe it has made a difference in my thinking and feelings toward others. God has helped me become more patient and to think before spouting the first thought that comes to mind."

"I just wish thee had said something to me before speaking in Meeting. That way I would have known how to respond to

Sylvia when she rushed out of Meeting to tell me thee was trying to be like the traveling evangelists."

Julia smiled. "I had no idea the Spirit would ask me to speak, Father. And even if I had known, you and I were not having many conversations, other than when to put Rachel to bed or what her first words were."

Charles smiled, the first time Julia had felt his warmth in a long time. "I thank thee for sharing of thy past. It helps me see why thee has been against my work with the freedmen. I shall let thee think about the forgiveness I believe thee needs to extend to that young man from thy past. I hope we will have other opportunities to visit before the time arrives for me to leave for Oskaloosa."

Julia rose, wishing to give her father time to reflect on what they had discussed. If only he could forgive the young man—and himself—and receive forgiveness, perhaps then he would once again be the warm and loving father she remembered from her childhood.

Charles was somber the next few days, though Julia was too busy to worry about him. She felt a calm assurance that in time all would be well between the two of them. He was not the sort of person to leap at a new idea, and Julia believed it would take time for him to pray and seek the Lord's guidance where forgiveness was concerned.

Supper with David and Hannah was a delight, though it was clear to Julia that Hannah's constant efforts to get comfortable meant she was not feeling as well as she wanted them to believe.

"When, exactly, is the baby due?" Julia asked curiously.

"As near as I can calculate, within the next week or so," David answered.

"I do so hope he or she arrives before I must leave for Yearly Meeting. I would feel awful if I did not get to see my new niece or nephew until he or she were half-grown."

"So thee is planning to return to Kansas?" David asked cautiously.

"Of course—why would thee ask?" There was something implied in David's simple question.

David looked at Hannah for guidance. Should he tell his little sister their father's plan? Hannah's slight nod was the only encouragement he needed.

"Father has other plans for thee," David said somewhat eagerly.

Julia frowned. What else could her father possibly do to disrupt her ministry in Kansas?

"He would like for thee to become a pastor in a Friends' Meeting in Iowa. He believes thee would be well-suited for such ministry."

"Whoa, David. Back up. For one thing, Friends do not have pastors. For another, I am committed to Elizabeth's work in Kansas. Besides, Father and I had a long talk yesterday and I believe you will see a change in his attitude toward my work in the near future."

Once again the young married couple looked at each other. Finally Hannah spoke. "It is wonderful thee had the opportunity to speak with Charles about thy work. I do not want to discourage thee, but thy father seems to have been driven by one and only one thing this past year: getting thee out of Kansas." Hannah paused a minute, a frown crossing her face. "David, I think I will go and lie down for a spell while thee tells Julia about the pastoral system Friends seem so determined to establish."

David jumped up from the straight-back wooden chair where he had been sitting during supper and their time of visiting. "I will help thee, Hannah, please wait." He lovingly extended a hand to help his wife, and with one arm around her waist and the other holding her hand he led her to the bedroom. Hannah did not speak as they left, which seemed unusual to Julia. But, she assured herself, David will know if there is something wrong with her.

Julia busied herself cleaning up the kitchen. Soon David joined her, reassuring her that Hannah was merely tired, not ill. Together they made swift work of the dishes, though David could not resist snapping at Julia with the dish towel now and then, a teasing gesture he had loved when they were growing up.

When they had settled in the living room for more visiting, Julia asked David to explain what was happening with Friends and the pastoral movement.

"I am surprised thee did not hear of this in Indiana, Julia. They are experiencing much more of a problem than we are here in Iowa."

Julia smiled sheepishly. "I did not always attend the business sessions," she admitted. "Thee knows how terribly monotonous they can be. And sometimes when I did attend I was thinking of other things."

"Or other people? Like Hosea, perhaps?" David's look was somber, not the teasing grin Julia was hoping to see.

"I think of Hosea now and then," she replied honestly, though some days she thought of him a great deal, "but mostly I spent the time in Indiana thinking of what I would report to the Friends there about our work in Kansas.

"Is that all? Thee seemed rather fond of the young man when I visited thee," David said.

Had David guessed her true feelings for Hosea when he was there last spring? Thoughts of her last words with Hosea opened raw wounds that were just now beginning to heal. She would not discuss Hosea with David.

"That is all, big brother. As I told thee last spring, I have a great deal of compassion for him and all he has been through. It might interest thee to know," she added, hoping to change the subject, "that Hosea accepted God's gift of salvation a few weeks ago and right now he is in the East with Elizabeth giving his testimony and helping raise money for our work."

"That is truly wonderful news, Julia," David said, relaxing a bit with the news of Hosea's salvation. "It is always a joyous celebration when any of God's children repents and becomes a believer. I wondered why Elizabeth was not with thee on this mission."

"But tell me about the pastoral debate," Julia implored, anxious to know what changes might be brewing in the Society of Friends.

"It is really quite a simple controversy. As thee has probably heard, the revivalists have brought great numbers of new members into our churches. These are not birthright Friends, merely sinners saved by grace."

"Like all of us," Julia reminded him.

"Exactly. But these new believers find sitting in the silence to be the closest thing to torture they have ever known. They have no experience worshiping and receiving from God in that manner. It was a preacher who brought them into the church, and they are not satisfied unless a preacher speaks to their needs each week."

"But what about our belief in the priesthood of believers? That *all* are called to ministry?"

"Well, the revivalists believe the true minister has a special call from God, a call to be a shepherd to a flock of believers in one community."

"Are these preachers who stay in one place paid a wage? I know traveling evangelists are paid. In fact, Elizabeth once said the only reason she thought some of the evangelists traveled was so that they could receive rather large sums of money for what they did."

"That is another problem, Julia. Friends have always believed that ministers should support themselves in a secular trade. But the revivalists are saying that if a man or woman is truly called to preach the Gospel, God intends all their energy and mind power be used in that direction. David Updegraff said that such a calling demands the dedication of one's entire life to spiritual work, and a complete separation from every secular pursuit. Some revivalists are even teaching that a regular preaching ministry is necessary for the growth and development of the Meeting, and that congregations cannot thrive on silent prayer and a few words spoken now and then by those present in silent worship."

"And what does thee believe, David?" Julia valued the opinion of her brother who often seemed wise beyond his years.

"I can understand the dilemma of those coming into silent meetings, but I have to respect the history of our forefathers who felt that man best received from God when waiting for Him in the silence. When a Meeting has a pastor it seems a necessity to have a programmed service. There is singing, vocal prayer, and preaching. In some of these new pastoral meetings I am told there is no silence or worshipful waiting whatsoever. The other problem I foresee is the loss of freedom in our meetings. When a pastor begins to feel more powerful than the congregation, he—or she—may begin a one-man rule. This will destroy everything George Fox sought to establish: freedom from church leaders who control one's spiritual life. I suppose that is the main reason I tend to support our tradition of silent worship. What does thee believe?"

"It seems a difficult question, David. I am speaking every morning in Meeting for Worship at the Association—when I am there, of course—in the manner of a preacher. But I was moved in a very powerful way to speak in the silence yesterday, so I am torn between the two methods of worship. Perhaps it is the occasion which should determine the manner of worship."

"It almost seems to me," David added thoughtfully, "that we would do well to include both in our worship. It seems reasonable to provide instruction for the new believers; it also seems a travesty to discard our heritage of worshiping in the silence.

"Which brings me back to our original discussion. Would thee be interested in being a Friends pastor in Iowa? I know there are only a few churches seeking pastors right now, but when thee goes to Yearly Meeting thee is certain to be asked by someone if thee would consider the opportunity."

"No," Julia said emphatically. "I am committed to the Association in Kansas. God called me to that specific work, David, not just to preach. Is there no one who understands what that means?"

"I am sorry, Julia. Although it would be nice to have thee closer to Salem, I truly believe thee knows what God is asking of thee. I told Father I would mention it to thee, but that I was fairly certain of thy answer."

"Does thee believe Salem will have a pastor some day?" she asked.

"I would hate to see that happen," he confessed, "but the revivalists are a forceful group and they seem intent on bringing all Friends around to their position on the necessity of pastors."

"David!" Hannah's sharp cry brought her husband instantly to his feet.

"Excuse me, Julia. I shall return in a moment."

What was happening? Was Hannah ready to deliver their child? Julia was both excited and anxious to know what might be taking place. In a few moments David returned.

"Looks like this might be the night, Julia," he said with a concerned grin. "Thee might as well go home and pray for a speedy and safe delivery. I will bring all of thee the news when the work is finished."

"But I could boil water, tear strips of cloth, anything thee might need," she protested, remembering the things she and their neighbor Will had done when Rachel was born. She wanted to be there when the new one arrived.

David smiled. "It will be some time before this baby arrives, I am afraid. The first child often takes its sweet time to enter this world, and I shall have no problem making the preparations. Besides, Mother and Father will be quite worried if thee does not return home shortly."

"All right, I suppose I can go now, but you have to promise to ride over with the news as soon as possible."

"It is a promise, Julia. Ride carefully—it is nearly dark and thee might not find thy way home."

Julia laughed, remembering how her suitors at the Academy had always insisted on walking her home to protect her from wild animals, which, of course, everyone knew did not exist in Pleasant Plain, Iowa. It was good to be home again, even if only for a visit. This was her family, and soon there would be a new member. Julia could not wait to tell everyone at home the news of the pending birth.

CHAPTER 15

'Git ON Board'

Although Julia and her mother tried to stay calm while they waited for news of the baby's arrival, both women found themselves fidgeting nervously. They rose to get a glass of water, went to check on the sleeping Rachel, and checked the fire. Anything to help the time pass more quickly. Charles remained in his home office reading yet another Friends' Review. He merely nodded when Julia gave him the news.

"I thought perhaps thee might want to be present—in case something goes wrong," Julia said.

"No," Charles replied, not even looking at her, "David has delivered numerous babies since returning here to practice medicine. He will know what to do should there be a problem. I would only be a meddling grandfather."

"But I believe—"

This time Charles looked up. "I said he can handle the situation, Julia." There was a sternness to his voice, reminding her once again of the unbending side of his nature. "By the way," he added, rather as an afterthought.

"Yes, Father?" Julia was nearly out of the room, but turned toward him.

"I just read a communication from Mrs. Comstock here in the Review. She writes that she received a letter from John Greenleaf Whittier saying he would send as much as he could for the work there. He has already raised a thousand dollars and he is asking those in St. Louis to do likewise. Does thee know anything about this?"

"Yes, Friend Whittier is one of our strongest supporters. Elizabeth visits him nearly every time she makes a trip near his home. Why does thee ask?"

"No reason, just curiosity I suppose." And with that he went back to his reading, effectively dismissing Julia. At least he had not mentioned her becoming a pastor in Iowa.

Julia returned to the kitchen to wait with her mother. Rebecca chatted aimlessly about Rachel and her birth and the births of both Julia and David. Although Julia had heard the stories numerous times in the past, she knew her mother needed an outlet for the tension she was feeling. Finally, around the tenth hour, only three hours after Hannah's cry for help, there came a knock on the door.

Rebecca jumped, startled at the sound, then quickly went to receive the news. David entered, grinning from ear to ear. "He's arrived! Our son—your grandson, Mother, and your nephew, Julia—arrived just over an hour ago. The delivery was much swifter than I expected and both Hannah and the baby are doing well."

"Has thee named him?" Rebecca asked.

"Yes, he shall be called Peter Charles Jones."

"Peter. I like that," Rebecca said, more to herself than the others.

"Peter was one of Christ's first followers, 'The Rock', Jesus called him, and both Hannah and I want to raise our son to be a firm believer, a rock of faith to lead others. Charles, of course, is in honor of Father. Where is he, by the way—has he gone to bed? I would like to give him the good news if he is still awake."

"I am certain he is waiting to hear of the birth, David," Rebecca answered. "He has been in his office since Julia returned home with the news." Rebecca motioned in the direction where David would find his father.

Soon both men emerged from the office, grinning from ear to ear. This was the happiest Julia had seen her father since she returned. "A grandson, Rebecca. What a wonderful way to celebrate Julia's return."

Julia slowly looked at her father, not knowing how to interpret his last statement. By "return" surely he meant "visit". Did she dare ask him to clarify his statement?

"Yes, it is," Julia said cautiously. "I am so happy I was able to be here when Peter arrived. A few more days and I would have missed this wonderful event." She hoped her words left no doubt as to her intentions. "Will we be able to see him in the morning?" she asked, turning toward David.

"Certainly. Just give me a few hours to get the house back in order. I am afraid I was a little more rattled than I would have liked when the child seemed determined to arrive in record time."

Everyone laughed and soon David left to return home and the others headed for their rooms. Julia had not minded sleeping with Rachel, though she knew subconsciously she was always aware of where the child was in the bed so as to not disturb her sleep. One night Rachel had awakened when Julia rolled too close and it took quite a while to get the little girl back to sleep. This night all was calm as Julia lay still, reflecting on the events of the day. Looking out the window she saw a sky full of stars, reminding her of God's promise to bless Abraham in such a way that his dependents would be as numerous as the stars in the heavens. Though her family fell far short of that mark, there was one bright new star to shine in their lives, one new blessing they would share. Perhaps this child would take Father's mind off her and her future. Finally, Julia began to pray for her father, a simple prayer that she might have grace to accept his ways, and a fervent plea for his release of the past that he might enjoy the present life to the fullest.

Though Julia had hoped for another opportunity to speak with her father about letting go of his past, Charles seemed determined to avoid such a confrontation. He left the house early each morning, returning just before supper, and then retiring to his office. The office had always been off limits to Julia and David as children, and for some reason even now Julia was reluctant to enter the doors without an invitation. I shall leave it to God, she decided. He is the One who can meet Father's need.

The visit with Hannah and baby Peter had been wonderful, though when Julia held him a yearning so powerful overwhelmed her she hardly knew what to do. Instinctively she longed for a family and motherhood. Peter was nearly perfect. The sight of his light hair with a touch of auburn thrilled her heart. Ten tiny fingers and toes, skin so soft, a perfect little mouth which puckered now and then in search of food. What would her own children look like? The longer she had been away from Hosea the less she thought of the young man with whom she had once been so determined to share a future. Had Hosea been right? Were her feelings born of compassion rather than the love of a woman and a man? Perhaps it was not meant to be, Julie finally had to admit. Perhaps, though whatever it was she felt for him still remained deep in her heart.

Julia's departure for Yearly Meeting was a tearful one. She had not realized how much she had missed her family while she had been in Kansas. Normally some of them would have been traveling to attend the sessions in Oskaloosa, but with the new baby David and Hannah had not wanted to journey that far, and Rebecca said it was too difficult to take a squirmy two-year-old to five days of meetings.

"What about Father?" Julia inquired. "He nearly always attends."

"Thy father has kept to himself these past few weeks. Something seems to be troubling him, though when I ask he merely says all is well. I truly do not know if he plans to attend any of the sessions. I will encourage him, however. I believe he would feel a great sense of pride in hearing thee speak of thy work in the joint session."

Julia was doubtful. Right now Charles seemed anything but proud of his daughter.

As her train rolled into Oskaloosa the day before Yearly Meeting was to begin, Julia was shocked to see Elizabeth and Hosea standing on the platform awaiting her arrival.

Julia embraced Elizabeth as soon as her feet hit the ground. She smiled at Hosea, a smile she hoped was warm and caring, but she did not approach him as she did Elizabeth. "Hello, Hosea," she finally said, unsure of his feelings, unsure of her own.

"'Lo, Julia," he said, his soft words once again tugging at her heart.

"However did thee manage to arrive here before Yearly Meeting?" Julia turned to Elizabeth as she spoke. "I thought thee would be in the East much longer than this." The excitement in Julia's voice was evident to everyone around them, and several strangers smiled at the animated young woman with the infectious smile.

"I will tell thee all about it over supper tonight. I trust thee had a good trip?"

"It has been interesting," she admitted, "and I, too, have much to share with thee. Both of thee," she added, not wanting to exclude Hosea.

"Then let us get thy luggage and get thee settled in the hotel."

Hosea picked up her suitcase and for some strange reason Julia wanted to grab it from him and insist on carrying it herself. It was the image of a slave carrying his owner's baggage that Julia could not escape.

"I can carry that, Hosea," she said.

Elizabeth's look of disbelief disturbed her, too. Could she not see that this picture was all wrong?

"I be happy ta carry this for you, Miz Julia."

"Just 'Julia,' Hosea, please. I suppose, if thee is certain thee wants to do this . . . "

Hosea did not know what to think. The woman he had thought of often the past three weeks was acting in a manner he could not understand. Had something happened to her in his absence? Had she not been the one who said not to give up, to pray about God's plan for the two of them? He had been praying every day that somehow God would provide a way for them to be together. And now, just when he was beginning to believe that perhaps their differences could be overcome, she was pulling away. Hosea was deeply troubled as he followed the two women to the hotel.

Hosea and Elizabeth had arrived the day before and already had rooms. "Would thee mind sharing a room with me?" Elizabeth asked as they approached the hotel.

"That would be wonderful," Julia said warmly, thinking of all the things she wanted to share with her mentor.

"Then it is settled." Quickly they climbed to the second story and when arrangements had been made with Hosea for the hour of dinner, Julia began to settle her things in the room where they would spend the next few days before heading back to Kansas.

"Now . . . tell me all about thy travels. Did thee have any difficulties in Indiana?"

Julia proceeded to share everything that had happened since the two had parted on the train platform in Richmond. They discussed sanctification and Elizabeth seemed pleased with Julia's desire for holiness, though she did have one comment on the subject.

"Sanctification, holiness, Inner Light, all are mere words we humans like to argue the meaning of. I believe thee to be sincere in thy desire to live each day in a manner pleasing to our Savior. But I would remind thee of the central task of those who call themselves believers: being servants here on this earth. There are so many needs and so many needless arguments over theological differences. Friends seem pleased to recite the day and hour of conversion, regeneration, consecration, or sanctification. Would it not be preferable to simply say 'whereas I was blind, now I see?' and spend our energies helping those less fortunate? I do not mean to make light of thy sanctification, Julia," she said hastily, seeing the hurt look on the young woman's face, "I simply want thee to see a broader picture of the whole of humanity, not just the small world of us as individual believers."

Julia thought about Elizabeth's words the entire course of Yearly Meeting. Perhaps she could help the Friends gathered see the bigger picture of the needs of others, especially the refugees.

When it came time for their report on the work of the Association, Elizabeth asked Julia and Hosea to accompany her to the front of the room where both men and women were gathered.

Hosea was the first to share his testimony. He spoke again of the injustices his people had endured, comparing their plight to that of the Israelites trying to escape Pharaoh in Egypt. The plagues, he said, could not have been any worse than the Negro's suffering at the hands of the white men in the South. Julia smiled, knowing Elizabeth must have shared that scripture story with Hosea in hopes he would use it in his messages to the various groups to whom he spoke.

When it was Julia's turn, she stood and spoke proudly. It gave her great joy to share the accomplishments she had been a part of. As she quickly scanned the faces of the representatives gathered, she was shocked to see her father sitting in the back row. When had he arrived? She was certain she would have noticed him had he been there when she entered the room. Julia realized how very much she wanted to please the man who had been a good father to her for so many years.

She began by telling the story of Julianna, omitting the part about wanting to adopt the little girl. She also told about leading the worship services each morning. She left most of the statistics about money raised and items donated and distributed for Elizabeth to share. When she finished her part, she took her seat next to Hosea, not daring to look at her father.

Then it was Elizabeth's turn. "Since 1879, sixty-thousand dollars has been contributed to the refugee work by compassionate Friends like yourselves," she began. "Also, since 1879, sixty-thousand Negroes have poured into the state of Kansas. If I calculate correctly, that is one dollar collected for each person arriving. What can each of thee do with one dollar? Ninety percent of those arriving need help to get started in their new lives, whether it is basic living supplies or job training and education. Yet even in their distress they still fervently and earnestly say 'God Bless You' when they receive even one bit of help from us. These are well-behaved, sober folks, eighty percent of whom voted to support prohibition in our state.

"It saddens my heart that we see very little of Friends in our Topeka work. Julia, Laura Haviland, and myself are the ones who must carry the load. That is why thy support is so needed. Last January I toured Cherokee County in the southeastern corner of Kansas, from Emporia to Parsons, Oswego to Baxter Springs. We have plans for a Normal School to educate the refugees in Parsons, and we are in need of a teacher for a year at the newly established Agricultural and Industrial Institute in Cherokee County. The needs are growing daily and workers are few. We have one doctor in Topeka—not even a Friend—who volunteers several hours of his time daily to treat those who come with frozen feet and hands, and diseases of every nature.

"Then there are the children. Fifteen thousand children need garments before winter sets in. Do you know how many pairs of socks and mittens it will take? I am no longer a young person with boundless energy to secure these needs. It grieves me to think of the little ones who will suffer this winter because I cannot provide for them.

"I do have one bit of good news to share with you. On my recent trip to Washington D.C., I, with the help of David Updegraff's brother, was able to secure passage of a bill to allow duty-free goods from overseas to enter this country. Friends in England have supported this work since its inception and it has been a most trying situation to see our Congress refuse to allow bedding, clothing, and household utensils to enter without a duty. This new bill will certainly be a boost to our work.

"What is God asking of each of thee this day?" she asked in closing. "Whether you give a gift of cash or clothing or bedding or utensils, God will bless your gift. Even more important, will you give of yourselves? Could you volunteer for a month? A year? God will bless you, my friends, He truly will. I am getting on in years and fear my health will not allow me to continue the work to which I have given every ounce of my energy. Someone must rise up and take on the challenge. Please pray for this mission field as we seek to do God's will."

Julia was stunned. Elizabeth seemed in fine health to her. Of course the nagging cough was always present, but she still seemed to be able to accomplish as much in a day as she ever had.

"Is Elizabeth ill?" Julia whispered to Hosea.

He simply shrugged his shoulders.

At the conclusion of Elizabeth's speech there was a long discussion by representatives from each of the meetings in Iowa. It was finally agreed to take an offering, which raised two hundred dollars, and to provide a teacher from the Yearly Meeting to work at least one year at the Agricultural and Industrial Institute in Cherokee County. Friends also agreed to support the erection of a normal school at Parsons, though just what that support would be was not determined.

Gathering her courage, Julia rose at the end of the session to find her father. She was amazed to see that he had cornered Elizabeth and was talking animatedly with her. Though she could not tell his mood, she prayed fervently that he was not angry with her and taking it out on Elizabeth.

Finally Elizabeth glanced Julia's way and motioned for her to join them. With heart pounding she made her way to where the two stood.

"Thy father has just given us the most wonderful news, Julia!"

Julia stared at her father. Whatever could Elizabeth mean?

"I have decided to give a year of my time to work either in Topeka or Cherokee County, whichever might need me the most."

Julia was speechless. Whatever for? she wondered. He had a wife and young child. What would he do with them? And why the sudden change of heart? And why Kansas? Surely there were other places he might volunteer his services.

"Julia, has thee nothing to say?" Elizabeth could not understand Julia's silence. Was the child not pleased with her father's change of heart? How many times had she prayed with Julia that her father would accept her ministry?

Finally Julia spoke. "I am surprised, that is all. I thought thee hated the Negroes, Father," she said, challenging his decision.

"Thy words were powerful, Julia. These past few days I have been able to think of little else than thy admonition that I forgive the young man from my past—as well as myself. I fought that suggestion. Oh, how I fought it, even though deep in my heart I knew thee was right. But the night thee left for Yearly Meeting I realized what I stood to lose: a wonderful daughter that I had every right to be proud of. I asked God to forgive me and lead me.

"I am also certain David has shared with thee my lack of fervor this past year for the practice of medicine. There seemed to be something missing. Oh, I enjoyed helping a new life enter the world, but the daily grind of patients and their complaints was wearing me down. There seemed to be no purpose in my being there when David and Matthew could so ably manage the practice without me.

"But when Elizabeth spoke this morning it was like the Spirit opened my heart and I was finally able to receive the message. God still has a use for my talents and abilities. What better way to use my training than to work with these poor souls who truly have needs I have never experienced."

"What about Mother and Rachel?" she asked.

"They will go with me, of course. We will stay for a year or two and then return before it is time for Rachel to enter grammar school."

"Then I am happy for thee." Though Julia spoke the words, she knew that for some reason she was not truly pleased with his decision.

Charles and Elizabeth both stared as the young woman they were both so fond of turned and ran from them. What in the world had happened, Charles wondered? He had thought she would be so pleased with the news: father and daughter, possibly working together with the Negroes. As he started to follow her he felt Elizabeth's hand on his arm.

"Let her go, Charles. She needs a little time to adjust to the news. I will speak with her this evening and hopefully all will be well by tomorrow."

"I hope so," was Charles's sad reply. "I certainly hope so."

CHAPTER 16

Good News

The last night of Iowa Yearly Meeting brought an invitation from Julia's Uncle Levi to dine with his family. She was anxious to catch up on the happenings of each family member, as well as hear all about Levi's teaching experiences at William Penn College. Memories of the year she lived with this wonderful family filled Julia with happiness as she thought of being with them once again. The family's log cabin had been a place of warmth and activity during her year of boarding as her two young cousins, twin boys, continually begged Julia to play with them. They would be nearly five by now and Julia wondered if they had changed. There was also their little girl, Grace Elizabeth, born to the family after their departure for Oskaloosa two and a half years earlier. Julia had only seen her once and could not wait to see how much she had grown.

The only fly in the ointment was the fact that her father would also be joining them for dinner. Julia was still unable to accept his decision to work in Kansas—*her* mission field. Although Charles had sought to have a conversation with his daughter several times since his announcement, Julia maintained her cool demeanor, her words affirming his decision, while her attitude suggested she was not the least bit happy with his plans.

Have I gotten so old I cannot understand young people any more? Charles wondered each time Julia seemed to avoid talking to him. His only hope was that with time, and Elizabeth's advocacy, Julia might come to the place where she actually looked forward to having him nearby. Had she realized how happy Rachel would be living so much closer to her big sister? He could not remember Julia being a selfish child and her present behavior confused him.

The meal prepared by Aunt Anna was delicious, and the conversation of the adults interesting. But, as always, it was the children to whom Julia was drawn. Timothy and Andrew had lost a bit of their rambunctious selves, but they still clamored for her attention. Little Grace tugged at Julia's skirt time and again, begging to be picked up. She was a beautiful little girl, thick, black hair in pigtails, dark, sparkling eyes, and skin the color of dark tea. There was something about her that reminded Julia of Julianna, and once again she felt the pain of losing the one she had so loved.

Julia helped Anna prepare the children for bed, Anna directing the boys' activities and Julia helping Grace. Before long each was tucked in bed, ready for a special short story from Cousin Julia. As they blew out the lanterns Julia gazed one last time at the beautiful faces of the three special children. When, Lord? When will I have an opportunity for children of my own to love?

Charles insisted on accompanying Elizabeth, Hosea, and Julia to the train station early the next morning. "I can haul all thy luggage in my carriage and once you are on the train I will depart for Salem. The Mendenhalls, our friends at Pleasant Plain, have invited me to spend the night with them. It will be an easy day's journey and I insist on seeing you off."

Julia wondered why she was feeling such animosity toward her father. She had wanted him to be free of the pain of his past, but why did he have to volunteer to come to Kansas? This was her work—hers and Elizabeth's and Laura's, of course—and she did not see the need for yet another doctor. Doc Samuels took care of their needs quite nicely. Perhaps Elizabeth will send Father to Cherokee County to work in that Association, she thought hopefully. At least there would be some distance between them and she would not be under his constant watch.

Why should it bother you so that I have called your father as well as you? I have given gifts to each of you and you are using them for my work. There seems to be a bit of pride within you—pride that causes you to want to keep this work for yourself.

Was it pride? Was that the reason she did not want Father coming to Kansas? But it is my work, she argued. I was the one who first responded to Elizabeth's plea for workers. Father was so opposed, yet now he believes the work is so wonderful that he has to help. Why? What changed?

His heart. My Spirit working within the human heart can produce miraculous changes. Remember Hosea? Remember how he hated me? And now his love for me grows stronger with each passing day.

But Hosea is different. My father has never suffered like Hosea. He has no idea what it has been like for the refugees.

All believers suffer in their own way, Julia. Please allow me to do my work in the lives of those who seek Me. All I ask is that you be faithful to my calling. Holiness will allow you to desire only what is best for each of my children.

I have been faithful. I do want what is best for Father, I just do not want him there to interfere in my life. She was not certain what he might do, but he would always be her father and she would never feel comfortable with him looking over her shoulder each day offering advice, or even worse—criticism. Holiness was becoming more difficult with each passing day.

Once the luggage was loaded on the train, Charles knew he could not let his special daughter leave without at least trying to mend the rift between them. Gathering her in his arms, he whispered, "Please pray about this, Julia. If thee receives confirmation from the Spirit that I should not come to Kansas, then I will remain in Salem."

Julia was surprised that her father would actually leave the decision to her. This was so unlike everything she knew about him. Pulling away she looked at him carefully to be sure he was serious. There seemed to be no anger or insincerity present.

"All right, Father, I will do as thee asks."

Elizabeth, overhearing the conversation, knew that in time all would be well between these two who had such strong, similar personalities. She knew how difficult it had been for Julia to move to Kansas against her father's will, and it was easy to understand why she resented Charles' sudden change of heart. An independent child would find it difficult to have her actions once again overseen by an overzealous parent.

Once they were settled in the passenger car, Julia asked Elizabeth if they could exchange seats at one of the stops down the tracks so she might have a chance to talk with Hosea. Though Elizabeth was not certain of the wisdom of such a conversation, she could see that Julia seemed intent on having some time with the young man and she finally agreed.

It was late in the afternoon when Elizabeth finally exchanged seats with Julia. This meant that Elizabeth was now across the aisle, and although it did not provide a great deal of privacy, Julia felt is was the best she could do. She had to talk to Hosea before they reached Kansas.

"Did thee get to meet the President?" she began, though from her conversations with Elizabeth in the hotel room she already knew the answer.

"You knows I did. You shorely talked ta Miz Comstock when da two of you was in da same room at da hotel," was his reply. This was not how Julia had wanted the conversation to begin.

"Well, she did mention it, but I was wondering if you got to speak with him."

"I don't say much. 'Lizabeth, she do most of da talkin'."

"What about meeting with some of the members of Congress . . . was that exciting?"

Hosea was puzzled. Why was Julia asking these meaningless questions? There was certainly something more than this on her mind or she would not have asked Elizabeth to allow them some time together. "Whats you really wanna say?" he asked quietly.

Julia hesitated, not wanting to plunge right in. But perhaps that was the best way. "Did thee think and pray on the things we talked about the night before we left?" She had to know what he was thinking and feeling.

"Yessum," he said slowly, "I do jist what you say. I pray and pray about it."

"And what was the answer?" she asked cautiously.

"Maybe you best tell me what God be sayin' ta you, Julia. You didn't seem ta be too happy ta see me in Oskyloosa, 'n you don't hardly say nothin' ta me da whole time we be there."

Julia felt the heat rise in her cheeks, remembering how she had begged Hosea to hang on to the hope for their future. She now knew—beyond a shadow of a doubt—that her previous feelings for the young man beside her were very real, but not the feelings a woman and man who were to share their lives. She also knew she could never have a ministry with Hosea, nor could her present ministry continue if the other Negroes knew she and Hosea had feelings for one another beyond friendship.

"I am sorry, Hosea," she began, silently begging God to intercede for her that somehow Hosea might be spared the pain she knew he was certain to feel. "I do not want to hurt you. You know how special you are to me."

"Like I's your little project? Da sinner who come to da Lord? I don' think I mean anythin' to you, Julia. I jist some poor black boy you feels sorry for."

"That is not true!" Julia realized her voice was louder than she intended. "I care very deeply for you!" This time her voice was passionate, though she merely whispered the words.

"*Care*, dat's da problem. You cares about me, but it be more like pity than somethin' with real meanin" . . . like love, he almost whispered.

"I am sorry, Hosea. I truly care for thee. I want thee to have a life of ministry to others, a chance to share thy faith. But I also want thee to be happy, and it could never happen with me."

Hosea looked out the window, afraid to look at the one he knew he loved in a special way.

"Julia," he finally said, hurt evident in his eyes. "Can I ask you jist one thing?"

"Anything," she said.

"If there wasn't no hatred between Negroes and whites, do you thinks you might have loved me enough to want to spend yer life with me?"

Julia's answer was a long time in coming. She wanted to be honest, but she did not want to further hurt the young man who had done nothing to deserve her rejection. "I do not honestly know, Hosea. What I do know is that you are a wonderful person who has suffered far more than any human being should have to endure. I know you will make a wonderful husband to some very lucky woman, and a great father to some lucky children."

Hosea turned away, resigned to the news. Julia sank deep in the seat, closing her eyes to keep the tears from spilling. What had she done? She had not wanted to hurt Hosea, truly she had not. Please, God, she prayed, please comfort Hosea and ease his pain. She continued praying until finally drifting off to sleep.

Kansas Yearly Meeting was very similar to the sessions in Indiana and Iowa. This time Julia and Elizabeth went alone to the gathering in Lawrence. Hosea was back in the barracks, working at the blacksmith shop during the days. He refused to accompany Elizabeth and Julia, telling Elizabeth he had more than paid his debt to her by the speeches he had made on their trip. Elizabeth let him go, sensing that speaking before a crowd was not the only thing bothering him. Julia had never shared a word of their conversation on the train, but Elizabeth was certain Hosea's somber mood in the days since their return had something to with whatever Julia had said to him.

Elizabeth's report to the Friends gathered in Lawrence was similar to her earlier reports in Iowa and Indiana. There was one bit of news, however, that surprised everyone.

"This will most likely be my last winter in Topeka. My health has been failing me the past two years and my doctor has recommended I have total bed rest until my lungs have had a chance to heal themselves. I do not know if I can follow those orders to the letter, but at this point it seems I have little choice.

"You have just spent an entire day reporting on the condition of the various Indian missions in this state, down to the number of bushels of corn harvested and hay cut by the Indians. I would ask that you give at least as much consideration to the Negro refugees who have been forced to flee for their very lives because of the injustices being perpetrated in the South.

"I do not mean to sound ungrateful. Your assistance in organizing and building the Agricultural and Industrial Institute for refugees in Cherokee County has been most generous. Without the help of T.E. Pickering, a man as near a saint as God created, many citizens would not have known about the refugee's needs. You sent him out to spread the word and hundreds responded liberally by giving supplies of meal, bacon, clothing, and bedding. We have distributed these as wisely as possible. There are others of you who have also contributed greatly to the work. Now I am asking that one of you rise and accept the challenge of supervising the ministry in Topeka in my absence. I have been praying about this for several months, and I believe God has chosen someone here this morning to take my place."

And with that statement Elizabeth sat down. There was a stunned silence as Friends considered her words. The presiding clerk seemed at a loss as to how to proceed. Surely it was not the duty of the yearly meeting to provide leadership for this work. The members had always supported the work, even formed a committee two years earlier to assist in any way possible. But surely it was not the representative's responsibility to find a replacement for this woman who had come years before of her own accord. Finally, one member suggested a time for silent seeking of the Spirit, and those gathered sat quietly, trying to center on the request.

Julia was stunned by Elizabeth's announcement. First, there was the news of her departure. Second, Elizabeth had not considered her for the position. Elizabeth had told her several times she had done a good job when she was left in charge. Did she think she was too young to be a permanent replacement? Why had she not even mentioned the possibility? Julia was flooded with disappointment.

Eventually a young man sitting in the row ahead of Elizabeth and Julia rose to speak. Julia looked up at the sound of the voice, smooth as butter and with deep resonance. A voice she would have recognized anywhere.

"I believe God is calling me to this work," he said. "My name is John Stanley and I am from Rose Hill Meeting. I have been in a state of mourning for the past year, ever since my beautiful wife was killed when a train hit her carriage one night at dusk. She left behind two wonderful children who have not known how to cope without the mother who did everything for them. I felt like God was punishing me, though I had no idea what I might have done to deserve it.

"A few months ago I began volunteering my time at the Association a couple of days each month. It has been a most rewarding experience and this morning, listening to Mrs. Comstock speak, I felt the Spirit nudging me. 'It is time to move forward,' it seemed to say. I am a hard worker and if Mrs. Comstock is willing to teach me every thing I'll need to know, I will do my best to continue the work in her absence."

Julia was appalled. John Stanley, the most sober, unhappy man she had ever met was going to be in charge of the Association. How would she ever be able to work for this man she found so unpleasant? Elizabeth was the thread that held them all together. She was able to take the pieces each of them brought to the Association and weave a beautiful quilt. This man knew very little about their work. How would any one with such a bitter personality ever persuade Friends to give one thin dime to their work? Julia just sat and shook her head. Surely some of the representatives knew this man well enough to know he did not have the leadership capabilities needed to oversee such a large operation.

The clerk called the meeting to a close after the representatives, much to Julia's displeasure, unanimously agreed to support Mr. Stanley in his desire to take over for Elizabeth. As they rose to leave, Julia could not help tapping the shoulder of the man who was going to be her overseer in the not too distant future.

"Excuse me," she began, "Perhaps thee does not remember me, but my name is Julia Jones and I am one of the workers at the Association."

As John turned to speak, Julia was startled by his eyes. They were aquamarine, such a contrast to his dark hair and beard. Strange she had never noticed them before. He seemed a bit friendlier than he had been in their previous encounters.

"Hello, Julia. Of course I remember thee. As I recall, the last time we met thee was teaching thy brother one of the Negro spirituals. By the way, how was that received?" Then he smiled. The first time Julia had ever seen anything besides a frown on his face. The smile reminded her of a mother's warm gaze at her child. So gentle, so kind. When Julia did not respond, he continued. "I am hoping thee will help me learn more about the work with the refugees. I have great admiration for all that Mrs. Comstock has done for the Negroes in this state, but I am certain those working for her have played a major role as well."

Who was this man? Surely not the same John Stanley who always seemed to carry the weight of the world on his shoulders. This man was kind and caring, and he had a smile.

"I am sorry," John said. "I did not mean to pry into thy work. Please be assured I will try to continue the work at the Association in much the same manner it is now conducted. I look forward to visiting with thee again in the near future."

Julia shook the hand he extended, so large it nearly swallowed hers. The handshake was firm, yet gentle.

"Fadder! Whad is taking dee so long?" a young boy asked as he burst into the meeting room. "We have been waiting and waiting for dee."

Smiling once again, John grabbed the boy and swung him around several times. A spitting image of his father, he appeared to be around the age of her twin cousins.

Just then a girl peeked around the corner of the door and shyly came toward her father. She was a little older than the boy, with fine features. Her light yellow hair must have been a gift from her mother. The eyes, however, were her father's.

"Julia, please meet my children, Caleb and Esther. Caleb will be five next month, and Esther is seven. They are the light of my life and I hope they will adjust to life at the Association. Children, this is Julia."

"Who is she?" Esther asked cautiously.

"I will tell thee all about her later."

"I will tell thee all about her later."

"Come on, Fadder," Caleb implored once again. "We are hungwy!"

"All right, sprout, it is past the dinner hour. Oh—Julia, would thee care to join us?"

Julia looked at the faces of the children. She was a stranger to them and they were wanting to be with their father. "Not this time, thank you. Perhaps in the future."

"Very well. Children, let us find some sustenance."

Julia watched the three of them leave. The children would certainly liven things up at the Association offices. And their father . . . what a man of contradictions. Would they be able to work together as well as she and Elizabeth? Things were changing. The possibility of her father's joining them, working with John Stanley and his children, and Elizabeth's leaving. A sense of sadness filled Julia. Changes she made of her own accord were one thing, but changes forced on her by others were more difficult to accept.

CHAPTER 17

Keep IN THE *Middle* OF THE *Road'*

*T*he winter swept in with sub-zero temperatures and howling prairie winds which gave anyone walking the sensation of being propelled along by an invisible force. Snow began to fall the first of December and continued on a regular basis. It was difficult to traverse the streets of Topeka much of the time, as the city workers were unable to keep the streets cleared of snow. In late November Laura announced she was returning to her home in hopes of regaining her health, leaving only Elizabeth and Julia to handle all the duties at the Association. Refugees continued to arrive from the South, often with frozen fingers or toes, emaciated, and weary. The daylight hours grew fewer, adding to the depression Julia felt.

In January Hosea came to the offices to announce his departure. He talked with Elizabeth for some time, about future employment, Julia guessed, and finally he approached her office door.

"Please come in, Hosea," she said warmly. They had remained cordial since returning to Topeka, though there had been no stolen moments in the evenings like in the past. There was still a tender place in her heart for the man she had once felt so close to, and a feeling of sorrow for the disappointment she knew she caused him. She hoped he harbored no ill feelings toward her, though she would not blame him if he did.

"I jist come ta say I's leavin' in da mornin' for Cherokee County. The refugees that come two days ago say they needs a blacksmith real bad cuz da one that do all da business gots layed up from a piece of flyin' iron. I 'speck I kin have lots a work soon's I kin get there."

The thought of Hosea being injured in a similar manner sent a chill down Julia's spine. "Please be careful!" she admonished.

Hosea looked at her for what he knew would probably be the last time they would ever see one another. "I's be careful, Julia," he finally said. "And Julia?"

"Yes, Hosea?"

"I don't think I ever thanked ya fer helping me find God's forgiveness."

"But it was Elizabeth . . ."

"No, it be you, Julia. That time you talked about that son who took all his money and then wanted to go back like a slave. His daddy took him back and forgave him. I wanted that, too. I jist had to be sure it was what I really wanted, and not somethin' I was doin' jist ta please you. Miz Elizabeth, she jist help me say da words. You be the one that preach da truth."

"I am the one who needs to offer thanks, Hosea. If it were not for your stories of torture in the South, and your willingness to teach me the spirituals, our worship services would still be as dry as dirt. You taught me everything I needed to know to have the compassion to love and care for everyone here."

Not caring whether or not it was appropriate, Julia walked over to Hosea and gave him a brief hug. "Please let us know how you are doing," she said, though they both knew there would be no future communication between the two of them. "I will never forget thee, Hosea. I wish thee the best."

After a final glance at the beautiful woman he knew he would never forget, Hosea left.

I'll never see him again, Julia thought, overwhelming sadness welling within her. When will I once again feel joyful?

Julia received a letter from her mother in February outlining the family's plan to arrive in Topeka in April or May, depending on how soon Charles could finish his work in the office. They would send most of their belongings ahead by freight train, and she asked Julia to make arrangements to secure them at the train station. At least that was one positive in this whole dark picture: they were not bringing everything with them so perhaps their stay would be short.

I knew Father would not consider my opinion, she thought. He asked me to affirm his coming to work here, and in spite of my lack of consent he is still coming.

You did not tell him not to come, she reminded herself. Still, it would have been more respectful if Father had sought her feelings before making plans to move. Perhaps she could persuade Elizabeth to send him to Cherokee County to work. There was certainly a great need there from the reports they were getting. Often refugees would stop at the Agricultural and Industrial Institute, as it was the first chance at life in a free state. Some would eventually move on to Topeka where the population was greater with more opportunities for employment. It was these refugees who spoke of the needs in Cherokee County. That is what I will do, she thought, mention these needs to Elizabeth and suggest Father be sent there to practice medicine.

Elizabeth was doing her best to make certain the record books were accurate. She even had two bankers in town look over the accounts to be certain there was no money unaccounted for. "The sixty-thousand dollars raised these past few years is a great sum of money, Julia," she had said, "and it is vital that every penny be accounted for." Julia admired her for wanting to make certain their work was beyond criticism.

Julia did not want to think what it would be like at the Association without its founder and leader. Elizabeth knew all the little details: where refugees might look for work, the names of Friends in Kansas she could call on when funds ran low, the future plans for the existing Associations, and those she hoped to construct in the future. Would John Stanley be able to learn everything there was to know about their work in a few short months?

Just as he promised, John came to the offices every few weeks. Once harvesting was finished he had more free time and his visits became weekly. Sometimes he brought his children along—to get used to their future home, he told Eliza-beth—and sometimes he left them with their grandparents who lived across the road from the Stanley home. Although there were still many times when John's expression was one of great sadness, Julia was growing accustomed to his ways and found that the more she got to know him the less sorrowful he seemed.

The first time he brought the children Julia was work-ing in her office and was startled by the high-pitched laugh-ter as they entered the hallway. As she went to the door to welcome them, they grew instantly quiet, Esther clinging to her father and Caleb staring at her.

"Good morning, Caleb and Esther," she said warmly. "How nice of you to visit us today."

Silence.

Finally John spoke for them. "I must apologize for my children, Julia. They are not adjusting to this move as well as I had hoped, and I thought perhaps a visit might help them see it is not such a terrifying place. They are not accustomed to being around strangers, having spent most of their lives with either their mother and I or their grandparents."

"I am certain they will be fine once thee makes the move." Julia tried to sound encouraging. "I could show them the area if thee would like."

"Children?" he asked. "Would thee like Julia to show thee where they help the refugees?"

"No thank you," Esther said politely. Even though her tone was very cool, Julia was certain she could win her confidence given enough time.

"Caleb, would thee like to go with Julia?"

"No sanks, Fadder. I want to stay wif you."

"I am sorry, Julia," John said apologetically. "This is all new to the children. They have been with me or with their grandparents since the time of their mother's death. I suppose it will take them a while to feel comfortable around others. Perhaps it is my fault for sheltering them. My grief was so great that at times I could think of no one's needs but my own."

"It is fine, John," Julia said, trying to hide the disappointment she felt. She had always gotten along so well with children, and it was hard to deal with rejection, even from two strangers.

"Caleb, Esther, before you leave I could show you a big wall where children can draw anything they wish—if you would like, of course."

There was a spark of interest in Esther's eyes, Julia was certain, though neither child responded to her invitation.

"That would be lovely, Julia. I will bring the children to thy office before we leave this afternoon."

Julia had hoped to have the children alone for a bit, but she supposed John would want to come with them. She thought perhaps he was clinging to them just a bit too tightly, though his protection was understandable considering the loss they had all suffered.

Around mid-afternoon the children and their father were once again in the offices. A timid knock on her door brought her face to face with seven-year-old Esther. "I would like to see the wall," she said quietly.

"Where is thy father?" Julia asked curiously.

"Talking with Miss Elizabeth. He said I might come on my own if I wanted. Caleb did not wish to come."

Julia smiled, hoping she conveyed the happiness she felt at the fragile trust exhibited by this little girl. She wanted to grab her and give her a big hug, but was afraid to shatter the fragile bond she hoped would only grow stronger.

Once they were in the infirmary Esther's eyes—John's eyes—grew big as saucers as she stared at the wall. Colorful people of all shapes and sizes, animals, trees, and words scattered here and there covered most of the wall. "Who painted this?" she asked."

"A little girl named Julianna."

"Your little girl?"

Julia smiled, remembering how badly she had wanted Julianna for her own.

"No, Julianna was a little mulatto girl who was very sick and came to live here until she was all better. Then she went to live with a new mother and father."

"What is a mulatto?" Esther asked.

"Someone with light brown skin." Julia did not think a seven-year-old needed explanations about mothers and fathers of a different race.

"Where was her mother? Why did she get a new mother and father?"

Questions. Another of Julianna's traits.

"Her mother was sick and could not take care of her." Well, that was mostly true, Julia reasoned. A mother who would abandon her child had to be sick in her mind.

"Where was her father?"

"He died." Murdered by white men, she wanted to add, but knew the inappropriateness of such a statement.

"So she got a new mother and father?"

"Yes, a father and mother who loved her very much and wanted to make a home for her."

"Will I get a new mother?" Esther asked innocently.

"Would you like that?"

"I think so. I cannot even remember what my real mother looked liked." The sad look in her eyes touched Julia's heart.

"Does thee remember some of the things she used to do with thee? Games thee played? Work thee did together?"

"Oh yes! She loved to play hide and seek with Caleb and me. We would hide in the prairie grass and she could never find us." Esther giggled. "Sometimes she would get angry when we did not come when she called."

"I imagine she was frightened and worried that something might happen to thee or Caleb."

"I know," Esther said seriously. "Then something happened to her. Julia, does thee believe God wanted my mother dead?"

Julia was quick with an answer. "No, Esther, I do not believe God wanted thy mother dead."

"Then why did she get killed?"

What should she say? That sometimes events happen that we have no control over? That God created humans with minds to think and invent things like locomotives that have the power to kill if we get in their way? Or should she tell her the truth— that she honestly did not know why.

"Sometimes, Esther, things happen in this world that we do not have answers for. One thing I know, though. God loved thy mother very, very, much. He was just as sad the day she died as thee was."

"Really?" Esther's eyes were big, never having considered God might have feelings.

"Truly. And I also know that thy mother is in heaven with God right now, and she is keeping an eye on thee every day."

"She is?" Esther asked incredulously.

"She is. And she wants thee to be happy."

"Will God give me a new mother to take her place?"

"No one can take her place, Esther, but perhaps some day thy father will find a woman who could be a mother to thee and Caleb."

"You could," Esther said hopefully.

Julia blushed. "I hardly know thy father, Esther, and I am sure he would want to find someone more his age."

"He is only twenty-five. How old is thee?"

"Twenty."

"That is almost the same age."

Julia could not argue with her. This was certainly an intelligent child.

"Would thee like to draw on the wall?" Julia asked, hoping to change the subject.

"I could ask father for thee," she continued. "I could ask him if he would like to have thee for a wife. Then we could have a mother."

"No! I mean . . . please do not mention this to him. He is trying to learn about the Association and I am certain he has no time to think of marriage right now."

Esther looked heavy-hearted. "All right, Julia," she said sadly.

"Let's draw a picture to show thy father and Caleb when they return," Julia implored, hoping to get the child's mind on a different subject.

"Yes. We could draw a rainbow. That was God's promise to Noah. I want it to be a promise from God that he will give father a wife and Caleb and me a mother."

"All right, Esther. A rainbow it shall be."

The two of them set to work, Esther losing her former shyness, chatting endlessly about life on the farm. John and Caleb came looking for them just as they were finishing the red stripe.

"There you two are!" he said warmly. "We are ready to leave, Esther."

Julia prayed fervently that Esther would make no mention of her becoming the children's mother.

"Do we have to, Father? Julia and I were just finishing our painting of a rainbow. A promise rainbow."

"It is beautiful," John said kindly.

Julia looked at him once again as he gathered his children to leave. Julia had been certain he was much older than twenty-five. Perhaps it was the beard. Julia had never been too fond of facial hair, though many of the Friends she knew, including her brother David, wore full beards. His eyes, however, still remained the focal point of his face, their aquamarine color so inviting.

"Julia?" John asked.

"Oh—yes, John?" Julia felt her face grow warm, embarrassed that she had been caught staring at him.

"I asked if thee might want to join us for supper. Elizabeth has asked me to stay over another day so that we might finish the accounting details. We will sleep here in the infirmary, and then go home tomorrow afternoon."

This was the second time John had asked her to dine with him and the children. Did she want to go? She was not sure.

"Please?" Esther asked imploringly. "Will thee please come with us?"

"She will come," Caleb said confidently. "Otherwise how will I tell her about Wildfire?"

"Now Caleb," John began, "we cannot expect Julia to join us if she has other plans."

"I would be delighted to join thee," she said simply. "But I must ask, who is Wildfire?"

"That is a very long story!" John said jokingly as the four of them set off for supper at the nearby hotel.

CHAPTER 18

'Chatter
WITH
THE *Angels'*

Both children warmed to Julia as they shared their evening meal. Caleb told her all about Wildfire, the colt his father had given him for his birthday. Wildfire, it seems, had been most uncooperative when John had broken him to ride. Caleb had said sparks like fire flew from his eyes when John climbed on his back, thus the name. Julia thoroughly enjoyed the conversation and too soon it was time to return to their respective places of lodging. As Julia's boarding house was the opposite direction from the Association, she informed John that she could walk the two blocks herself so that he might get the children back and to bed at a reasonable hour. John, however, would have nothing of it.

"We will walk with thee, won't we children?"

The answer was affirmed with Esther taking one of Julia's hands and Caleb the other. "Tell us a story, Julia," Esther begged as they headed down the street.

"Now children," John began.

"John, it will be fine. I love telling stories."

"Then perhaps thee would not mind telling them a story from the Bible. I seem to have neglected that area of their lives these past months."

Julia told them how Jesus was always asking questions, questions, questions, when he was their age. "His parents even had to go back to the temple to look for him because he was too busy talking to the elders to realize his parents had already left without him," she told them.

"What is an elder?" Esther inquired.

"Just like Jesus!" Julia said fondly. "Always asking questions."

"Esther, it is not polite to be constantly badgering adults with thy questions," her father scolded.

"John, please," Julia said, slightly disturbed by the man's stern words. "I am delighted when children ask questions of me. It means they are seeking to know more about their world. It is as natural as bees seeking pollen to make honey."

John stared at the woman walking with his children. His wife would never have spoken to him in such a way. She had been quiet, obedient, and attentive to his every word. This girl was as bold as any man he had ever known. He was not certain he liked Julia's forward manner.

Disgust . . . is that the look on John's face? Julia wondered. Surely he could not object to her answering a few of the children's questions.

Ignoring John's admonition to the children, Julia continued. "An elder is one of the older, wiser members in a Meeting, Esther. In the temple where Jesus worshipped, some of the elders lived in the temple and spent all their time studying God's word and trying to help people understand God."

"I would never want to live at the Meeting House," Esther said emphatically. "It is too cold."

Julia and John both laughed at the thought of Esther living alone in the poorly heated meetinghouses they had both experienced.

"We would never let thee live there, either." Julia stopped. "I mean . . . thy *father* would never allow thee to live apart from him." What was she thinking? This was not her child. In the future she would need to be more respectful where John's children were concerned.

"We will see thee to the door," John announced as they approached Maggie's front porch.

Not wishing to start an argument, Julia simply opened the door with no further comment. She thought perhaps she had been outspoken enough for one night.

"Maggie, I'm home," she called, opening the front door. Announcing yourself had been one of Maggie's rules since the day she moved in. Announce your comings and goings so I don't have to worry my fool head off, she had declared.

"It's about time!" came the gruff, but loving response. Maggie came around the corner of the kitchen just in time to see the young man and two children with Julia.

"John? Is that you?"

"Maggie! How art thou?"

Julia looked from the old woman to the man. They knew each other?

The two began visiting as if old friends. The children stood still, obviously trained to remain silent when in the presence of their father and another adult.

"I am sorry, Julia, I was so surprised to see Aunt Maggie that I nearly forgot about thee."

"The two of you are related?" she asked, amazed.

"Yes, this is my wife's Aunt Maggie. She used to come visit us before Carolyn passed—when the children were younger."

"That reminds me. How's come ya never been ta see me since Carolyn passed away? I'm still a great aunt to those two children of yours, you know. I ain't been able to travel like I used to, but that don't excuse you from comin' ta see me." Maggie, as always, was blunt with her questioning.

"I am sorry, Maggie. I have not felt like socializing since Carolyn's death. The children and I have spent most of our time this past year working on the farm."

"That ain't right, John, and you know it. Those children need to be around others. You'll do harm to 'em if ya don't get 'em out some."

"I know that, Maggie, but it is just so difficult. I do, however, have a bit of good news for thee. God has finally spoken to my heart and I am going to begin working at the Association in June."

"You don't say! That mean you're takin' Lizzy's place?"

"Yes, as a matter of fact I am." John could not help but smile at Maggie's nickname for the woman he would never think of calling 'Lizzy.'

"Well I'll be! Lizzy said she's been trainin' a young man, but she never once said your name. Ain't that somethin'? My great niece and nephew comin' to live with me."

"Oh, no—I mean," John sputtered. "We will not be moving *here*, Aunt Maggie. We will find a home of our own here in Topeka."

"Nonsense. I got plenty of room, even for the youngsters. Julia here will still have a room, but there's two others up there—Lizzy's, and Laura's old room that I keep as a spare fer guests that show up now and then."

"No." John's voice was a more stern than Julia would have liked. "I am sorry, but we need a place of our own. The children can be loud and boisterous at times and I am not certain of my hours. I may be out late at night patching problems that might come up at the Association."

"So what? It ain't like Lizzy and Julia get here any certain hours. That's why I insist they announce their comin's and goin's. As fer the children, why it's a child's laughter that keeps an old woman like me feelin' alive."

"No, Aunt Maggie, I would not think of moving these children in with thee. We will visit thee, of course, but we will not live here. Children, we must get back to the Association. Julia, I thank thee for joining us for supper." John firmly took both of the children by the hand and with a final goodbye was gone.

"What is the matter with that man?" Julia exploded. "Did you see the way he treated those children? They were stiff as statues the whole time he was talking. And the way he talked to you, Maggie . . . why, it was simply rude. Outside of a few times when the man actually smiled about something involving the children, he has been the most downcast person I have ever seen."

"Now Julia, don't you worry 'bout John. He'll be fine ta work for. He's got a heart o' gold and he loves those children, too. He's just still mournin' over Carolyn's death. You don't know what it's like ta lose your husband, no matter whether he dies or runs off like mine did."

"No, I have never lost a husband," Julia said slowly, "but I do not believe I would bury myself and my children in work in hopes of forgetting the one I loved."

She remembered Hosea and the pain she still felt at the thought of never seeing him again. But she certainly had not let it affect her whole life like John had allowed Carolyn's death to do.

"I am so happy ta hear he's gonna be takin' Lizzy's place. Be just the thing that boy needs to start livin' again. And those poor youngins . . . they need to be in school, learnin' how ta git along with others."

"I am sorry, Maggie, I know he is your relative—well, sort of, anyway—but I just wish he would let the children be children. He even gets upset when they ask too many questions."

"I know, Julia, I know. I'm worried 'bout 'em, too, but this move'll do 'em all good. I can't wait fer 'em to move in here."

"But—"

"I heard what he said, Julia, but he can be won over, I'm sure. I'll find out from Lizzy next time he's comin' to town and I'll fix him and the youngin's a fine meal. I don't s'pose John's ever learned how ta do much cookin' since Carolyn passed on. I'll help 'im remember just what it's like to eat a home-cooked meal, and then we'll see how he feels 'bout livin' here."

Julia smiled. Good old Maggie. She had a heart of gold. Maybe she was right. Maybe she could convince John to move in with them. But was that what she wanted? And what would the neighbors think about a man and two children living under

the same roof as a young, unmarried woman and their outspoken landlady.

The warm weather of spring was a welcome relief from the
woes of winter, and the additional hours of sunlight were a
boost to Julia's spirits. Even the daily messages she prepared for
Meeting for Worship were easier. The refugees seemed to enjoy the services more than in the winter; the singing was livelier, and the time of open worship often lasted for nearly an
hour as member after member told of the changes God was
making in their lives.

John had not brought the children back to the Association
with him, and when Julia asked about them his answer was
always the same: they were doing well. John Stanley . . . now
there was a man Julia did not understand at all. His eyes were
warm and inviting, but his tone of voice was often cold and
unfeeling. And those adorable children. He seemed to love
them dearly, but he also seemed afraid to let them be the seven
and five-year-olds they were.

Maggie kept working on Elizabeth to invite John and the
children to dine with her, and finally, the last of April, John
agreed to bring the children and join them for supper.

"I want the two of ya here as well," Maggie informed Elizabeth and Julia the night before the expected arrival of their
guests.

"I am sorry, Maggie," Elizabeth said, "but I am planning to
leave in a few short weeks and I have too many things to do."

Maggie, however, would not take no for an answer. "You
been livin' here now fer three years, Lizzy, an' I ain't asked ya ta

do too much, now have I? So I ain't gonna let ya turn me down on this one. I want John and the children to relax and enjoy themselves durin' dinner. He knows you better 'n he knows us two, so I want you here."

"All right, Maggie, if it means that much to thee."

"It's the youngin's I'm worried about. They deserve a warm home that I don't think that man kin give 'em."

Julia was surprised at Maggie's words. Maggie and John had seemed to be cordial enough the night he walked her home. Maggie must know something about him I do not, Julia thought.

John and the children walked from the Association to Maggie's the next evening with Elizabeth. Julia had left early to help Maggie with the preparations. She was also hoping to ask the old woman a few questions that might shed some light on the puzzling young man that had been Maggie's nephew by marriage.

"Maggie," she began as she peeled potatoes, "tell me about John. Esther told me he is only twenty-five, but he seems ten years older to me. And sometimes he is warm and kind with the children, and other times he is stern and rigid. I just do not understand him at all."

Maggie looked curiously at Julia. She hadn't thought of John and the children for several months before they showed up that one evening. She had to admit the possibility of Julia becoming a mother to those children had crossed her mind since that time. They were so different, though. John was more quiet, reserved, but with a sternness that sometimes even scared her. Julie, on the other hand, was a precious young woman who was never afraid to speak her mind. She would never be the submissive wife her niece Carolyn had been.

"I will tell ya what I know, but it ain't that much," she began. "Most o' what I know came from Carolyn when she used ta bring the children ta see me. John was always too busy in the fields to find time for a visit."

"Whatever thee can tell me will be helpful," Julia said. "Anything would be better than nothing.

"Well, it seems that John's father was one to believe that beatin' a child was the only way you could make 'em mind. Carolyn said John told her his daddy beat him every time he did the least little thing he didn't approve of. I reckon that's why John seems stern with the children. But I believe the man has a good heart, Julie, and I think he dearly loves those two youngin's."

"You do not believe he would ever hurt them, do you?"

"No, I asked Carolyn 'bout that very thing one time and she said he never laid a hand on Caleb or Esther. But I know she was a little afraid of him herself, sometimes. She always seemed to try to do her best to please him and do whatever he asked. I never heard her speak up to him even one time."

Julia remembered the way she had spoken to John about the children's questions. I suppose I am nothing like his first wife, she thought.

All during supper Julia thought about Maggie's words as she tried to interact with the children quietly, in a way John would approve. After the dishes were cleared John insisted on drying them for Maggie. Elizabeth had excused herself, saying she was not feeling well, and Julia took the opportunity to spend some time alone with the children.

"John, would thee mind if I took the children to see my room? I have a few things I brought with me from Salem that I think they might enjoy seeing."

John seemed hesitant, though he finally consented. Once they were in the room Julia impulsively hugged first Esther and then Caleb. "I am so glad to see thee both again," she said warmly.

Both children smiled gratefully, as though they had just received a gift from heaven. "Does thy father hug thee often?" she could not help but ask.

"Sometimes," Esther said.

"Not very much," Caleb spoke truthfully.

"That is too bad. Thee should be hugged many times a day," Julia told them.

After they had looked at the dolls and pictures Julia had brought from Salem, Caleb posed the question she had been expecting one of them to eventually ask.

"Will thee be our new mother?"

"Is that what thy father said?" she asked.

"He said we should not ask such questions," Esther reported.

"Thee likes us, yes?" Caleb asked eagerly.

"Of course I do," she replied. "Has thy father said anything about me being thy new mother?" For some reason it was important for her to know if John had any thoughts similar to his children's.

"No," Esther said. "He does not talk of anyone who might be our mother. Am I a bad person for wanting a mother?"

"Thee could never be a bad person," Julia assured her, angry at the thought that John might have planted such an idea in her head. "Everyone wants a mother and father when they are a child. I am certain you will have a new mother some day."

"Father said thee is too bossy," Caleb blurted out.

"Caleb!" Esther admonished her little brother. "I told thee not to tell Julia what Father said."

"It is all right, Caleb," she assured him. "Thy father is right—I can be bossy sometimes."

"Thee does not seem bossy to me," he said innocently.

Once again Julia drew the stocky little boy close to her. "I thank thee, Caleb, for thy kind words. I do think it would be best if thee did not speak of me to thy father for a time. He has other things to think about right now. The most wonderful thing is that in a few weeks you will be living in Topeka, and I will get to see you every day!"

The eyes of both children lit up. "Will thee give us hugs each day?" Caleb asked.

"Of course I will. And thee can give them to me as well."

"Father says we must live in the infirmary until he can find a suitable place to live," Esther reported.

Julia smiled. John had not yet met the challenge of a determined Maggie. We shall see if you live in the infirmary, she thought.

"Children," John called from downstairs. "It is time we left for home. It will be well past dark when we arrive as it is."

"You kin always stay here," Julia heard Maggie pipe in.

"Now Maggie, I told thee I would consider thy offer, but for now it is best that the children and I return home."

So Maggie had at least gotten him to consider living with them. That woman never ceased to amaze Julia. And John thought she was bossy!

Once the family had said goodbye and were on their way, Julia could not help but quiz Maggie about her talk with John.

"Did thee actually get him to consider living here?" she asked, wanting to make certain she had heard him correctly.

"Let's jist say I made him an offer."

"That you'd make homemade pies and noodles every day?" Julia teased.

"No," Maggie seemed quite serious. "That I would love and watch after the youngin's when he was workin', and that I'd see to it they got to school each day and home safely."

"But Maggie, you're almost sixty-five years old! How will you care for two young children?"

"With your help," she said with a twinkle in her eye. "I figure you kin' help me give those youngin's the love they oughta be gettin' from the mother they ain't got."

"But I do not believe John—"

"You leave John ta me, dear. I'll take care of him."

Yes, Julia thought, I just bet you will. She began to warm at the thought of living with the two children. She would ask Maggie to give them the room that shared a door with hers. That way if they needed something she could help them so as not to disturb their father. This might work out after all, she decided. Esther and Caleb would be a wonderful addition to their home, and surely she and John could accept each other's differences enough to live peacefully under the same roof. And I shall be a wonderful friend to the children, even if their father does believe I am bossy.

Chapter 19

'Rock-a my Soul'

A telegram arrived the first week, fifth month, announcing that Charles, Rebecca, and Rachel would arrive the twentieth day of that month. Julia felt torn between wanting to see her mother and Rachel, but not wanting to work with her father. As Elizabeth's health continued to deteriorate, she was only able to work an hour or two each day. Julia had not found the right time to persuade her to send her father to the southeast corner of Kansas to work. How did one explain something that one did not understand herself?

Much to Julia's relief, the day before her family's arrival Elizabeth announced that she had decided that for now Charles' labors were needed in Cherokee County. Julia's feelings must have been evident as Elizabeth asked her to sit for a moment. *Sit for a moment* was Elizabeth's way of saying *there is something thee is doing I am not too pleased with and we need to discuss it.*

Julia sat. Elizabeth stood and began to pace back and forth across the room. "Julia," she finally said, "I must tell thee I am concerned about thy attitude regarding thy father. I had imagined thee would be thrilled when thy father made his commitment to come to Kansas. Instead, thee has been as sour as three-day-old milk these last few months." Elizabeth's weariness was evident and she finally sat down next to Julia on the bench along one wall, placing her hand on Julia's arm. "What is bothering thee, dear? Thee needs to consider thy feelings before thy family arrives."

What could she say? She had gone over it and over it in her mind, but the reasons for her unhappiness were never clear. "I am not certain why I feel this way, Elizabeth. I just know I have feelings of anger when I think that Father made my life so miserable when I wanted to answer God's call."

"What about thy prayer for holiness and thy desire to see thy father in a different light?" Elizabeth asked gently.

Julia blushed. "I know that was my desire, but can thee not understand? Father would never even consider the possibility that God could use me. He plotted and schemed to keep me in Salem. He used two wonderful older ladies in our Meeting to try and convince me the work would be too dangerous. He even asked a young man—Will Clark—to ask for my hand in marriage to sabotage my plans. I cannot begin to tell thee how many hours I spent in prayer, not wanting to disobey my father, but at the same time wanting to answer God's call.

"It nearly broke my heart when he would not give his blessing to my departure, and I worried for days after I left that I had somehow hurt him terribly by my actions. Did he ever apologize for any of his actions? No. Not once. And now all of a sudden he believes refugee work does, indeed, have value and

FOR THE BLESSINGS OF A FRIEND

that he wants to be a part of it. *My* work. The work God called *me* to do. I feel like he not only rejected my call, but somehow he rejected me as well."

"Julia, does thee remember the parable Jesus taught of the workers in the vineyard, where the laborers who signed up to work the last hour were paid the same as those who had worked the entire day?"

Julia squirmed. Of course she knew that parable, but it was one she never used in her messages because it did not seem fair!

"Yes, I know the parable."

"What message does thee believe Jesus was trying to convey to the disciples with this parable?"

"I suppose that we each have different rewards and we should not look at what others receive."

"That might be a part of it, but I believe it is more about grace than rewards. Tell me, dear, what did thee do to deserve God's forgiveness of thy sins?"

Again Julia was uncomfortable with Elizabeth's question.

"I suppose nothing."

"Exactly. None of us is deserving of the gift of salvation we receive by merely asking."

"But I do not see what this has to do with Father," she protested.

"Should thee begrudge thy father's change of heart toward our work, even if it took him longer than thee? If God calls him in the ninth hour, as he did some of the workers in the vineyard, is it right for thee to feel jealous?"

"But I do not believe I am jealous of—" Julia began.

"Yes, Julia, I believe jealousy is the underlying reason for thy anger—jealousy that God wants to also use thy father in this work. Does thee not feel a bit of pride about thy work here? Pride that thee was willing to leave thy home and family to come to Kansas, pride that swells in thy chest when thee speaks to Friends about this work? It would seem to me that thee does not want thy father to give his time to this work because it might take some of the glory away from thee. Am I anywhere near the truth, Julia?" Elizabeth paused, the wracking cough once again consuming her.

Julia thought about Elizabeth's words. It was true that it did not seem fair that Father had come at the last minute and received praise from other Friends for his 'sacrifice.' And if she were truly honest with herself, she knew jealousy and pride were also a reason for her dissatisfaction. But the part about grace was the real humbler. Julia knew it was only by God's grace that she had received salvation and the many other blessings she had been given in her life.

Once the coughing spell subsided, Elizabeth continued. "Perhaps if thee can focus on God's gracious benefits to thee it will be easier to accept the gifts he has given thy father. God knows thy heart, dear one, and He knows thee loves thy father. Ask Him for the courage to graciously accept thy father's gifts and then thee will experience God's peace in the matter."

Julia sighed. Why was it so hard to admit when one was wrong?

"Julia? What does thee think?"

"I know thee is right, Elizabeth," she admitted. "Please pray for me that I will be able to be gracious to Father. Holiness is certainly a lot harder than it seemed that night in Indiana."

"I know thy father hurt thee with his actions two years ago," she said softly, "but if thee will look at God's grace, his graciousness to each of us, I believe it will not be as difficult as it seems now."

Julia hoped not. Time spent in prayer was in order for this evening, not only where Father was concerned, but also for the cough that seemed to be taking more and more of the spirit and life from Elizabeth.

"Juwea!" came the excited cry from the crowd departing from the train.

Julia knew Rachel's voice and scanned the faces for the cherub she loved. "I see thee!" she said happily as she reached to take Rachel from her Father's arms. "How did thee like the train ride?"

"It was smelly!" Rachel said, wrinkling her nose.

Julia laughed. Coal-burning steam engines were indeed 'smelly' when the windows of the passenger cars were open.

"If thee will follow me," she said to her father after greeting both parents, "I will take thee to the baggage area, and also to the place where the belongings thee sent ahead are being stored. Elizabeth asked John Stanley to bring his wagon and help thee bring thy things to the Association. John is over by the station," she finished, pointing a few yards to their left.

Julia saw her father look curiously at the bearded young man sitting in the wagon.

"And who might this John Stanley be? To thee, I mean," he asked with a grin and a suspicious look in his eye.

Julia shook her head and smiled. This was the father she remembered, a father who loved to tease her about the men she might some day marry, a father with a smile on his face. He seemed happier and more relaxed than she had seen him for a long time.

"John is going to take Elizabeth's place—next week, in fact. It was my understanding Elizabeth told thee of the plans for the Association when she knew she would be leaving."

"Oh, well, I suppose she did mention she might be leaving, but I did not believe she would actually go," Charles admitted. "You say she is leaving next week?"

"Yes, she is going to New York. Her doctor has arranged for her to stay in a sanitarium until the infection in her lungs is gone and the tissue is healed. Even now she is only working an hour or two a day."

"I see. Is her doctor trustworthy?"

Julia laughed. "Only thee would ask that question, Father! I am certain Elizabeth would allow thee to examine her if thee feels she has not been given a proper diagnosis."

Charles grinned. "I do not believe that will be necessary. But I must admit I am a bit disappointed. I was looking forward to learning about this work from her."

"John will be able to answer thy questions. He has been coming here for six months now and knows most everything there is to know."

"And this John Stanley . . . is he married, perchance?"

"Charles!" Rebecca spoke for the first time. "Thee promised not to meddle in Julia's life once we came here."

Julia smiled lovingly at her mother. Leave it to her mother to prepare the way for her.

"For thy information, John is a widower with two young children. And no, I do not intend to marry him." This time there was no anger toward her father. She was determined to focus on her blessings, thanking God for the return of good feelings where her father was concerned.

Once the belongings had been gathered Julia announced that she, Rebecca, and Rachel would walk the few blocks to the Association as the wagon was nearly full with the family's belongings. As they walked Julia answered the questions of the happy little girl swinging her hand, while also trying to visit with her mother. In no time at all they were in front of the main offices.

"Elizabeth is not here this afternoon," John informed Charles as he tied the horse to the hitching post, "but she said for thee to store thy belongings in the warehouse. We have not had many shipments this winter and there is plenty of space there. When thee is ready to move to Cherokee County I will be happy to haul these things for thee."

Charles looked stunned. "I know nothing about Cherokee County," he said gruffly.

"Oh, well, uh," John stumbled, not knowing what, if anything, Elizabeth had told the doctor about her plans for his services. "I am certain she will tell thee what she has in mind when she comes to the office in the morning. She is nearly always here by seven."

"What is it, Charles," Rachel asked as the three approached the somewhat distraught husband and father.

"John says we may be working in Cherokee County. I am certain there must be some sort of mistake, however, because I specifically said I would work here, in Topeka. I am certain I can straighten everything out with Mrs. Comstock in the morning."

Though Julia was somewhat amused at her father's befuddlement, she knew a straight face was in order. If Father thought he was going to make Elizabeth's decisions for her, he did not know the woman very well. Not at all, in fact. Although Elizabeth was the most compassionate woman Julie had ever known, there was also a backbone of steel that would stand up to any man if she thought her way was best.

"Would thee like to dine at the hotel?" Julia asked when they had carried everything into the warehouse. "It is just down the street. Then thee can get settled in the infirmary for the evening. I made the beds up fresh for thee this morning."

"I wanna sweep wif thee," Rachel said imploringly, pulling on Julia's skirt.

"I have plenty of room in my bed at Maggie's if Mother and Father will allow thee to spend the night with me."

"Pwease? Pwease?" Rachel begged her mother.

"I suppose, but just this one time. Julia needs her sleep and thee is as wiggly as a worm after it rains."

Julia remembered their nights together last fall and had to agree with their mother. But it would be fun to have Rachel meet Maggie and show her where her big sister lived.

"John, would thee like to join us for supper?" Charles asked.

"No, I must get home to pick up my children from my parents. They have been keeping them a great deal while I learn the work here, and they will be expecting me even before I get there."

"Then be on thy way, good Friend, and I thank thee for bringing thy wagon and helping load our belongings," Charles said warmly, shaking John's hand. "By the way . . . has thee ever tasted Julia's cherry pie?"

"Father! Charles!" Julia and Rebecca chimed in together.

Charles just grinned. "I noticed the cherries on the tree behind the warehouse when we pulled up. Thee really should make him a pie some day, Julia. Thee is a wonderful cook!"

Julia blushed. John just smiled. "That would be wonderful, Julia. I look forward to it." And with that he left.

Julia stood staring at Charles. What had ever possessed him to make that comment about her cooking?

"He seems like a nice young man," Charles countered, not wanting to break their fragile new beginnings. "But I would never try to influence thy choice of a future husband."

Both Julia and Rebecca laughed. They both new better.

Julia would never forget her father's conversation with Elizabeth the next morning. She had never seen her father cowered by anyone, let alone a woman, but Elizabeth told him in no uncertain terms that he was needed in Cherokee County, especially since more and more refugees were settling just inside the state's border. It would be no problem for Doc Samuels to continue to take care of the work in Topeka.

"But I supposed Julia and I would be working together," he countered.

"Julia is needed here, thee in Cherokee County. Is there a problem with this arrangement?" she challenged. Even though Julia knew the woman was quite ill, she had to admire the way she had an answer for each of Charles' protests.

"Well, I suppose if I am not needed here," he continued.

"Thee is needed *there*, Charles," she said kindly. "When God spoke to thee about this work, did He say 'go to Topeka,' or was it merely, 'I need thee, Charles, for my work with the refugees'?"

"I suppose I did imagine the work here when I answered the call. But I am willing to go wherever the need is greatest."

"Fine!" Elizabeth beamed. "They are expecting thee at the end of the week."

"But I—I mean I had hoped to spend some time with Julia."

"Thee will have today and tomorrow and then thee will need to catch the six a.m. train to Columbus. One of the workers from the Agricultural Institute will meet thy family at the station. John has offered to haul thy goods in his wagon, but it would certainly be preferable if thee would have them shipped as before—if thee can afford it, that is. I know thee has volunteered thy services at thy own expense and I would not want thee to be pressed financially."

"I will have them shipped by rail," Charles said emphatically. Julia struggled to keep from laughing. Her father was one of the most frugal men she knew, and although he was always generous with his gifts and tithes, she knew finances would not be a problem.

"Good. It is settled then. I hope thee has a good visit with Julia while thee is here. Now, if thee will excuse me, I believe my work is finished for the day."

Julia glanced at the clock on the bookcase in Elizabeth's office. It was not yet the ninth hour and already the woman was worn out. She was not leaving a day too soon, Julia feared.

Julia enjoyed the time she spent with Rachel the next two days, and of course the conversations with her mother. Charles was busy learning as much about the work of the Association as he could from John and Doc Samuels. Julia and Rebecca spent part of their days helping Elizabeth pack. Elizabeth's face was pale and her breathing shallow, lapsing into a coughing fit every time she said more than a few words. Most of the time she directed their activities from the chair where she sat. Maggie bustled in and out making sure everyone was well-fed and had plenty of hot tea to drink. Julia had never learned to like the beverage, but her mother gratefully accepted several cups while they worked. Finally the packing was complete and within a day of each other both Julia's family and her surrogate mother were gone.

Julia felt the loss of Elizabeth more than she had imagined as she sat at meals with Maggie trying to be cheerful. She knew Maggie also missed Elizabeth terribly and she encouraged her to talk about the times they had spent together discussing the various happenings at the Association.

"Ya know," Maggie sad sadly, "the thing I liked the most 'bout that woman was the way she always made me feel like I was important. Didn't seem ta matter ta Lizzy that I was an old woman that never done much 'cept be a homebody. She treated me like I was the smartest woman on earth."

Yes, Julia thought proudly, that's the kind of woman she is. At her suggestion, both she and Maggie prayed for the safe journey and full recovery of the one they loved.

Julia missed her family, as well, but she had been away from them for two years and had grown used to the distance. As always it was difficult to say good-bye to the clinging Rachel. If only they had been closer in age and been able to grow up together, playing and sharing each other's lives.

The Association seemed emptier than ever with both Elizabeth and Laura gone. John was quiet, seldom speaking unless spoken to. He and the children would not be moving into Maggie's home for a few weeks as he wanted time to sort through their belongings once operations were running smoothly at the offices. Julia went about her work methodically, preparing the messages for each morning's services, sorting clothing and bedding, doing some of the paperwork for John, and returning to Maggie's for their somewhat lonely supper.

"Won't be long, now, we'll be havin' us a gay ol' time with them youngins here," she said happily one evening.

Julia laughed. "I do not know about a 'gay old time,' but it will be livelier around here, that is for certain. But I still do not understand how you ever convinced John to move in with us. He was so opposed when you first mentioned it."

"Well, like I told ya, I jist told him those youngins of his needed to be mothered a bit, and with both you 'n me here we could do what he couldn't in that department. And I also told him you was good at makin' pies."

"Surely you did not say that, Maggie," Julie gasped.

There was a twinkle in Maggie's eye as she replied. "Well, no, I reckon I didn't, but after talkin' to that daddy of yours I reckon I should a said jist that."

"Do not ever say that, Maggie Hollingsworth. Please!"

"Then you better do some convincin' on yer own, Missy. That's a right nice man, even if he is a bit sober most of the time. I think he'd be a good man fer ya."

First her father, now Maggie. Was a young, single woman such an abnormality that everyone thought it a duty to find her a mate? Julia shook her head. No mate needed, she said firmly. I am doing just fine on my own.

CHAPTER 20

'Swing LOW, SWEET Chariot'

The summer months were as hot as the winter had been cold. John and his children were finally settled into Maggie's home, much to the old woman's delight. Esther and Caleb were a wonderful addition to their home, providing Julia with several opportunities a day for nurturing. Rather than spend his spare time in the Hollingsworth home, John preferred to throw himself into his work, leaving before anyone was awake and often returning later in the evening when supper dishes were finished and Julia and the children were reading books or telling stories. Julia's heart was sad for the man who was obviously still grieving the loss of his wife. It will soon be two years since her death, she thought, and he should be enjoying the life he now has. But I have not lost a husband, she reminded herself, not even knowing how to approach the subject with him.

"Swimming!" Caleb said excitedly one hot July afternoon.

"Thee would take us swimming? That would be wonderful. Grandmother used to take us swimming when father was busy in the fields, if we promised not to tell him."

"What does thee mean?" Julia asked, curious about his comment.

"Father would not permit us to go swimming unless he was with us and took us one at a time, and he never let go of our hands," Esther explained. "Grandmother said he was going to smother us and we could go with her if we promised not to tell Father."

"I see," Julia said with a smile, thinking how angry John would have been had he known about his mother's doings. "We will not go without thy father's permission," she said firmly, not wanting to upset the man who seemed to carry the weight of the world on his shoulders most of the time.

"Swimming?" John said when Julia approached him with the idea.

"Yes, swimming. Thee has heard of the activity?" she teased. "I thought I would fix a picnic lunch and the children and I could walk to the lake about a mile east of here. I will watch them carefully, John. I am good with children."

He looked at her for the first time in several weeks. He remembered the first time he had seen her at the Association . . . she had seemed like a porcelain doll, skin so pure and creamy, hair such a warm color, and a beautiful smile nearly always on her face. Perhaps he should have spent more time getting to know her, he lamented, seeing how well the children responded to her—and her to them.

But Julia seemed too pretty to care to frolic in the water with a couple of children—his children. And the children could not swim well enough to be allowed in the water on their own. No, this did not seem like a good idea to him. "I am sorry, children," he addressed his answer to them rather than Julia. "Neither of thee can swim well enough for such a venture. Even if Julia could watch thee closely I am afraid one of thee might wander off and be in danger."

Esther and Caleb's faces fell. Once again their melancholy father had spoiled an opportunity for fun.

Julia felt her anger rising. She also knew a comment out of that anger would not accomplish her purpose. Taking a deep breath, she offered another solution.

"Then thee will join us. It is time thee got away from thy work for a day, John. Thee spends far too many hours at the Association. Why, I am surprised we could function at all before thee came. Thee works more hours than Elizabeth and I worked together the past year or so. I will not take 'no' for an answer," she said firmly. "We will go tomorrow. I know thee does not have so much to do thee cannot take a few hours on the seventh day to spend with thy children."

"Now Julia," John began.

"Yes, Father, please come with us!" Caleb said excitedly. "Thee can teach me how to swim better."

"Will the water be warm?" Esther wanted to know.

"As warm as your bath water," Julia replied.

"I do not believe the water will be that warm," John said dryly.

"Then thee will go?" she asked.

John looked at the expectant faces of the two he loved more than life. How could he disappoint them yet another time? So often in the past they had asked him to take them swimming, or go riding with them, or play games. On a few occasions he would consent, but usually he was too tired to do much with them.

"All right, children, we will go on a picnic and swimming." Then, turning to Julia, "It was a lovely idea. Thee is welcome to come with us, but if thee would prefer I could take them myself."

Julia's face must have shown her disappointment. It was my idea, she thought. I was the one who wanted to take the children swimming.

"Oh please, Julia," Esther's big eyes looked imploringly at the young woman she adored.

"Juwea, come. Pwease?" Caleb added.

"All right, children, I will come." John might as well know it was only because of the children that she would accompany them to the lake.

"Then it is settled," John said. "I will ask Maggie to pack a lunch for us in the morning."

"But I was planning—"

"Nonsense. Maggie will want to help since she cannot go with us. I will go speak to her now."

Julia felt helpless around the man sometimes. He always had to have the final word. Maybe that was the way it had been with Carolyn, but he need not think he could tell her what to do. I will talk to Maggie myself, she vowed. If I want to fix the children and myself a lunch, I will do so. If Maggie wants to fix John's lunch, then so be it.

The next day was sunny and warm, perfect for swimming. When Maggie heard Julia's story about the lunch, she just chuckled. "You go right ahead, Missy, and fix the lunches. Heaven knows I won't be grievin' over the loss of one picnic lunch I ain't gotta fix!"

Julia laughed. Why could everyone not be as open and honest as Maggie? There would sure be a lot less hurt in the world, she thought, especially for John, and even for her father.

The walk to the lake was pleasant, John talking more than Julia had heard in months. He included Julia in the conversation, asking about her family and her childhood years in Salem. He seemed warm and caring, unlike their previous encounters. It was almost a metamorphosis, this change in the withdrawn man who always seemed old beyond his years. Julia wanted to ask about Carolyn, but never knew the right words to broach the fragile subject.

Once they arrived at the lake they spread the blanket Julia had brought and the children helped take the food Julia had prepared out of the basket. There were slices of chicken from the previous night's supper, rolls slathered with creamy butter and fresh rhubarb jam, a jar of pickles Maggie had suggested Julia pack, Jonathan apples from the tree behind the house, and the cherry pie Julia had gotten up early to bake. I cannot believe I actually baked a cherry pie for this, she chided herself. That, too, had been Maggie's suggestion. Cherries jist rottin' on the tree, she had said when she and Julia discussed what she might fix for the lunch. Might as well make a pie, I reckon.

Maggie could not fool anyone, let alone Julia. There was more to her wanting Julia to make a pie than just overripe cherries!

"My, but this is good cherry pie!" John exclaimed. "That Maggie is one fine cook."

"Juwea made it," Caleb piped up. He had been up at the crack of dawn in anticipation of the day at the lake. He even helped pit the cherries as he chatted about swimming and the fun it would be.

Julia blushed. She would have preferred John believe the pie to be Maggie's work.

"Julia? Thee made this?" John asked, surprised.

"Yes, John, I can do a little cooking." What did he think she was? A woman with no homemaking skills whatsoever?

John looked at her again and shook his head. The girl was full of surprises. Of course one would have to be blind not to see what a beauty she was. That thick, wavy red hair, her creamy complexion, small nose and chin, a waist so slim he knew it would fit in his two hands. But he had discovered other things about her, too, things that were a pleasant surprise. He had gone to Meeting for Worship a few times and listened to her speak. A real fine deliverer of God's word, that she was. And she was good with the children. They were constantly talking about the things she did with them. She was also full of ideas to help their work at the Association, and now he discovered she was a good cook.

But there were things about her that bothered him as well. She looked straight at him and was not the least bit submissive; she held her head in a way that almost defied anyone to challenge her words or actions; and she seemed to care less whether or not he was in her presence. So unlike his Carolyn.

After lunch the children were allowed to wade into the lake, but only up to their knees. Julia had insisted they bring other clothes to change into after their swim, even though John was emphatic they not venture far into the water. "I probably should be there with them," he said uneasily as he sat beside Julia to watch.

"They are children, John, they need to get into the water and splash and have a good time. Surely thee was allowed to do more than just stand in the water at that age."

John seemed to consider her words, though she supposed she had spoken in haste—again. It was such a shame to waste the opportunity, in her opinion.

"These are my children, Julia, and I must think of their safety above pleasure. But I suppose it would not hurt for them to go a bit further into the water." After he instructed the children on exactly what they might and might not do, he seemed to relax a bit on the blanket next to Julia. They had moved the blanket closer to the water's edge after their lunch so John could keep a closer watch on the two splashing and playing in the water.

John seemed to relax a bit, telling Julia of a time when he and Carolyn and the children had gone to a Meeting picnic where they sold pies to the highest bidder to raise funds for the Indian mission work. "Carolyn's brought the highest bid," he said proudly, a far off look in his eyes.

"I am certain she was a good cook, John, and no doubt a wonderful wife for thee." Did she dare continue? Should she tell him what she thought of his constant mourning for the wife he would never see again?

"I know thee misses her a great deal," she began.

"Thee has no idea how much," he said emphatically. "I loved her more than I loved my own life. She was the most wonderful woman God ever created." He stared off at the horizon, once again transported to another time and place.

"If only I had not allowed her to visit her friend," he lamented. "I had a premonition that day, and I should have told her to wait and go another time. But she was so insistent. Amanda, her friend, had a new baby she had not yet seen, and she so wanted to go and help out for a day. My mother said she would watch our children, so I relented. It was the worst mistake of my life."

His story was so like the feelings her father had expressed when describing the day he lost his wife. The helplessness of their situations, the belief that somehow each should have been able to foresee the future was all too familiar.

"Thee had no way of knowing what would happen, John," Julia said quietly. "None of us knows what the future holds. Who of us would not change our actions if we could foresee danger or tragedy? God gave us a free will and the ability to make choices. There are times when we blame ourselves for the unfortunate things that happen to us, but we forget that God has allowed us, as humans, to live without his hand dictating our lives. We experience joys that way, but also sorrows. It is a part of life. I realize I am not old in years, but I believe God has shown me some truths about this life that have helped me live in the present, not the past or future."

John looked up, tears in his eyes. "I can never have true happiness without Carolyn," he said sadly. "I have tried to forget her, but the memories are always there to remind me. And Esther. She looks so much like her mother. I want to protect her and keep her from all harm."

Julia's heart went out to the forlorn soul beside her. "Perhaps thee needs to release thy wife to God. The tighter thee clings to her the harder it will be to find fulfillment in this life. Thee has many years to live. Thy children need a father who is living in the present. Someone to laugh and tease them, not someone clutching at the shadows of the past."

John sat with his head buried in his arms, the broad shoulders shaking with silent sobs. What had she done? She had meant to help, not harm. Will I ever say the right thing to this man, she wondered.

"Father! Caleb is gone!" came Esther's loud shriek.

John looked up in a daze while Julia had already jumped to her feet and was headed toward the water.

Esther was screaming hysterically when she reached her. "Thee must be calm Esther. Now show me. Where was he?" Julia implored. "Right over there," she pointed, choking out the words. "He was playing and he was in too deep. I told him to come back, but he said he was going to catch a fish. And then his head disappeared. Help him, Julia, help him!"

"Go to the blanket," she commanded. "Thy father and I will find him." By this time John was also in the water, frantically moving toward her. "Over there," Julia pointed, diving into the area Esther had indicated. The water was somewhat murky from a recent rain, and it was impossible to see anything—or anyone. But Julia thought she could hear water churning to her left. Instinctively she moved toward the sound. Within a few seconds she had located Caleb in water well over his head—and hers. He had stepped in a hole several feet deep. Grasping him around the waist, Julia fought to bring him to the surface for air. Caleb was still frantically thrashing his arms and legs, making it difficult for Julia to get either of them above water. Finally, when it seemed her lungs would burst, she felt two strong hands grasping her waist, pulling both her and Caleb to shallower water.

In a matter of minutes they were all on the blanket again. Esther continued to sob while Caleb coughed and sputtered as John continued to pound him on the back. He had ingested quite a lot of water, but was breathing as normally as possible with lungs still containing part of the lake. John's hands were shaking, and as soon as Caleb was lying more comfortably, he began to scold the young boy.

"I told thee not to go above thy waist, Caleb. When thee disobeys, this is what happens. Did thee want to die, too?"

"John!" Julia could not help but interrupt. "It was an accident. He is a young boy. Perhaps thy love is needed more than thy scolding."

Caleb looked into the anguished face of his father. "At least I would be with Mother," he said, now sobbing. "That is where thee wishes thee could be."

John was stunned. What a thing for a child to say. He raised his hand to silence the young boy and then slowly put it back down. No, he reminded himself. I will never touch my children in anger. Hitting his son never worked for my father,

Was that how he acted? Like he would rather be dead with Carolyn than alive with his own living flesh and blood?

"I believe we need to go home," he finally said. "Esther, Caleb, put on the dry clothing thee brought."

"What about thee and Julia?" Esther asked, "Both of thee are soaking wet."

"We will be fine," Julia assured her.

John looked at Julia for the first time since dragging her and Caleb from the water. Her wet clothes clinging to her cold body sent feelings through him he had not felt in two years. Look away, John, he told himself. But his eyes remained riveted on the figure before him.

Julia, too, seemed mesmerized by muscles so clearly outlined under the soaked clothing. John somehow seemed younger just then, more vulnerable than she had ever seen him.

Quickly both adults looked away to where the children were changing.

"I appreciate thy help," John said hesitantly. "It was as if I had lead in my shoes when Esther cried for help. If thee had not gotten there so quickly we might not have found him."

"We would have found him, John. Esther called for help the instant Caleb went under. He could not have gotten that far away. And besides, if thee had not gotten there when thee did I am not certain how long it would have taken to get Caleb to safety. He was frantic for air and he is certainly strong for a six-year-old."

"It was still a brave thing for thee to do," John insisted. "Caleb owes his life to thee—and so do I."

The look John gave her was more than gratitude. It was a look of understanding, as if a great truth had finally dawned on him. He swiftly moved to embrace her but Julia stepped back, hearing the children approaching. "I would have done it for anyone needing help, John," she said matter-of-factly.

John seemed to understand her message and hastily picked up the remains of their picnic.

One would never have guessed Caleb had just had a brush with death as he chatted happily on the way home. Esther, too, seemed to have recovered from the ordeal and happily walked hand-in-hand with Julia and her father. Caleb was on Julia's other side, telling her about the fish he had been trying to catch when he stepped in the hole. John was quiet most of the way, answering the children's questions now and then, but adding nothing to the conversation.

Once at Maggie's, the children quickly filled her in on the events of the day, though one look at the two adults who were only beginning to dry out told her a good deal before even one word was spoken.

"And Julia saved Caleb's life," Esther said, her eyes glowing with admiration.

"Actually, thy father saved us both," Julia corrected, wanting John to have the credit he deserved.

"But thee was the one who found Caleb," Esther argued, "and thee would have gotten him out even if Father had not been there." A look of adoration filled the little girl's face and Julia did not want to disappoint her by discrediting her words.

"I am just thanking God thee called so quickly when he went under."

"And I am thankful God opened my eyes to new truths today," John said.

"My, my," Maggie exclaimed. "Seems like y'all had quite a day! By the way—how was the pie?" Julia saw the twitch of Maggie's mouth as she asked the question.

"Best cherry pie I ever had," John said with a smile, knowing Maggie's intent. And it truly was, he thought. Carolyn made good pies, but this one had been extra special, just like the woman who baked it.

CHAPTER 21

'He's GOT THE Whole World IN HIS Hands'

As the end of summer neared Julia saw changes daily at the Association. Fewer and fewer refugees were coming for emergency supplies, and even fewer for housing and training. The school had been prepared for the fall session and Julia spent much of her time teaching the refugee children since there was not enough to keep her busy in the warehouse. Many of the faces she was used to seeing in Meeting for Worship had moved on, living in new communities in the area. Though she did not want to admit it, Julia could see the handwriting on the wall: there would be a time when the refugees would no longer need the help of the Kansas Freedmen's Relief Association.

Julia had volunteered to take Esther and Caleb to the school near Maggie's on the first day. Maggie had reluctantly agreed, as the arthritis that crippled her knees made the five-block walk nearly impossible.

Esther was so excited she could hardly contain herself. "What will we do all day?" she asked Julia on the way.

"Thee will have a time of singing and Bible reading and prayer. Then thee will recite the Pledge of Allegiance and begin thy lessons."

"What kind of lessons will we learn?" Caleb asked innocently.

Julia smiled, remembering her earlier school days.

"There will be reading, of course, and numbers. Thee will have to memorize and recite poetry, and when thee is older there will be lessons on government and science."

"That sounds hard," Caleb said soberly.

"But it is not, Caleb," she said encouragingly. "Thy teacher will give thee just what thee can learn each year."

"Will Caleb and I be in the same class?" Esther asked. "Even though I am seven I have never been to school."

"But remember what I have taught thee? All the letters of the alphabet and the sounds they make? And thee knows some of the little words like 'the' and 'it' and 'at'. Thee knows the cat family, too."

"Cat, rat, bat, sat, hat, mat, fat, pat, tat, vat," Esther rattled off.

"Correct! Thee will do well, Esther, and I would not be surprised if thy teacher moves thee rapidly ahead."

"But I want to be with her," Caleb pleaded.

"There will be other boys thy age," Julia assured him. "And do the two of you know what the best part of school is?"

"No, what?" they asked in unison.

"Recess! You will play hide-and-seek, and tag, and have foot races . . . oh, you will both love recess!"

Julia made certain the teacher knew their names and the other important information required for entry in their new neighborhood school.

"And you are their mother?" she asked.

"Oh, no. Their mother was killed in an accident nearly three years ago. I am . . . I am a friend of their father's—I mean, we work together."

"I see," the woman said with a smile.

Once the paperwork was finished Julia said goodbye to the children.

"Now work hard, both of you, and I will come and pick you up at three. Do not leave the school yard before I get here," she warned.

"We will wait for thee, Julia," Esther said for both of them. "We promise we will be here when thee returns. Won't we Caleb?"

"Yep," he said, throwing his arms around Julia's waist and burying his head in her stomach. "I'm gonna miss thee, Juwea."

Julia knelt and hugged both of them. *Oh how I love these two adorable children,* she thought as they returned her embrace. *Their mother would be so proud of them. I am proud of them.*

"I will miss thee, too, but I know thee will both learn so many new things. Work hard," she called as they ran in response to the morning bell.

"We will. Bye."

"Bye," she said more to herself than them.

In early fall a letter from Julia's mother arrived telling her of their work at the Agricultural and Industrial Institute in Cherokee County. She was teaching in the school and Charles was volunteering with the refugees, as well as helping a local doctor who had more patients than he could properly care for. They were living in a rented home a few blocks from their work, and Rachel had met several friends in the neighborhood where one of the mothers had volunteered to keep her so Rebecca could be free to teach. The letter was friendly and full of news of her family, leaving Julia with a feeling of emptiness, unlike she had felt in the past. Her family had moved on and she was no longer a part of their lives.

John had been more cordial since the day of Caleb's near drowning, but he still worked feverishly and traveled several times a month to various Friends meetings seeking support for the work. His appearance had changed, too. Without a word of explanation his beard disappeared the day after Caleb's mishap. Julia hoped it was John's way of symbolizing his desire to put the past behind him and begin living in the present. She liked the new younger-looking man whose features appeared more boyish without all the dark facial hair.

"Friends do not seem as interested in the work as they once were," he lamented one evening as the two sat conversing in Maggie's parlor following supper. The children were playing outside under the watchful eye of Maggie who gently glided back and forth on the porch swing.

"Friends see the numbers of new refugees declining," he continued, "and they believe nothing more is needed of them."

And thee is not the motivational speaker thy predecessor was, Julia wanted to add, but kept silent knowing Elizabeth had a gift for raising funds that few others possessed.

"What will thee do when the work is finished here?" Julia asked curiously.

"Oh, I do not believe that will happen for some time," he said quickly. "As long as there is oppression in the South there will be refugees fleeing north."

Julia was surprised that John could not see the changes that had taken place in the past year alone. He has not been here as long as thee, she reminded herself. She could remember when there were lines of people waiting for tickets to secure food, clothing, bedding, and eating utensils. She could not remember a day the past year when there had been even two or three waiting in line for assistance. Within several years she imagined there would be little work for either of them to do at the Association.

"Will thee return to thy farm some day?" she persisted, wondering if he had thought beyond his present work.

"I really cannot say for certain," he said after a moment's pause. "I suppose the farm will always be there, but it holds so many memories . . ."

"Memories of Carolyn?"

"Yes, of her and that phase of my life. This life here seems so different, so detached from the other. Being here has helped me put some of the hurt and sorrow behind—that, and the words of my son that day at the lake. I realized what harm I must be doing to my children by continuing to harbor the old feelings of bitterness and sorrow. That is the reason I shaved my beard . . . it was a part of who I was when Carolyn and I were married, and I wanted a new beginning. It is only when I return to my parent's home that the feelings of hopelessness resurface."

Julia felt suddenly warmed by his words. He truly did want to put the past behind.

"Then it would seem that perhaps finding another occupation might be best for thee. Would thee consider another mission work after this? Perhaps with the Indians?"

John looked curiously at the questioning young woman. What did she want to know? Perhaps he should ask what her plans were. She would certainly want something to do once this work was finished.

"What about thee? Would thee be interested in being a traveling evangelist?" he asked. "Or perhaps even a paid pastor in a Friends Meeting? I have found thy words to be very inspirational in Meeting for Worship."

"I suppose those are possibilities," she said slowly, never imagining John had an opinion about her messages.

"What would thee like to do with thy life?" he asked quietly.

Julia looked distant, as if this were the first time she had actually thought of the possibilities. He was certain she had thought of her future, but she was still young and perhaps the Kansas mission had been her only destination.

"I suppose in all honesty what I desire most is a family of my own, a husband and children."

"And this husband . . . has thee thought of what God might be offering thee?"

Julia stared at John's eyes they seemed more open and honest than in the past. Why was he asking this of her?

"I am sorry," John said after several moments of silence. "I did not mean to offend thee." He never seemed to say quite the right thing to her.

"It is funny thee should ask such a question, John, and no, thee did not offend me. In the past four years I have been asked to consider a life with three different men." She proceeded to tell him about Jonathan White and the feelings they had for one another while attending the Academy, and of Will Clark, her Hicksite neighbor who was now married and managing the hotel in Salem. And finally, after some deliberation, she spoke of Hosea.

"I know thee will probably not understand how such a thing could happen, but my feelings for Hosea, whether they were borne of compassion or something else, were very real. With Hosea I could say whatever was on my mind without fear of being too forward. As I look back on those feelings, I can say with some certainty that it was not the kind of love a man and woman have for each other that allows them to become one flesh. But he was an important part of my life for several months, and I miss him, nonetheless."

John was reflective. How had he loved Carolyn? He thought it was a deep love, but had she truly ever shared what was on her heart? They had been so young, he sixteen, she fifteen, their marriage following a brief courtship. He had been anxious to leave the home where his father ruled with an iron fist. Carolyn had not been a beautiful woman, but she had seemed to love and want him. He thought about the conversations they had. They were mostly about the farm, and then the children. Had Carolyn ever dreamed about what she would do with her life, other than be a wife and mother? It saddened him to think that he had never asked about her dreams and ambitions. She and Julia were so very different.

But there was something about Julia, something that had touched him the day they saved Caleb. What he had once thought of as impudence he now saw in a different light. It was definitely a part of who she was, this young woman who always said exactly what was on her mind and was not afraid to do what needed done no matter the consequences. How would it be to live with such a woman, he wondered. It would never be dull, he thought with a smile. This was not the first time he had thought of a life with Julia. Many times since their outing to the lake the vision of her body outlined so clearly under the wet clothing evoked deep longings: the longing to hold and be held, the longing to be joined with a woman as one flesh, and the longing to share the everyday happenings of their lives.

There were also the children. Esther and Caleb already thought of Julia as a mother. She helped them with their studies, gave them their baths each night and got them ready for bed. She told them stories and kissed them good night. She would be, no, she *was*, a wonderful mother to them.

"John, is thee all right?" Julia asked, concerned when he did not answer her question.

"Yes, I am fine. In fact, I think I am better than I have been for a long time." His face was radiant and Julia wondered what had caused the sudden euphoria.

"What is it? What has made thee so happy?" she asked.

"Thee," he said simply.

"I do not understand."

He told her everything he had been thinking. "I admire thy spirit and love for life, Julia. Though thee is different from Carolyn in that respect, there is a sense of adventure when I am with thee which makes me feel young and alive. Of course the children adore thee and think of thee as their mother. Thee makes all of us very happy, Julia."

Julia was surprised, though not shocked. She had seen his occasional look across the table during supper that revealed the feelings she thought might be developing.

"Julia, Father, come see the stars," Esther burst into the parlor.

"In a moment, dear," Julia said kindly. "Your father and I were talking about something very important and we need to finish. Then we will come and see the stars with thee."

"Hurry," she said, rushing back out. "Maggie showed us a dipper and a bear and a house and a snake. There are pictures in the sky!"

Both adults laughed, then remembered what they had been discussing.

"What I am trying to say, Julia, is that I believe I would like to have thee for my wife, if thee would consider me, of course. I know I am not educated, like thee, but I am a hard worker and I believe together we might accomplish great things for God's kingdom. Most important, I have grown to love thee for the wonderful young woman thee is."

Now Julia was stunned. He wanted her to be his wife? Of course she loved the children, and had since the day they were introduced. But marry their father? Be their mother forever? Was that what she really wanted? He had certainly changed in the time they had lived under the same roof, but did she have those feelings of love a woman needed for a man? She honestly did not know.

"Just pray about it, Julia. God will not fail thee. He will guide and direct thee. I would never push thee into making a decision this enormous, and unless thee is assured this is God's plan for thee—for us—it would be a mistake."

Julia sensed the love and care in his words. John gently took her hand and pulled her to her feet. "Stars await us," he said simply. Then, for one brief moment, he held her in his arms.

Julia was shocked at the electricity that seemed to shoot through her veins. As he caressed her back with his hand, she yearned for more. His body was so solid, so very much like a rock. He would be there for her. She looked once more at his face. The eyes. Oh, how beautiful were those eyes.

"I will make it a matter of prayer, John," she finally said, not moving from his embrace. "It is important to know God's will in the matter, not just our own desires." Her smile was all he needed. "Thank you, Jesus," he said, more of a prayer than a response to her words.

Though no more was spoken of their encounter, both Julia and John knew something had happened between them. Julia found herself seeking him during the day, often for no other reason than to just stare at his wonderfully carved body. John began coming home earlier and earlier in the day, and his eyes seldom left the woman he thought God created to perfection.

As Julia lay in bed a few weeks after John's proposal, she admitted she still had a few lingering doubts about the prospect of marriage to a man she was not certain she knew very well. Though she had met John nearly two years earlier, they had only begun to relate to one another the past three months. This was a decision that would affect the rest of her life. She thought of the stories her mother had told her of the few months she and her father had courted. They had certainly not needed months or years to make the decision to marry. In fact, most all of the marriages she had witnessed had taken place after brief periods of courtship.

But what about God's call on my life? she asked herself. God called me to work with the refugees, not to come and find a husband.

But the refugee work will not last forever, she argued with herself. And here is a man who wants to offer me a home and two adorable children to love and nurture. Might that not be a calling as well?

Finally, her mind in a turmoil, Julia slipped out of bed and knelt in prayer. The moonlight streamed through the windows, illuminating the children sleeping peacefully in the adjacent room. Julia felt an overwhelming sense of love for the two cherubs who even now thought of her as their mother. Can I leave them? she asked herself. Do I want to leave them?

"Lord," she prayed, "I need to know thy will for my life. I have asked thee for guidance in the past, and thee has always given it to me. I think I love John, but I have no idea if it is enough love wherein two shall become one flesh. I know he has many fine qualities, and I believe he loves me. And the children . . . well, you know how much I love them. Please help me make the right decision."

Julia felt at peace as she crawled back in bed. She was confident God would answer her prayer for wisdom. Just as she was about to drift off to sleep, the voice returned to her thoughts.

Julia, you are more precious to me that you can ever imagine. I only want what will make you happy. Do you remember your longings for a husband and children? You have wanted a family for many years now. You were willing to give your life to my work, and I have blessed your faithfulness. Now I am offering you the fulfillment of your hopes and dreams. A man who loves you, and children for you to love and train up in the way they should go. Trust me to know what is best for you, my child. A new world awaits you.

Julia began to cry softly, finally understanding God's plan for her life more fully, believing she and John were, indeed, to become one flesh. Wiping her tears she quietly made her way to John's room. She laughed, thinking about Maggie's bedroom being directly beneath John's, and hoping the old woman's hearing was not too keen that night.

"John," she whispered, gently shaking the snoring form.

John bolted up, grabbing Julia's arm. "What is it? Is one of the children ill?"

"Shhh," Julia admonished. "The children are fine. I just could not wait until morning to share what God has just revealed to me." She proceeded to tell the man sitting beside her of the longings for a family she had carried for several years, and how God had shown her that this was the answer to her prayers.

John wiped the tears from his eyes as he wrapped his arms around the angel who sat glowing beside him. "Thee has made me the happiest man in the world!" he said fiercely. "And if Maggie weren't right below us, and of course if it were not against God's laws, I would take thee in my arms and show thee just how happy I am!"

"John!" Julia scolded. "I can see it is time for me to return to my room."

"I do not not believe God would object to one kiss to seal our engagement."

The kiss was tender, yet passionate. An ending to past feelings and a mark of the new life they would share. Julia could not remember a time she felt any more joy than in the arms of the man she would marry.

The next morning the glow surrounding the newly engaged couple was still evident in their faces and the way they kept looking at one another.

Finally Maggie could stand it no more.

"All right, you two, what's goin' on with ya's? Ya been moonin' at each other fer weeks now, but this mornin' somethin's different."

Caleb and Esther both perked up, looking from their father to Julia.

"John—thy father," she added, looking at the children, "has asked me to become his wife. What would thee think of that?"

"Really?" Esther asked excitedly. "Truly? Would thee be our mother for real and forever?"

Julia laughed. "For real and forever."

"Maggie, what does thee think?" John teased the older woman. "Think thee could stand it if Julia and I shared the guest room? That would give thee another room to rent."

"Don't need no more renters, heavenly days! Got more now 'n I know what ta do with! Seems ta me Esther needs that room. She's gettin' too big ta share a room with Caleb anyway." Though her tone was sharp, as always, the happiness was evident as well. "Only thing I can't figure out is what took ya so long?!"

Everyone laughed. "Sometimes it takes a while to see what has been there all along," John said quietly.

"And some of us need a little help discovering our true feelings," Julia added.

"When is the wedding?" Esther wanted to know.

"Slow down, sweetie," John told her. "We just made the announcement five minutes ago and you want to know when the wedding is!"

"Well, when is it? I want us to be a family as soon as possible."

"Thy mother will have to work on those details," John said warmly.

"We will have to work on them together, John," she said steadily.

"I want that, truly I do. I want us to share our lives—all of our lives." John reached over and covered Julia's small hand with his much larger one.

"'Scuse me, but I believe our breakfist is gettin' cold," Maggie interrupted, always the practical one. "And when we git finished, I believe there's a pie waitin' in the pie safe."

"Pie? In the morning? Wouldn't be cherry, by any chance?" John asked jokingly.

"Nope, apple. But that wife—I mean future wife, makes a mean apple pie, too. Guess I been considerin' you two bein' already married, ya both livin' here 'n all."

"Now Maggie, that would be living in sin, I do believe," John said solemnly. Maggie saw the gleam in his eye.

"Only sin is ya took so dad-blamed long to figure out ya belonged tagether!"

Everyone laughed as the soon-to-be family broke bread together in true fellowship with one another.